IF THESE FLAMES COULD TALK

MICHAEL BURNHAM

Mansfield Bound

Special Thanks

To my fundraiser contributors

Sean Conley, Krystle Blakeney, Jason Flye, Michael Schromm, Maryanne Sarazin, Victoria Prouty, Jessica Saladino, Erin Napp, Tina Spencer, Tarin Sarazin, Carol Spencer, Chris Clough, Donna Packard, Pam Peterson, Bob Peterson, Terri Tucker, Thom Burnham, Loretta Sarazin

To my beta readers
Jason Lafontaine, Rachel Roy
&
Haley Tucker, my first beta and partner in crime

This book is dedicated to
my parents, Thom and Loretta
and my brothers, Christopher and Mark

CONTENTS

CHAPTER I:
WELCOME TO THE JUNCTION

It would be easy to liken the life of a fire to that of a human. It breathes, it eats, and eventually, it dies. Its resemblance to human nature more purely reveals itself as a flame dancing when it's high, and crackling when it's low.

Felix Robinson, a man whose spark was often contained in a baggie and sold after dark, found himself at neither extreme, caught waltzing instead on the sizzling line between.

On the morning of June 12th, 1999, Felix woke with a headache, dry mouth, and blood on his hands.

"God dammit," he muttered as he closed his eyes again and began combing his body for cuts. "What the hell did I do now?"

As his hands moved over his chest and reached his arms, he realized just how heavy his eyes felt—like he had never slept an hour in his life. He felt the track marks, and while they were not the healthiest part of his body, they were also not the source of the blood, so he continued searching for this mystery wound. As he reached his throbbing skull, he felt what he thought was blood, but the grainy texture he felt as he rubbed his fingers together urged his eyes open. He saw only loose hair, and mud.

"What the fuck?" he said again, louder, feeling more awake with every inch his hands moved. With his eyes now wide open, Felix could see that his hands were not the only thing covered in blood—so were his clothes, shoes, and the unfamiliar couch beneath him.

He bolted upright, intent on getting his bearings and making sense of his surroundings. He spun his head around and immediately recognized the clamshell pattern wallpaper and yellowing lamp fixtures. He was at the Shady Acre Motel.

His mind then jumped to the next question: *How did I get here?*

But the motion of standing and spinning had been too fast. He got what he would have described as "static of the brain" and folded back onto the couch. Questions rushed into his mind at an impossible rate: *Is that MY blood? Did I hurt someone? Did I KILL someone?*

He felt sick to his stomach and began dry heaving next to the couch. He was ashamed of the next thought, but couldn't invalidate it either: *This would all go away if I got high.*

When the static finally started to abate and the dry heaving stopped, Felix began sobbing and covered his face with his hands. *What did I DO?*

"You're going to want to get changed as soon as you can," a man's voice said, startling Felix and making him stand up once again, this time with less static. "That's not your blood."

"WH—WHO THE HELL ARE YOU?" Felix yelled as he stumbled backward, keeping his eyes fixed to the man who had spoken.

The expressionless look he saw staring back from a face probably ten years his senior terrified him, quickly planting the idea that the man was there to hurt him somehow. He instinctively reached for any object he could use to protect himself, his trembling hands landing on what appeared to be a large, old-fashioned television remote. It wasn't a very formidable weapon, but he held it up to defend himself anyway. He searched his mind, trying to remember the man in front of him, but nothing surfaced. He was sure he didn't know him.

"WHO THE HELL ARE YOU? AND WHY ARE YOU HERE?"

"Whoa, whoa, whoa. Easy. You mean you... you don't remember?"

Felix flinched as the man put up his hands in an I-mean-no-harm stance.

"I, uh... I can explain, but can you please sit down?"

The man slowly sat in a chair and motioned toward the couch with his right hand. "Please, just um... sit."

Felix hesitated, then sat, keeping the remote gripped tight. The man sat silent for a moment, unsure how to begin the conversation. He then nervously laced his hands over his head and asked, "What, um... do you remember about last night?"

Felix thought about it for a few seconds, then dropped the remote onto the floor. He put his face in his hands. The only thing he could remember was scoring heroin and shooting up, and this had to be the old you-got-high-and-fucked-up routine he'd heard more times than he could count.

"I don't know. I... I must have relapsed," he choked out before dropping his hands and looking at the stranger again. "Whatever happened, I'm sorry. Okay? I'll get help, I swear. Please just let me fix it."

"Well, ya see, I don't think that's gunna be possible," the man said, causing Felix's frown lines to deepen further. "You stole my car last night, and hit someone with it."

The man paused. "It was a cop, and... he's dead."

Felix looked back at the man in shock. "No," he said. "No, no. NO!"

Felix felt devastatingly ill and doubled over, dry heaving again. This time it hurt worse, and his thoughts were racing faster than bullets. *I DID kill someone, I'm going to jail, my life is over. And maybe this would go away if I got another fix.* His stomach felt like *he* was the one who got hit by a car, and his head felt the same. He pounded his fist on the couch and buried his face in the cushion, one that now smelled like Febreze and pennies. He screamed as loud as his battered lungs would allow, then wept as the last of his energy drained into the upholstery. When he finally lifted his head and sat up, the man across the room had a cell phone in his hands.

"Are they on their way?" Felix asked, sure that any minute sirens would pierce the air and solidify his future as an African American statistic.

"No," the man said. "Not yet."

2

Nicole Schaffer ashed out a cigarette just before hitting the Interstate 91 off-ramp toward White River Junction, an unincorporated village in the town of Hartford, Vermont—the Green Mountain State. The year was 2019, and she hadn't seen these rolling hills since she'd left home almost fourteen years ago.

The signs are new, she thought as a burst of wind sent her dark brown hair into an interpretative dance across her face, but her feelings about the town remained old and bitter. She turned down the radio as she hit the thirty-five-mile-per-hour stretch, the fleeting voice of an overly confident DJ exclaiming, "Get ready for another thirty minutes of the greatest nonstop rock, brought to you by Fairlee Ford and your favorite rock station, 106.1!"

"Yeah," she said, "the greatest rock a grandma could ask for!" Satisfied with this burn, she laughed to herself, one part amusement and two parts anxious wreck.

She rode into town and parked at the Petro Mart—the same one that had always been there and probably always would. The signs read, "Two hotdogs and a bag of chips $3.99, NICE PRICE!!" and "5 cents off a gallon, cash customers only!" There was a couple arguing in the parking lot; both appeared to be slightly intoxicated, judging by their sloppy movements and clear lack of social awareness. When the man got in the woman's face to yell, Nicole imagined he could have been a pal of her father's. She was reminded of something her grandfather used to say back in Arkansas:

5

"Not my rodeo, not my clowns." She shook her head and allowed herself a half-amused smile, wearing it as she opened the gas station door and walked inside.

The girl behind the counter looked like she was twelve years old, and, after spending what seemed like an hour studying her identification, handed over the smokes Nicole had requested. Up until last week, Nicole had quit smoking for a solid eight years, but the thought of coming home was enough for her to temporarily disregard the Surgeon General's warnings. As Nicole pulled out a twenty-dollar bill, she saw a police car pull into the parking lot next to the arguing couple. *Your clowns now*, she thought as an officer exited the vehicle and began talking to the woman. At first, Nicole was amused by the woman's flashy hand gestures and obviously un-ladylike language, but as the officer turned and his face became visible, Nicole instantly recognized him. It was her old flame, David Demick Junior.

"Ma'am, your chan..." the girl behind the counter started, but didn't get to finish. Nicole was already moving toward the door, deaf to the sound of twelve-year-old gas clerks. She'd known the moment would come at some point while she was in town, but she didn't think it would be so soon.

"... I don't *care* what they told you, he never touched me, and you can't arrest someone for being *loud*. That's against his rights!" The woman in the parking lot yelled and pointed at the man next to her. "So, unless he's being detained, you *have* to let us go! Why are you always HARASSING US? HE DIDN'T DO IT!"

The officer took a step back from the woman, recognizing a losing battle. He was about to tell the man that the next time he received a call, he'd be asking the questions from the station, but his eye caught the woman standing under the "WE SELL VAPE PODS" sign, and he hastily issued the disgruntled woman his contact card instead. "I'll be seeing you," was the last thing he said before walking up to an ancient memory.

"Jeez, well, howdy, ma'am. I haven't seen you for a *coooon's age!*" David said in an exaggerated country voice.

He remembered the phony accent used to get a laugh or two back when his job was still sharpening pencils and researching Mesopotamia. He hadn't seen or heard from Nicole since she'd gotten emancipated and left town on her sixteenth birthday. The surprise showed on his face as he met the green eyes looking out from behind a set of white sunglasses. He had a short-lived fear that the joking voice was too kiddy for the situation, but the smile that appeared on her face told him the impression was still effective.

"Hey, I know it's been forever!" Nicole replied, half-happy and half-nervous.

She let out a laugh too as she remembered the country voice. She thought she'd heard it probably a hundred times too many and a thousand times too few. She reached out her arms and they hugged. It was weird, and warm, and stirred up memories of a time when that type of embrace had meant everything to her.

"God, how ARE you?" she asked as they stepped apart.

As she looked at his clean-cut hair and shaved face, a shimmering wave of energy enveloped her body like a freshly cracked glow stick. She had always found David handsome,

7

but the grown-up version carried a smooth and comforting sense of strength.

Then she eyed his uniform with its Hartford Police Department badge. "I see you finally got the dream job."

"Almost!" he replied. "Still working on that detective shield. Sort of a quiet day aside from the guys who think they can beat up on their girlfriends and get away with it."

He glanced over at the couple, who had since crossed the street and started act two. "But yeah, I finished school and the academy, and here I am, *servin' up possum pie with a side of justice.*"

The last part he said in a country voice again. *This time it's overkill,* he thought, but domestic violence wasn't the best icebreaker.

"That seemed kinda intense," she said, looking across the street at the couple David had been questioning a moment before. "Is that the guy? The one who…"

Nicole's voice trailed off. She wanted to say, "the one who claimed he killed your father then took it back and said he didn't," but she knew she didn't have to. David's father had been a detective back then, and when he was murdered in an unsolved hit-and-run accident, it had left a deep red stain on the town that even time couldn't wash away.

She did the math in her head and realized it was close to twenty years ago, and though she was happy to see David had followed his father's footsteps into law enforcement, she wished she hadn't brought it up and potentially spoiled her current encounter with him.

"Yeah, that's Cooper." David replied, looking at the couple.

"But that's great you got onto the force, just like you always wanted!" Nicole said, trying to salvage the conversation.

"Thank you, ma'am," he replied, to her relief. "And, jeez, what are you up to these days? I haven't seen you in, oh, what's it been now? Fifteen years?"

"Fourteen years, yeah," she said. "I'm actually a nurse now, believe it or not."

She watched as a smile formed on his face and his eyes told her to continue. "I lived with my grandparents in Arkansas while I finished up school, then I cut hair for a long time after that, but it never really felt meaningful, ya know? So, I went back to school so I could help people, kinda like you always said I should!"

"I cuff 'em, you cure 'em."

"Oh, now that's gold! Comedy your side gig these days?"

"No, that would still be singing in the shower... thinking about going pro, actually." He put one hand on his hip and raised the other towards the sky with his palm up, as if he were belting out an operatic composition.

They both laughed. Then, returning his hands to his belt, David asked, "So what brings you back to the ole' White River? Surely there's enough sick people in Arkansas to keep you busy."

"Well," she paused, "it's actually my birthday next Sunday. The big 3-0."

"Oh, well, happy non-belated birthday," he said, and immediately wished he hadn't. *Stupid, stupid, stupid.*

"Thank you," she said. "It's a big one, and I figured it was probably time to come home and..."

She paused again, this time unable to hide the concern on her face. "... try to make amends."

David recognized the look. It lived on a much more mature face than it had years ago, but still, it brought him back. He remembered seeing it while visiting Nicole at home after her parents had found out he and she were doing more than swapping math answers on the bus. *Pure organic stress.*

"Ahh," was all David could muster, taking his turn searching for something to break the tension while looking at his boots.

"So you haven't talked to him in all this time, either?" he added finally.

"No... I mean, I meant to, but I just couldn't bring myself to think about this place and everything that happened. He used to say he was just protecting me the way my mother would have wanted, but it didn't feel that way, and... I just needed a chance to figure it out myself, ya know? I took a couple weeks off work so I could come up and at least try. If nothing else I can head over to Hampton and be a beach bum like I told everyone at home I was."

"I get it, I really do. His parenting was a bit much—a lot more rigid than your mom's—and hell, if I were in your shoes, I would have left too! But hey, that's all behind you. It sounds like you got all your ducks in a row down there, and even that's more than most of the people in this town can say!"

Nicole grinned at the last part; she'd never really felt like she had her "ducks in a row," but she guessed that was probably just her own insecurities and the thought of unfinished business lingering in the back of her mind.

"The big 3-0 though, that's either exciting or… terrifying?"

"Both, actually. I can't decide if I'm just getting started or if I'm halfway to being a crazy old cat lady."

"No, not a crazy old cat lady," David decided. "If I remember correctly, you'd be a crazy old *dog* lady?"

"Yes! Cats are the spawn of Satan, and dogs are angels sent from heaven!" Nicole sighed in relief. She had played versions of this conversation with David in her mind millions of times while she was away, and none of them had included him remembering her pet preferences.

"Hey now, easy, I had a cat named Pickle once, and he was the greatest pet this side of the Mississippi," David said as he looked into Nicole's eyes. She was calling his bluff with an incredulous smirk that he couldn't help but laugh at. "No, no he wasn't. He was a *nightmare,* and was probably plotting my demise!"

They laughed for a minute until the radio in David's cruiser began spouting out the voice of a dispatcher. David held up his pointer fingers as if to say, "Just a minute," and got in his car to respond.

Nicole watched as he went, thinking about how much he had changed from the gangly teenager with a Mountain Dew t-shirt she remembered. She wondered if he had been able to have an actual girlfriend after she left, one he could be around without sneaking through windows and pretending to be *"just friends."* She remembered her own attempts at entering the dating world, all starting with a hope for something different and ending with the old "it's not you, it's me" routine.

11

David returned a minute later looking slightly annoyed and said, "I have to get back at it—there was a call that came in about a guy who was refusing to leave a grocery store after his card got declined and who is now demanding that someone fix the machine or he's going to take all the stuff and leave without paying!"

He rolled his eyes. *Leave it to criminals to ruin a perfectly good reunion.* "Hey, listen, I know you just got into town and probably haven't figured out anything yet, but I would love to meet up again and maybe talk some more. I'm not sure where you're staying or what your plans are, but I'm off the clock at nine tonight, if that's not too forward or too late?"

"Neither," Nicole said with a warm smile. She was glad she had bumped into David so early and that it hadn't gone as terribly as her mind had made her believe it would. "I'm not sure I had much of a plan, but I was going to stay at the Shady Acre, if that's still a thing?"

"Oof," David said with comedic pain on his face. "It's still there, but it definitely wouldn't be my first choice. I think I get called down there to play 'Who's stealing drugs from who?' twice a week."

"Well, at least I know who to call if I see it in action," she said, then smiled again. The truth was that although being a nurse helped her self-esteem, it didn't necessarily make the Hilton an option either, so the Shady Acre, in all its marijuana and glory, would have to make due.

"I'm here to protect and serve, helping damsels in distress and *servin' up a slice uh justice to the vegetable-isle outlaws*," David said, sneaking in one final country voice and handing Nicole his business card.

12

"Fancy," she said, looking at the logo of the Hartford Police Department and his contact information in shiny black ink.

"It was so great to see you," David said. "And I know you probably thought things would be weird between us, but I understand why everything happened the way it did, and I would be happy just to get to know the new you. I hope everything goes well when you talk to your dad. I'm sure that's going to be tough, but you're a different person now, and that's gotta count for something!"

That was hard for Nicole to imagine, but she supposed that since she was an adult and made her own decisions now, her father didn't really have a choice but to listen. She reached out to give David another hug. "It was great to see you too."

And it wasn't weird at all, she thought. "I'll call you tonight."

David walked back to his cruiser, tipped his hat, and mouthed the word *ma'am* as he drove away. Nicole opened the pack of cigarettes she was clutching and lit one up, sitting down on the bench outside the Petro Mart.

She wished she would have thought about this scenario playing out—David being so understanding and all. Maybe she would have come back sooner if she'd known it were going to be that simple. Maybe FDR was right about only fearing fear itself.

She pondered this for a few minutes, then watched the couple across the street walking away, now holding hands and apparently in love again.

Not my rodeo, she thought as she walked to her car and prepared for her journey to the Shady Acre, *not my clowns.*

13

3

One week before Nicole's arrival, a group of eight gathered inside the meeting chamber of the Riverside Methodist Church. They found their seats around a large, circular wooden table and began trading salutations, gossip, and news they'd heard since their meeting the month before. The usual "Did you hear who got picked up?" and "Looks like it's gonna be hot next week," wafted through the air, mixing with the smell of burnt coffee from the recovery meeting earlier that day.

The group was comprised of local business owners and their designees, all of whom were bestowed with the task of selecting the winner of their monthly charity drive, which had been informally dubbed The Hobo Lottery.

Among those seated around the table was an overdressed man in his late twenties named Adrian Emerson. He was the Assistant Funeral Director of the Peace at Last Funeral Home and Crematorium, as well as the part-time groundskeeper at the local cemetery; the suit he wore was an expensive, yet self-proclaimed necessity, of the former.

Some of the local women shared similar stories of failed attempts at flirting with the quiet and attractive "man in black." Each swooned at the thick dark hair that occasionally hung down his face in tempting strands, but most failed to capture more than a passing moment of his attention. Some quietly ventured as far as to say he was secretly homosexual, but the few who'd managed to find themselves exposed to his keeping of faith assured people that was a foolish assumption.

He now glanced at the clock, the door, and the clock again, wondering when the pastor would arrive to begin the selection process.

His father, Scott Emerson, was seated next to him, describing in great detail the temperature of his Dunkin' Donuts coffee to the woman next to him.

Adrian assisted his father with services, setting up flowers, playing light piano, and handing out tissues to family members. He was also the better record keeper of the two and the main operator of the cremation oven, which—since the business had upgraded to hydraulic lifts and steel rollers—he could manage by himself, barring the occasional, as his father put it, "contestant for who could eat the most fried chicken in one lifetime."

Because his father was one of the original members of the Hobo Lottery selection board, Adrian had been given a seat at the table, and while he was the youngest member at the table, he believed he was also the least dull-witted. There were a few brains between the whole lot, and Brent Fleurry, a retired police officer turned hardware-store owner with a fidgeting problem, had probably half of them to himself.

"I wasn't sure this coffee was going to get me, A-WAKE," chimed Scott as the door opened. Adrian rolled his eyes and fixed them on the final member of the meeting, Pastor Felix Robinson.

Felix entered the room wearing a white clergy robe trimmed with gold seams and buttons. Beneath his left arm, he carried a Bible and a stack of blue-covered folders. He looked at his fellow board members through a set of red-rimmed reading glasses before taking them off and letting them rest around his neck. It revealed his approach to being "over the hill" as well as, if not better than, the liver spots that seemed to come as they pleased.

"Sorry, sorry I'm late, everyone. I swear the traffic lights weren't made with patience in mind," Felix said as he took his seat at the head of the table and began passing out a pile of applications and folders, each containing the names and current standings of the three potential winners for the month of July. "Forgive me for being late, but let's get started. Are there any updates anyone wants to share?"

Everyone shook their heads no. Two out of the three candidates had been arrested for petty theft the week before, so the meeting was essentially a formality, as their only other candidate, Morgan Sandberg, was actively working as a dishwasher at a restaurant downtown, attending services on weekends, and turning in negative drug tests.

"No, nothing? Alright, well, I'm sure you all have heard the news that Jamie and Cooper have gotten themselves into a bit of trouble," Felix said, looking around the room. "And while I know that doesn't come as a shock, I'm also sure that will effectively make our decision for us."

Felix knew he could speak to the value of redemption and make a case for the other two, but he also knew this group needed to believe their money would not be foolishly wasted on under qualified candidates, such as repeat losers Jamie and Cooper, or they may not want to contribute in the future. "So, let us vote, then. All in favor of Morgan Sandberg, the Hartford, Connecticut native to be the recipient of gifts and services for the month of July, 2019?"

Seven hands went up in an instant, causing a few voters to chuckle and eliciting a "duh" from one.

"I too vote for Morgan," Felix said as he raised his hand, "and, with a unanimous vote, he will be our winner." The room erupted with applause as Felix took a cell phone and gift cards out of his pocket and placed them on Morgan's file. Adrian eyed them as he clapped his hands together; the next item was what he'd come for, and he hoped he could clap for that too.

"In speaking with Morgan," Felix said as he waved his hands to quiet the applause, "I have learned that, while he appreciates the help he's gotten in our town, his wish, were he to win, is to return to Connecticut and make things right with his family. He believes he now has the strength to stay sober, and with the help of God, he will stay on the path he's begun walking here with us, bringing the light back home. He wanted to express his thanks to you, Vincent, for allowing him to work under your supervision these past few months, and to you, Adrian, for giving him transportation to do so. Thank you both from Morgan."

"That's my son," Scott said as the room once again filled with applause. Adrian clapped his hands together and grinned at the mention of his work as a transporter. *Necessary,* he thought.

"With that being said, I will purchase bus tickets to Hartford, and if you're up for it, Adrian, you can give him one final ride to the stop. I know how much you enjoy playing chauffeur!"

"Absolutely I do, and I can," Adrian replied. "When does he leave?"

"I will be calling him tonight to let him know he has won, so, most likely, the end of next week."

"Hey now, I expect my dishwashers to give AT LEAST two weeks' notice before they up and quit on me," Vincent said, looking around the room. After a couple seconds of reading the shocked faces of the other members, he belted out a deep laugh and waved his hands, yelling, "Ahh, I'm only kiddin', he's a good kid!"

The rest of the meeting consisted of Felix bringing out new folders with potential candidates for August, along with resubmitting the folders of Jamie and Cooper for consideration. "We all make mistakes," he said as the other members begrudgingly added them to their stacks.

Everyone in town knew Jamie and Cooper were never going to win; they were a couple who tried once or twice a year to get sober, but always seemed to find a reverse loophole that got them disqualified instead.

At the end of the night, Adrian stayed to help Felix stack chairs and set aside the tables to make way for a youth dance happening the next day. "I appreciate all you do for the cause," Felix said. "I know you and your father are busy men."

"Never too busy to do the Lord's work," Adrian replied as he reached out to shake the hand Felix had extended.

As a kid who had been hastily thrust into religion by his father to help cope with the loss of his mother, Adrian admired the way faith had transformed Felix from a regular man to a full-on symbol of God's acceptance. It was incredible. After joining his mentoring project, Felix had spent countless hours reading the Bible, reciting passages, and learning what it meant to truly live in the light. Through those lessons, Adrian had finally found a path through the pain, and a purposeful life in service of a higher power.

Adrian finished up and left the church with both a feeling of accomplishment and excitement. The next day, he got two phone calls—one from Felix confirming the departure for Morgan's bus the following Thursday, and one from Morgan himself, who called to arrange a pickup time and to say thank you.

"See you then, Morgan," Adrian replied. "And congratulations!"

4

Nicole finished unpacking her things at the Shady Acre and flopped down on a sofa she imagined had been the recipient of at least five hundred naked butts in its day. She eyed a cigarette burn on the cushion next to her, which made her light up one of her own.

She hadn't been sure if she was prepared to face her father yet, but after meeting with David, she felt confident that it would be easier than she had expected on the drive up from Arkansas. She tapped her foot on the floor as she took in another drag; the room was "smoke free" apparently, but she figured that sign was just for show—the proof showed on the couch, the floor, and the ashtrays.

She finished the smoke and got to her feet as the sound of mumbled yelling came from the room next door. It didn't surprise her much; the motel may have been a little less sketchy when she was younger, but it'd always had a reputation for attracting winners. She was glad she was only there for a few days—a week, tops.

She got in her car and drove to South Main street, a name that implied an abundance of life, but was usually as quiet as a mousetrap in a cat store. She gripped the steering wheel as she drove closer to her old home, passing the tree that had claimed at least three arm bones in their clumsy childhood climbing years, the fire hydrant that had never exploded with water during hot summers like the movies said it would, and the bus stop where she used to rendez-vous with David.

She lit up another smoke just before she entered the driveway, needing that extra motivation to push out the thoughts of driving home to Arkansas. She rounded the corner and was both relieved and puzzled to see not a single car parked in the driveway. She put her own car in park and got out.

At first, she thought that maybe they had moved, but after seeing her mother's old "Welcome All Who Wander" sign still firmly attached to the side of the door, she concluded she was probably wrong. She thought about knocking, but couldn't bring herself to go to the door. Instead, she waited outside for a minute, only half-hoping someone was home.

When no one appeared in the windows or opened the door, she took a deep breath and decided to leave. She got back in her car and drove back on South Main, thinking again, as she passed the bus stop, about those sweet getaways with David. Shortly after she signaled to turn into the Shady Acre once again, she had a thought. *Maybe he's at work? Yes, if I meet him there, it's common ground. It will HAVE to be civil.*

She turned off her blinker, *Fuck it, I'll go,* she thought as she pressed the gas and passed the motel.

Nicole made her way across town with no less than two moments of panic and anger. *What am I afraid of? HE'S the one who should be sweating this, not me!* The thought manifested as a cigarette being crushed into the ashtray with a little too much force, sending painful red-hot ashes down the side of her leg. Swiping at her leg to cool it, she gripped the wheel harder and took a deep breath as she finally saw the old white van she knew belonged to her father.

She got out of her car and eyed the van for a second before walking to the door, amazed the old thing was still running after so long.

"Hello?" she said as she waited in an empty front room. No response. "Is anybody here?"

After a second silence, Nicole decided that, rather than forcing a hasty conversation, she would take the night to settle in at the motel and save the reunion for the next day. *Maybe a mutual setting WITHOUT a corpse.*

She was going to leave and began walking towards the front door when a muffled crash from the floor below made her stop and listen. A few seconds passed: nothing. She knew it was too late for a client to walk in off the street, so whoever was working probably wasn't aware that anyone else was in the building.

"Shit," she said as the sound made the inevitable more real in her mind and convinced her to turn back around. *Just get it over with.*

The quiet crept back in as she made her way down the hallway and began descending the stairs, freezing in her steps as the sound of a man sobbing cut through the air. The man was saying something that Nicole couldn't quite make out, so she slowly continued walking down the rest of the way, clutching at the cell phone in her pocket. *Maybe it's a family member,* she thought. *Or maybe he's hurt.*

She stopped again when she heard the voice speaking from the room next to her—the cremation room. She looked through the glass on the top half of the door and saw the incinerator had a disposable casket labeled "Human Remains" on top of its metal conveyance rollers.

"Please," the man's voice cried out again.

Nicole couldn't see who was speaking, but the sorrow embedded in his words reverberated down her spine as though they had been whispered directly onto her skin. *"Please just let me out."*

The empty seconds between wails stacked on top of one another like an eager horde of beasts, clawing at her chest and impaling her with dread.

Then, as a tremor surged through her lower back, the reality struck. She slowly raised her hand and covered her mouth to stifle a scream.

The voice is coming from inside the box.

She pushed her way through the door and ran to the back of the rollers, her limbs springing to action and doing their work before her brain could even comprehend what was happening. She could feel the heat beginning to radiate off the incinerator, contrasting with the cold chills playing chutes and ladders on her back like a campfire in December.

He's been mistaken for dead—I have to help him! She had heard about things like this. *But how did it happen in the modern era? How could someone be cremated alive?*

She frantically grabbed at the top of the box and tried to pull it open. No such luck.

A second later, she noticed why her efforts were fruitless: the box was wrapped tightly with several loops of clear tape. She pushed against the inside lip of the lid, harder this time, hoping she could get enough leverage to get one or two strands of tape loose and grab the bottom of the lid. She set her feet and pushed up with everything she had, lifting

23

the end of the box off the roller a few inches before drop-ping it back down with a *clang*.

It didn't work.

"No, please, I told you! I'll do anything you want, just let me out!"

"I'M TRYING TO GET YOU OUT. STAY CALM!" Nicole yelled.

Then she noticed that on top of the box there were what seemed like credit cards, and next to them a bus ticket with that day's date. Destination: *Hartford, Connecticut*. She took her keys out of her pocket and began cutting the tape with one hand, holding up her phone to dial 911 with the other. She had only entered two numbers when the man in the box cried out again, startling her and making her drop her phone.

"Just let me go... PLEASE!" the man begged. "My name is Morgan Sandberg. I don't want to die."

"My name is Nicole. I'm a nurse and I'm going to try to get you out. Just keep breathing." She sawed at the tape again, this time making it through one of the strands successfully.

Suddenly, Nicole realized she had heard wrong.

He wasn't saying, *"Let me out,"* like he was trapped. He was saying, *"Let me go"*—like he was...

Nicole never saw the man standing next to the door, and never heard him walk up behind her as she struggled with the tape.

Just as she had realized what the man was saying, she was struck in the back of the head with a metal object and fell to the floor, her foot kicking her phone across the room as she fell. As she drifted out of consciousness, she heard the screams getting louder and felt the heat of the incinerator getting hotter on her skin.

A metal pole dropped out of a man's hand and fell on the floor as he watched Nicole's lights fade out. He closed his eyes and drew in a deep breath.

"One for the Father," he said, pushing the box into the incinerator.

He took a second deep breath. "One for the son," he said, and walked to the control box on the side of the machine.

"And one for your ghost, Mother," he said as he opened his eyes and pressed the red button on the control panel. As he looked down at the floor, the door closed and locked with a grinding metallic clash.

Orange light poured out of the incinerator window as Adrian knelt and brushed the hair out of Nicole's eyes.

"And what am I supposed to do with you, sis?"

CHAPTER II:
THE RECEIVING VAULT

Nicole opened her eyes—at least, she thought she did. She blinked, trying to figure out her surroundings, and when she saw only darkness, her chest tightened. It wasn't her eyes deceiving her. She was in the dark.

She tried to stand up and figure out where she was, but found her hands were bound by some type of hard leather that gripped tightly around each of her wrists and was weighed down by something heavy. Her heart raced and her muscles tensed as she raised her arms in front of her. The motion was accompanied by the sound of clinking metal, which told her she was also in chains.

She screamed, realizing she had been kidnapped by the same person who likely killed the man in the box. And who would probably be back to finish her off next.

"LET ME OUT OF HERE!" Nicole screamed as she stood up.

She took her left hand and felt the restraint on her right. It was a wrist cuff with metal loops. *Definitely leather.* She scratched at the sides and tried to dig her nails underneath the edges. When she couldn't, she tried the other side with the same result.

She shook her arms violently and tugged at her chains with all her strength. The chains rattled against the walls and her wrists began to ache from the vibrations, but nothing was budging.

She followed the chains to their beginning and felt that they were attached to larger metal loops set into the wall—eye hooks, she thought they were called. After trying to dig at the sides and finding them set in concrete, her face became hot with rage. She beat her fists against the wall and tried running as fast as she could to break the chains, but was immediately yanked backwards forcefully by the chains after a pace and a half.

As the energy left her body, tears began rolling down her cheeks, and she began speaking to the darkness. "Please just let me out," she said softly.

But she was met only with the cool feeling of the dirt as she lay down, defeated.

After a few hopeless minutes had passed, Nicole felt around on the floor, scratching at the dirt and trying to imagine where she was. The dirt felt hard, as if it had been packed down.

Maybe a basement? She stood up and walked to her right side, feeling around on the walls, this time being careful of the chains.

On her left side, her hands came across something that wasn't soil. She held her breath as the feeling of smooth woodgrain swept beneath her fingers, separated from the soil by a thin, straight crack.

A door!

Her chains kept her from fully turning to her left, but after pulling them to their max, she quickly found the handle and twisted it. *Locked.*

She felt the end of the knob, her heart dropping at the absence of a sweet little metal tab. *From the outside.*

She slammed her fist against the door and heard an echo on the other side dissipating upward as the idea that she was somewhere in the middle of nowhere sank itself into her brain. *Where else do they have doors made to keep people IN?*

She reached past the door, and after finding the corner of the room, began inching her hands forward. She came across another hard object she guessed was three or four feet away from the wall. She could barely feel it with the tips of her fingers, but the smoothness told her it was made of stone. She couldn't reach the top of it, so she wasn't sure exactly how tall it was, only that it was taller than her.

She got down on the ground and reached out her leg, finding she had a little more reach this way, and put her foot directly on its surface. It was cold, and felt polished, like it was marble or some other millionaire's delight.

She reached her foot out again, trying to explore the edge, and was able to reach it around to the object's front. She moved her foot up and felt another layer of stone, and after that, another opening. *Not a door,* she thought. *Some sort of... shelf?*

She tried reaching straight out from her starting point and found nothing but empty space, kicking the air as if in a wild imaginary soccer game. She pulled back and moved against the wall to give her wrist restraints a rest.

Knowing what furniture was in the room didn't do her any good. She was trapped.

As the thought began to suffocate her ability to think clearly, she became aware of a dull buzzing sound coming from somewhere above her. She listened closely—it seemed to get slightly louder, then quieter again, as if whatever was making the sound was moving. She kept listening as it got steadily closer.

"I'M DOWN HERE!" she yelled, hoping whatever was making that sound was attached to a human being. Then, as it occurred to her, she screamed, "I'M UNDERGROUND! I'M DOWN HERE, IN... IN THE BASEMENT! Help me, PLEASE!"

Nothing.

"HELLLLP MEEEEE!" she screamed with the last of her breath. She tugged at the chains with a halfhearted effort and sat back down when it became clear it was a fool's errand.

She wiped the tears from her eyes and crossed her arms. Not only was she trapped in some maniac's basement, and probably going to die soon, she was also getting cold. She listened to the buzzing as it slowly faded away to almost nothing, then rolled onto her side and closed her eyes.

She thought about David—how happy she had been to finally see him after all these years and have it NOT be a total train wreck. She wished so badly she could go back to

30

that talk and say, "No, I don't have any plans tonight."

Maybe if she had waited one more day, she would be sitting on that awful and beautiful couch right now, listening to that country voice over the phone, or better yet, in person. "But yer' not," she hears David say in her head. "Yer' gunna be flame-broiled like a raccoon burger."

While Nicole replayed the conversation in her mind, the buzzing started up again. She paid it little attention at first, but soon it became louder than it had before, passing above her head in the opposite direction of the door she had found. She opened her eyes and got to her feet. "Hello-o, can you hear me up there?"

The next sound she heard was different—not a buzz, but more of a muffled scrape.

"Hey! I'm down here! Help me, PLEASE!" she cried out.

No answer came, and the minute of quiet that followed convinced her that whoever had been the source of the noise had left. She balled up her fists and was about to sit again when footsteps began echoing through the room.

The hair stood up on her arms as the whining objections of stair boards grew steadily louder.

There's another door up there, and those aren't the hurried steps of someone coming to help. They're the steps of someone who's been here before.

2

The footsteps stopped at the bottom of the stairs.

Nicole backed herself as close to the wall as she could. "Oh God, please," she whispered as the sound of a latch clicked. She heard the hinges of the door creak open, accompanied by a dim light cast down from the top of the stairs. She was able to quickly make out the silhouette of a man before the door closed, returning the room to darkness.

"Please," Nicole called out. "Please, I don't know what you want, but I won't tell anybody what I saw, I SWEAR."

She still couldn't see, but she could hear the man moving around, his feet crushing the dirt beneath his boots with each menacing step. She whimpered and raised her hands up in what she felt would inevitably be a futile defensive pose. She knew she'd seen too much, and that the killer never believed that line.

"I guess you never outgrew messing things up for me."

Nicole heard the words as a kerosene lamp flickered to life, illuminating the room with a sick yellow tint.

It wasn't a maniac with a gun or a knife—it was worse.

It was her *brother?*

He stood over what she could now see was a small wooden table in the center of the room. It was what must have been only inches outside her foot's reach before. The table was set with two wooden chairs, and in the corner behind him stood another object covered in a dusty white cloth. Her eyes found his and she stared at him in shock.

"A... Adrian?" she said. "But... I don't understand. Why are..."

"Don't," Adrian interjected, putting up his hand to indicate he wanted silence. "Don't ask me STUPID questions, Nicole... Schaffer is it now?" he said, then produced Nicole's driver's license from his pocket. "Things were so bad here you had to move away, and leave the Emerson name behind too?"

"Adrian please I don't know what you want from..."

"I don't have answers you're going to like," Adrian interjected while tossing the license onto the table, "so just shut up and watch."

Nicole wanted to reply, but his eyes had something in them she didn't remember from her kid brother, who used to ride his bike up and down the street and call her "Sickole" when he was mad.

She ducked his piercing gaze and recognized the stone feature she'd touched before. It *was* shelves—the kind made to store bodies.

She had seen places like this before. Catacombs, she was sure they were called, but the ones she was looking at were filled with what looked like jars, not corpses. She counted eleven poorly crafted jars, like things a child might have made at school to give to their faux-enthusiastic parents.

Adrian saw where she was looking, "They don't look special, but it's what's inside that counts," he said as he reached down below the table and grabbed what appeared to be a plain white paper bag.

"You just had to come home, after all these years. For what? To clear your conscience? Can't you see that's just as selfish as abandoning us in the first place?"

Nicole took a deep breath and let it out slowly, trying to sort out the storm of guilt and fear fighting each other inside her chest. She knew her brother hadn't taken her leaving well all those years ago, but what was she supposed to do? He was too young to go to Arkansas with her, and their father would have never agreed to let him go anyway. *Did he go crazy after I left? Did I do this to him?*

"Yes, that's it," he said, stroking the side of the white bag. "That's the look of ignorance I remember.

"And now," he said, "you've seen a bit too much."

He stepped out from the side of the table.

"Adrian, PLEASE." She didn't know what kind of hell he had gone through being the only one left for their father to take out his anger on, but in that moment, she knew it was enough to drive a person mad. Enough to make a person kill.

He took another step in her direction, then stopped.

"Do you remember…" he said as he grabbed a jar from the stone shelf. He stared at it momentarily, running his fingers along the edges and closing his eyes. "… when Mother died?"

Nicole felt sick to her stomach. Of course she did. How could she forget?

Their mother and Adrian had gotten into an argument—something about his grades and how he needed to "spend less time on his bike and more time on his homework." Adrian had lost control, and their mother had ended up at the bottom of their porch steps with a shattered collarbone. She was prescribed Percocet for the pain, and two weeks later, the pills were identified as the cause of death in her suicide.

"Yeah, I thought so," he said as the disgust washed over her face. "So you must remember who killed her, Nicole."

"Adrian, no, it wasn't your fault. You *know* that—you were just a kid, and she was the one..."

"NO!" Adrian yelled as he slammed the jar on the table. He removed the lid. "No. It wasn't *her* fault. It was *my* choices that cleared that path."

Adrian opened the white bag and began pouring out the contents onto the table. Nicole watched, horrified, as what could only be ashes flowed down like sand.

She realized that the things on the shelves weren't jars, but urns.

She heard something bounce off the table with a *tink*. It landed on the ground near her feet. She turned her head and vomited as its substance wrote its name inside her mind in bold, gruesome letters: *BONE FRAGMENTS.*

"Yes, it IS disgusting. VILE, even!" Adrian said with a laugh. He replaced the lid on the urn. "Who would have thought that the boy who killed his mommy could grow up to be so fucked-up?"

He laughed again as the ashes and bones continued falling like burnt snowflakes. "But that doesn't matter, does it, Nicole? The only thing that matters is *you!*"

Nicole's hands had gone numb from lack of blood flowing through her tensed muscles. She thought about the nights she'd spent wishing she could have brought him with her—to *save* him. Didn't he know she would have stayed if she could have? That she wouldn't have sacrificed everything if she'd thought it would have made a difference? Their father had hated that she was so independent, and if anything, he'd blamed *her* the most for not being a better role model for Adrian.

"I... I didn't... know..."

"You didn't know." Adrian cut her off. "And you clearly didn't care."

They both watched as the ashfall finally came to an end. "But you're not the only one. See, this man didn't care, either," he said, looking at the pile of ash and bone.

"His name was Morgan. He was a homeless drug addict begging for a second chance at life. *Begging* for it. And do you know what he did when he got it? When we gave him the opportunity to rise from his despair and make something of himself? He threw it all away for a quick fix! We don't all get the luxury of second chances—our mother is proof of that—and he certainly wasn't going to get THREE! No, he was given everything, and STILL chose the path of sin. Don't you see? He needed to be cleansed," he said, moving his hand and motioning for her to look at the rest of the urns. "They ALL needed to be cleansed to save them from temptation."

Nicole closed her eyes and dropped her head. *Who are THEY? Second chances?*

She thought again about her little brother, the one she used to call a doofus and punch in the arm when he tattled on her and David. She thought too about her poor mother— how she must have felt in those final days of pain, and what had gone through her mind in that final moment of clarity.

She heard Adrian walking towards to her, then his jeans rubbed against her leg as he knelt and lifted her head with his hands. "I ... don't understand," she said as she opened her eyes. The light was behind him, but she swore she could see its reflection in his eyes.

"My, oh my," Adrian replied with pity. He wiped a tear from her face. "You sure did grow up to be a stupid bitch."

Adrian stood up and walked back to the table without speaking. He folded the bag, placed it in his back pocket, and swept the last of the ashes off the table. He left, turning out the light as he went, the last specks of ash dancing in the sickly yellow rays, then disappearing in a flicker.

Nicole screamed and begged him to come back, promising to try harder to understand, but it was no use. The door latch clicked behind him.

He was gone.

Nicole wrestled with her restraints again, this time with full acceptance of the futility of trying. She slowly inhaled the cold, wet air, trying to focus on something, anything, other than the sight of those urns, and the glow she'd seen in Adrian's eyes.

The silence brought her reminders of the man in the box.

"Please just let me go," she could hear him say. *"Let me go."*

The minutes passed like days, and the hours like eternities. At one point, she thought she heard an engine firing up, but that too passed. She felt tired, and restless, but every time she closed her eyes, though it made little difference, she could see the glow.

Adrian returned that night with another bag in his hand. He didn't say a word, just turned on the light and sat at the table. Nicole braced herself as his hands entered the top and rifled through the contents. *Bone fragments* crossed her mind

37

again as he revealed what was inside: french fries. He pulled out two more items covered in tinfoil that turned out to be hamburgers. He went back to the top of the stairs momentarily and brought down a Styrofoam cup filled with soda and a bottle of water.

"I know you're probably not all that hungry right now," he said while placing the items at her feet, "but you will be."

3

On March 26, 1953, Dr. Jonas Salk changed the world when he announced that he had successfully tested a vaccine to treat Poliomyelitis, the Polio virus. A year before his words were broadcasted on national radio stations, cases had been at an all-time high, and reported deaths were in the thousands. These numbers prompted Lieutenant Governor Joseph B. Johnson to come up with a plan not only to keep the public safe, but to prepare to store corpses, were the pandemic to continue on its deadly warpath. His solution was simple: expand on the size of cemetery-receiving vaults.

Project grants had been provided to local towns, and, while some of the more densely populated areas were able to accomplish lavish masterpieces of ground-level stonework and iron, smaller towns like White River Junction had been forced to dig deeper in the earth and build less-than-impressive storage rooms for the dead. Short of a year later, the radio waves echoing Salk's message had once again rendered the spare rooms obsolete—we had beaten polio. In the following decade, many of the additional vaults had either been filled in or boarded off to the public, ceasing to exist except in town records and campfire tales.

David Demick briefly admired the architecture of the receiving vault in White River as he drove by the cemetery on his way to work, seeing Adrian Emerson at the far end, cutting the grass as he passed. *Creep,* he thought as he took a sip of his coffee and continued to the Hartford Police Station.

He checked his phone before putting on his uniform. He was used to seeing the "no new messages" readout, but part of him was disappointed he'd never heard from Nicole the night before. *"Is comedy your side gig?"* he heard her say in his head, making him smile as he buttoned up his shirt.

He suspected the meetup with her father had been as hard as imagined, but he thought Scott had lightened up over the years, and she was, at that moment, more than likely listening to him tell terrible jokes over eggs and bacon. He wished he would have gotten her number and not just given his contact card, but he knew she would call him when she was ready, so he erased the thought and put his phone in his pocket.

"You thought I was mad, what about the chicken who laid these eggs?" David impersonated Scott again as he buckled his tactical belt and started his shift. *"And don't get me started on the bacon!"*

Over the next few days, David became increasingly disappointed when he didn't hear from Nicole. He was concerned he had been too breezy in their conversation, and that maybe she'd gotten the sense that he could swing either way on continuing their reunion efforts. He had driven past the Shady Acre at least two dozen times between his transit and patrols, secretly hoping to run into her again. *Stupid stupid stupid.*

On the Sunday after their interaction, David once again read the "no new messages" readout on his way into the Petro Mart to get his caffeine fix for the day. He was half thinking about Nicole and half thinking of the million things he had to accomplish on his day off when he saw her father Scott chatting up the clerk.

"… you're not stupid, I didn't mean that, I just don't think anyone here really knows how to make a breakfast sandwich, that's all," David heard Scott say. It wasn't his normal chipper attitude, but David walked up behind him in line and waited for him to finish cashing out.

"Rick Flair says the sausage, egg, and cheese at Cumberland Farms is good enough to wrestle over," David said. He had kept his distance from Scott over the years, never quite being able to let go of the things that happened when he was a teenager, but White River was a small town, and keepers of the peace generally had to be peaceful.

Scott turned around, and after recognizing the owner of the voice, decided his rant was over and grabbed his tinfoil-wrapped trigger from the counter.

"Hey, David, I thought that was you," he said as he stepped out. "... yeah, Rick Flair, I would have thought those crocodile shoes would make him live forever!"

He laughed out loud, then added, "So how's the crime rate today?"

"Well, if *they* ever figure out how to make sandwiches, I'm sure it will go wayyy down," David replied. He nodded in the direction of the heated breakfast cabinet and thought he could go for one about now. *How bad can you mess up English muffins and eggs?*

"How are things down at the ash factory?"

"Well, if they ever DO lower the crime rate, I'm sure I'll be out of business too," Scott replied with a nod towards the door. David turned and saw his nod's intended recipient was the cruiser parked outside.

"We do what we can, but hey, now that I see you, I wanted to ask you something," David replied, confident the saturation of matching jokes was enough to lubricate the conversation. He put a pair of one-dollar bills on the counter for his coffee and mouthed the words "thank you" to the cashier.

"I'll walk you out," he said, then opened the door and invited Scott into the parking lot.

David thought about what he wanted to say to Scott as he walked out the door, not sure exactly how to tackle the father-daughter-friend-cop-citizen conversation, and deciding to just be straight, to talk like men.

"I know Nicole came back the other night and went up to see you, I know that probably wasn't easy, and hey, I'm not involving myself in that at all." He put his hands in the air to show he wasn't there to play judge. "I just wanted to know if she went back to Arkansas yet."

"Nicole... was *here?*" Scott asked, clearly confused. "What do you mean? She came up to see *me?* What are you talking about?"

"Oh," David replied, unsure which question to address first. "I thought..."

Why would she lie about seeing her father?

"She said she was going to, uh..." he thought for a second. "Thursday, I saw her on Thursday."

"She never came to see *me,*" Scott replied, this time with a hint of anger. "Did she say *why?*"

For a moment, Scott searched David's face for answers, then opened his eyes wide with understanding. "Oh... her birthday."

"Yeah, next week, she told me," David added. He felt awkward having jumped directly into such a heavy subject unknowingly. "The big three-oh."

"Jesus, that's right. Did she give you her number? Can you call her?"

"She didn't, but she said she was going to see you, so I'm sure she just wants to make sure the timing is right, you know? It's gotta be tough for her coming back here after all this time. I only happened to see her by accident, really, so I didn't have time to ask her for her number."

"Shit. Did she say where she was staying?"

"No," David lied. If Nicole really wasn't ready to see him, David didn't want to make that choice harder for her. "I saw Adrian out cutting the grass at the cemetery, though. Maybe she went to see him first?"

"No, no, he woulda told me if she was here. He didn't take her leaving half as well as I did, if that tells ya anything."

David tilted his head to the side and nodded. It was common knowledge that the Emerson clan weren't the type to take change without a fight.

"Well, thanks for letting me know, David. If you DO see her, and she's ready, she can swing by the house or the parlor any time." Scott took one more glance at David, sizing him up, before getting in his car. "I gotta go. Who knows, she could be there now!"

David watched as Scott drove away. Part of him felt bad for Scott, losing his wife and essentially his daughter too, but part of him knew that underneath the jokes and suits, there was a man who just plain didn't like him, and the selfish part of him hoped Nicole had thought better of herself and driven back to Arkansas.

4

David spent the rest of the morning and most of the afternoon patching up holes in the fence that separated his little patch of grass from his neighbors. As he swung his hammer, he thought about the sweet summer kisses he and Nicole used to share, and how they'd seemed to make time freeze in its tracks.

Seeing her again after all that time had awoken a part of him that he thought he had outgrown, one soaked in the drool of puppy love and the fragility of adolescent romance. He wondered if she ever thought about those embraces while she was gone, if they'd had any lasting impact on the way she thought about life and love, or if they'd gotten swept up in the madness with everything else and been lost somewhere in the shadow of guilt cast by her sudden departure.

He liked to think she did think about him, and that the idea of truly connecting to another person was placed way up high on a shelf where only worthy men could reach, and that she hadn't compromised away the things that made her beautiful and unique.

David remembered, too, the last conversation he'd had with Nicole's mother Kate, way back when his arms and legs had seemed unnaturally long for his body.

It was around eleven-thirty on a school night, and he was climbing out of Nicole's window, feeling like a modern-day Romeo, when he saw the flash of a cigarette lighter under the porch cover. He froze at first—he didn't know anybody smoked in the house, and he'd been sure everyone was sleeping when he first crept up to the mailbox and saw only Nicole's bedroom light glowing.

A billow of smoke rose out from the porch as David began moving away from the edge, hoping to wait out whoever was under him. *I hope it's not Scott, or I'm toast.* A second billow of smoke rose, along with the sound of steps. David closed his eyes and gripped the edge of the shingles beneath him, listening for the sound of a shotgun loading and praying for the sound of the door opening and shutting.

Instead, he heard a voice. "Well, David, are you coming down or what?"

David opened his eyes and saw that Mrs. Emerson had walked off the porch and was now looking directly at him, cigarette in hand. "You can't sleep up there, so you might as well come down before Scott wakes up."

"Ye-yes ma'am," David replied as he slowly crawled to the edge of the porch and jumped down. "I'm sorry. I didn't know anyone was awake. We didn't do anything, I swear. We were just..."

"David, David, David," Kate said as she took another drag off her cigarette. "You don't need to lie to me—I know exactly what you were doing."

David blushed. He was sure there was no way she could know they were kissing and talking about what would happen if they got rich and bought an island to live on with a house full of dogs.

"I'm going to have to tell him," Kate said, to David's dismay.

"So, climbing up our house like some sort of burglar isn't going to happen anymore, but," she said, stopping to flick her cigarette, "before you leave and try to figure out the next way to play Prince Charming, I want to show you something."

She reached inside the pocket of her oversized jacket and pulled out a picture. It was Nicole and Adrian when they were just little kids.

"Is this her?" David asked as he took the picture and studied it. Nicole had a giant smile on her face, and her hands, along with Adrian's face, were covered in what looked like birthday cake. They looked like they were having the time of their lives—like they were happy.

"Yes," Kate replied. "It's certainly not a picture from *my* childhood. It would have to be in black and white."

David smiled. It felt weird that not only was she NOT mad at him, but she was apparently in a joking mood. He looked down at the cake disaster again. "Why are you showing me this?"

"I know boys your age think they know what they want, and what women want, too," she said as she put out her cigarette, "but you never consider what others *need*."

"I don't think I know any of that," David said, feeling slightly offended by the implication that he was unable to think things through.

"DO you know what young women need, David? Do you know the one thing that truly evades them, the thing that could make them feel safe, and loved, and capable of making it in this crazy world?"

David's face got red as he lowered his head and averted her gaze. He didn't know the answer, and he was sure it probably wasn't a private island with a house full of dogs. "No," he said finally.

"Friends," Kate said as she got to her feet and walked close to David, stopping just a few feet away from him. She reached out to touch his shoulder.

"She has friends," David replied. "Danni, and Anna, and…"

"REAL friends. The kind that will choose her future over their own without question, every time. The loyal kind that will make her feel safe, and secure, and always have her back, no matter what. Now, I know you consider yourself her friend, David, and I do appreciate how sweet you are to her, but I just don't think you understand that what she needs right now isn't some boy climbing the side of her house and convincing her that all she needs is love to make it in this world. That's wrong, and selfish. What she needs is someone who she can cry with when she's upset, but who won't take away the lessons in those tears by trying to be her hero. I know how hard all that must sound, David, but if there's anyone who could find the strength inside themselves to be that friend, it's you."

David thought about those words now, and how powerful they had been to the teenager who received them. Of course, he'd wanted to be that friend, but he'd also wanted to protect her, to keep her from having to learn those lessons in the first place. He had heard Nicole got a stern talking-to after the porch incident and was grounded for two months. He thought about Kate's words every time he saw Nicole after that, always feeling torn between his wants and her needs. *Does she need me to help make all this coming-home stuff easier? Or is that what I want?*

He swung his hammer and hit the last nail on the head, then wiped the sweat from his forehead and stood up. He was glad Nicole was strong enough to make it in Arkansas alone, and, regardless of a want or a need, something was bothering him about her return to White River.

She'd seemed like she was in a good place when they spoke, and that she was confident she was going to get things sorted out with her father. So why hadn't she? David thought about the calls he'd been on to the Shady Acre in the past few months—from the occasional noise complaint to drug dealing to assault—and decided he wanted to swing by and check in on her. To trust his cop instincts and be a good friend.

Before leaving, David walked into his basement and opened an old plastic tote he had stuffed away under boxes of Christmas lights. The words, *"I see you got your dream job,"* had reminded him of a gift Nicole had given him the Christmas before her mother passed.

The tote was mostly full of toys and gadgets he'd had when he was a kid, a Bop-It that somehow still had battery life, and a set of walkie-talkies that had made their debut as kid detective essentials, but mixed in with those was a metal badge made to look like the sheriff's badges of the Wild West. Inscribed on the front was "Detective Demik." When the manufacturers had refused to replace it due to the mis-spelled name on the front, Nicole decided to give it to David anyway to *remind him of his future.*

He polished the front with his shirt and ran his fingers across the inscription before putting it in his pocket and closing the tote. He knew it would get a laugh if he got the opportunity to show it to her, to thank her for that reminder, and maybe even remind HER of the good times they'd shared before life had come along and done what it did.

David got into his car, and on the way to the motel, opened his glove box and saw that his father's revolver was still there. A saying coined by some of the local high school kids in town popped into his mind: *A beer to take 'er at the Shady Acre.*

He pulled up to the motel and got out in the parking lot. There were empty beer cans on the ground, oil spots in over a dozen spaces, and an annoyed-looking teenager staring at him from behind a rusty table outside one of the rooms. He gestured a two-finger wave at the boy, who couldn't be older than seventeen, and walked inside the front entrance when, as expected, he didn't receive the same in return.

The woman behind the counter was watching TV. *One of those shows that examines human behavior in extreme conditions,* he guessed as a character made their way through swampy terrain. The woman didn't acknowledge his entrance aside from a simple, "Help you?"

She spoke, but didn't turn immediately—a man had appeared on the screen and was explaining the animal trap he built while ignoring the fact that his genitalia were out, censored, to the woman's obvious amusement.

"Hello, Mrs. Carter," David said. He had been in that room at least a dozen times while in uniform, most of them ending with verbal standoffs regarding cooperation and willful ignorance.

The woman behind the desk turned and looked at David over the top of her glasses. She rolled her eyes and let out a small sigh. "Who called you? Was it Lenny? Cause he's just an old fool. You know that, D."

"Actually, I got a call that there was a noise complaint. It was a woman, says she just got into town a few days ago, and her neighbor's been keeping her awake at night threatening to kill someone. Said she hasn't seen anything suspicious, but wanted someone to check in. She said her name was Nicole."

"Emerson," the woman said. She had been thumbing through her records as David spoke, knowing from experience he wasn't going away without some form of an answer. "Nicole Emerson, room 47. Checked in on Thursday."

She turned her head toward the TV again as the sound of intense music began to play, signifying the naked man must be about to face some sort of challenge.

"Thank you, Bev." David began to walk towards the door. *Well, that was simple.*

He'd made it to the door and taken a step out when, from behind him, he heard, "Why aren't you in uniform? I thought you guys had to be in uniform for these things. You undercover or something? Everyone knows you, David. That's never going to work."

Shit, he thought to himself as he turned. "Headed out of town, actually. Prostitution ring up north and I signed up to help. Just taking this last call and I'll be off to Scary-Barre."

She laughed at that, so David thought it had worked. He thanked her again and walked outside. On his way to room 47, he realized that "signing up to go undercover for a

50

prostitution ring" sounded a bit creepy, but it didn't matter—
he'd gotten what he needed, and Mrs. Carter had done some
pretty creepy stuff herself, including allowing criminals to
rent rooms off the books if they paid enough.

David got to the door and took a breath. He'd thought
about what he was going to say on the ride over, but forgot
entirely now, unable to shake the mental image of the naked
man squatting down to set his trap.

He knocked on the door and waited. Nothing. He
knocked again, and a third time. Still no answer. He decided
she must be in town and was about to leave when the next
door opened and three people walked out. It was the town
junkies, Jamie and Cooper, and their guest, Pastor Robinson.

"... So please call me anytime. I know you have the
strength to walk the path of good, and I'm here if you need
help taking the next step," Felix said to the couple as they
looked at David with the same enthusiasm Mrs. Carter had.

"What the hell are you doing here?" Cooper asked with
an angry downturn of his greying eyebrows.

"Now, Cooper, this is what I'm talking about. I'm sure
Officer Demick has a perfectly legitimate reason to be here,
and you haven't done anything wrong, have you?"

"Actually, I came to speak with your neighbor," David interrupted. He thought about including the bit he'd said to Mrs.
Carter about the noise complaint, but decided there was probably some actual truth to that, and didn't. "Have you seen her?"

Jamie spoke up. "No, she's gone. I saw her a few nights
ago when she first got here, but that's it. She didn't kill herself in there, did she? HOLY SHIT!"

51

"No, no, nothing like that," David replied. "Just a follow-up, nothing serious."

For a moment, he thought about the possibility, but quickly erased it on the belief that Nicole wouldn't have driven all the way here just to end her own life in a dingy bathroom at the Shady Acre.

"Well, we haven't seen her for a few days, like I said. Haven't heard her in there either. That's her car right there, though," the woman added. "The black one."

She pointed to a little black Honda Civic. "She was parked in front of the door when she first came. I don't know when she moved it there, but it's been sitting in that spot for a few days." She motioned to Cooper to go back inside and leave David to his business, then thanked Felix again before pulling the door shut, squeezing in one last curious glance at Nicole's motel room door as it closed. David suspected that her helpful words were more of an act put on for their guest, but that thought fell short of the question on his mind: *Where DID she go?*

"I'll walk with you," Felix said to David as they left the couple's doorstep and moved toward the parking lot.

"Do you think they're telling the truth?" David asked as they walked up to the little black car. He knew they didn't really have any perceivable reason to lie, but David had learned over the years that there was always something criminals could gain from someone else's misfortune.

"Yes, I do," Felix replied firmly.

"I see you're not really here on official police business, though," he said, eying David's casual clothing. "So can I ask what's really going on, son?"

David decided to forgo telling the pastor his lie about being an upcoming star in "who can arrest the most perverts" and instead told him about his run-in with Nicole. He shared the suspicion raised by her lack of calling, and how she had never followed through with her plans to see Scott.

"... So, I really don't know what to make of this, but something isn't right. She wouldn't just take off back to Arkansas and leave her car behind. She would have called me and told me that, I *know it.*"

"That is troubling," Felix replied. "And you're sure Scott was telling you the truth? You're sure he wasn't leaving something out, or that he would even tell you if he had seen her?"

"Yeah, he was telling the truth. I could see it on his face, he was surprised, and a little angry that I saw her first, I think."

"I don't believe the ability to hide anger is a trait that exists in the Emerson family tree," Felix replied.

"You're right about that." David thought about Scott and how good he'd gotten at covering up his rage with jokes and small talk.

"And what about Adrian? I know he's not generally an open book, but maybe she decided to start small and see her little brother before walking into the hornet's nest?"

"I haven't spoken to him yet, but Scott doesn't think so. Maybe I should go there next," David said, shielding his eyes to investigate Nicole's car. It appeared to be clean, aside from the ashtray and remnants of road snacks. He thought about his run-in with Nicole at Petro and how he might have asked about the pack of Camels she'd had in her hand if he'd had more time.

He noticed that all the carpets were spotless, as if they had been vacuumed recently. *Why would you vacuum the carpets and leave Doritos crumbs on the seat?*

David then saw little white spots on the dashboard. *Cigarette ashes.* He saw that they specked the entire dashboard except the area on top of the steering wheel. He rubbed the window with his sleeve to clean it off and looked closer, seeing that the ashes were also missing from the shifting lever and the turn signal.

His mind began to race as he thought about Nicole, and how half-ass cleaning your car seemed like an unlikely activity for someone to engage in shortly after returning home after fourteen years.

Someone else drove this car and wiped it for prints.

"I have to go," David said hurriedly. He couldn't be sure it wasn't just a bout of paranoia, but his gut was telling him something was off about all this and that Nicole may be in real danger. He jumped back in his car and exited the parking lot, leaving Felix with a brief, perfunctory hand wave.

Felix returned the wave, then took his own turn looking inside the little black car. When he couldn't see what had made David's demeanor change so rapidly, he got into his own vehicle, pausing after the engine came to life.

He thought about the night he'd spent in the hotel room just a few yards from where he was parked, about how far he had come since waking up that morning with his life—and David's life, for that matter—changed forever. He wished he could have had someone to pull him out of the struggle before it got so bad.

He put his hands together and prayed Nicole would be found, possibly enjoying the latest additions to the thriving small-business district across the bridge on main street. He then prayed for David, that he would find the answers he was looking for.

As he pulled out of the Shady Acre, he thought about the other man who'd accompanied him in the hotel room that night.

Not yet, he thought. *Not yet.*

CHAPTER III:
A SHARD OF HOPE

While David spent his time mending fences, Nicole used the solitary morning hours to continue exploring the vault—an exercise that had produced zero results in the previous days.

She had woken feeling nauseous, throwing up a small puddle of bile and Sprite before getting to work. She found the smooth edge of the wooden shelves with her toes, and, while her mind continuously jolted her with images of the man in the box pleading for his life, she was able to push them aside and focus on trying to save her own.

She had spent the first few days unwilling to eat or drink, unable to shake the ridiculous thought of a bony hand reaching out from the darkness to offer her breadsticks, like some sort of grim waiter. Adrian had forced her to drink water one night, which had gone down like cement and come back up the same.

As she strained her leg muscles and came up with yet another empty attempt at finding some sort of escape-worthy leverage, she began to question why he would even bother—why hadn't he just gotten it over with and killed her already?

She asked herself this over and over until Adrian arrived on Saturday afternoon, this time without any bags, bottles, or cups.

The door creaked open, then closed again, and the light came on, just as it had every day before. Adrian sat at the table and said nothing, just closed his eyes and covered his face with his palms.

Then he began talking in whispered sentences to himself. Nicole breathed heavily as the thought of her own demise crept inside her head and told her *this must be what he does right before...*

"What am I going to do with you, Nicole?" Adrian asked after a long pause. He slid his hands down to reveal his eyes were now open and fixed on her. "I don't think Mother would be pleased if I killed you."

"I... you could..."

"Let you go, right?" Adrian interrupted as he got to his feet and looked down at her, his hip hitting the table with enough force to move it off the ground with a *THUD*. "Let you go, and you'll never tell anyone about this, and you'll go back to Arkansas, and everything will be just fan-fucking-tastic. Is that what I *could* do?"

Nicole wanted to say yes, to agree with everything and make any promise she could to get free, but the anger in Adrian's voice assured her that he would never make that mistake.

What happened to my little brother? she thought as his shadow loomed over her. Adrian had not only grown taller in her absence, but much darker to boot. *Did Mother's death catch up and turn him into a psycho, or was my leaving the straw that did it?*

She looked away. Either answer was painful, and she would never be able to keep his secret. She briefly imagined trying to live with the knowledge of what she'd seen at the crematorium, the guilt surrendering to the fear for her life, and she couldn't.

She envisioned also the police arresting him if she somehow made it out and came forward—a thought that was met with the reality of what would happen to her if Adrian caught wind, emptied this place of evidence, and walked away, free to hunt.

"You know as well as I do that's just a bunch of bullshit. You'd call your old boyfriend the second you walked out of here."

"He's not my..." Nicole started, but didn't finish, understanding he meant only to affirm her connection to law enforcement.

She thought about her phone. She knew she'd had it when she went into the crematorium; she remembered the light her background picture had cast on the stairwell moments before she'd been hit on the head. She thought that it must have gotten lost when she'd hit the floor, and if Adrian didn't have it, then maybe it was still there for the police to find.

If they ever figured out she was missing.

59

Adrian walked to the wooden rack and began touching the urns. His hands landed on a piece on the bottom row, which he picked up and placed on the table. Nicole noticed this one was shinier than the others, like it was made of a different material.

As he opened the lid, he closed his eyes and took a breath. "One for your ghost, Mother," he whispered before opening his eyes again and picking it up. He peered inside for a second, then dumped the contents out on the table.

Nicole watched as he used his fingers to stir the ash around, like he was playing with sand or silly putty. It seemed to calm him, and a smile crept onto his face.

"Do you know who this is? Adrian asked, then laughed out loud. "What am I saying? Of COURSE you don't!"

He laughed again and continued swirling. "His name was Ricky, and he was the very first person to sit where you're sitting now."

"Stop... please," Nicole begged. She didn't want to know anything else about this place or whom her brother had killed. The more she knew, the less she felt like a way out existed.

"Stop? I'm sorry. Am I *bothering* you, Nicole? Wouldn't want to do that! No, we can't have Nicole feeling bothered! You are my guest, after all! What do you think, Ricky, should we let her go?"

He put his ear to the urn. "What's that? YOU won't tell anybody about me either? Ricky, you're the best! Thank you for understanding. If you weren't dead, I'd shake your hand." She watched as the smile on his face widened and he began picking up the ashes and letting them fall on the table as if they were a toy, rather than the remains of a man he murdered.

"Who is he, Adrian?" Nicole asked when she couldn't stand the sight of his disgusting pastime any longer. "Who's Ricky?"

Adrian let the last of the ashes fall back to the table and swept them into a single pile. "He was a nobody," he said, using his hand to brush the ashes back into the urn.

"A drug dealer who thought that the world revolved around him, and when he almost died from an overdose, he thought maybe he could be a somebody. He asked for our help. Oh, he really had them fooled. But once the check cleared, he thought maybe being a drug dealer *was* his future after all. So he fell to temptation and used the money to start up his old business up again. Surprise, surprise! That's when I decided he needed more help than the lottery could provide—help from God himself to save his soul. He sat right there and told me he could change, but when I took his arm and gave him that final shot, I knew he would never be strong enough to withstand the power of temptation."

Nicole watched as Adrian pulled a small brown pouch out of his pocket. He unzipped the side and pulled out a small bag and a needle. "We never really change, Nicole. We say we will, and we work real hard at calling our flaws different names, but in the end, we're still the same bags of flesh with new tricks."

Adrian lit a lighter and put it to the bottom of a loaded spoon. After a few seconds, he took the needle and filled it, tapping the side and smiling. "Fortunately, some of us found a way past all that. A way to give God's children back, reborn."

She had seen this preparation acted out in countless TV shows and movies. It was heroin in the syringe. She couldn't be sure, but it fit as a substance that would make his victims unable to fight back, unable to comprehend the horror surrounding them and the sadistic play in which they'd been cast to play the leading role.

"But what about YOUR soul?" she spit out in a panic. She didn't think it would change anything, but she needed to try. "What happens to your soul after all this?"

Adrian stared at her for a moment, then let out a small chuckle as the grin on his face widened further. "Well, if you would have paid attention to Pastor Robinson back before you left us, you might remember the old saying, 'It's more blessed to give than to receive.'"

"Felix?" Nicole said, searching her mind to remember a Pastor Robinson.

"Oh, of course. You weren't around long enough to see him leave his civilian life behind, but that's your fault, isn't it? I tried to forget what happened to our mother, to forgive myself, but she was always there, reminding me of my mistakes. Felix used to tell me that didn't matter, that the best way to feel God's presence was to do his work and give until it hurt. Well, after Ricky here took advantage of the good in this town and tried stealing what we'd worked so hard to provide, well, I hurt. And just when I thought the pain was going to be the end of me, Mother came to me and gave me what I had been missing all along: her forgiveness. It opened my eyes, and I finally understood that God had an even more powerful task for me: to ensure the gift of salvation was never wasted again. You see, I forgave Ricky and gave him the gift of eternal light, and in turn, he gave it to me."

Nicole closed her eyes and felt another tear escape down her face. Her brother was gone. She thought again about his earlier words. *Mother wouldn't be pleased.*

While it was little comfort to think about the events that had triggered the unravelling of her entire family, she began to suspect it also meant that Adrian *couldn't* justify killing her the way he had the others. At least not yet.

She wanted to feel relieved at the thought, but an image of her little brother growing and molding into a disfigured, smiling monster overtook her mind and swirled around like an oversized carnival prize.

Adrian walked toward her with the needle in his hand and knelt at her side. "I saved them all. I'm just not sure how to save you," he whispered as he put the needle to her arm.

"Adrian, you don't have to do this," Nicole begged. "Please just wait. We can..." But the feeling of metal sliding through her skin stopped her mid-sentence. The drugs rushed into her system, and she knew immediately how someone could get addicted.

She felt her veins pump with excitement and her head explode with the release of endorphins. A swirl of emotions blanketed her—a mixture of euphoria, pain, happiness, and sorrow, all in one fluid form that squeezed her heart and seared her skin.

She watched as he backed away in a dizzying blur. Instead of a smile brought on by what she thought would be the thrill of absolute dominance, Adrian wore a frown.

2

Nicole thought about that initial hour of darkness as the micro-dose of heroine she had been given wore off a few hours later. Her mind had painted the walls with blood and deceived her ears with the sound of deafening lawn mowers. She remembered the look on her brother's face as she exhibited the same reaction he had elicited from the previous tenants of the vault: fear.

She was determined to escape, so she turned and kicked at the wooden shelves. Her kick was met with the strength of hardwood lumber and fastening ties. It wouldn't budge. She kicked it again, and again, with nothing but a *THUMP* with each strike.

Her face began to drip with sweat as the reality of her situation sank in again, the thought of dying in that hole driving each blow. She pleaded with the wood to break and give her an edge, to splinter, to do anything but sit there and remind her of her capture.

After a few dozen attempts, she finally stopped, her legs hitting the ground, defeated. Her face was flush from adrenaline and false ambition, and her foot numb from the barrage of fruitless blows. She rolled over and took a breath, thinking again about the man Adrian had called Ricky. He must have had the same idea, and he wound up as a psychopath's fidget toy anyway.

He CAN'T! she thought as she pulled her leg back and kicked toward the space where her brother sat with a sick grin. *HE CAN'T!*

As her foot reached the apex of her kick, it was unexpectedly met with something that hadn't been there before Adrian's manic display—*the table*. The joint where the tabletop met the leg squealed as it bent inward, giving Nicole another surge of energy. She began kicking until she heard the wood splinter, then break in two. The table then fell to the floor, followed by a shattering sound that scared Nicole at first before she realized it was Ricky's urn.

He forgot him on the table, she thought as she remembered the frown she'd seen in her drugged-up state. *He couldn't stand to see me like that, so he left, and forgot him.*

Nicole began moving her foot around on the floor until she felt the broken table leg. She stretched her foot out beyond the wood and it came across something cold and sharp.

She dragged it back towards her with her toes, having to readjust every time it got snagged in the dirt. After a minute, it was there, with her at the wall: a large shard of broken pottery.

She thought about her mother, how she used to make pottery at their home when Adrian and Nicole were kids. They'd had a kiln built right into their house so their mom had something to do while their dad was out running the funeral parlor. On rainy afternoons, she could often be found glazing vases or making clay flowers and moons.

Nicole recalled that Adrian hated having to spend time in that room, that, as he grew into his adolescent body, he avoided every attempt their mother made to spend time together there, and outwardly expressed an exaggerated teenage hatred for anything related to pottery or art.

Nicole felt the edges of the pottery shard and understood why Ricky's urn had looked different than the rest. It was actual pottery clay. *The rest*, she figured, *must be the user-friendly "air-dry" stuff*, which was used mainly by lazy art teachers to keep from having to tell students their precious elephant statue had exploded.

This one was fired in a kiln—or. . . She thought she knew better. *An oven.*

Nicole gripped the shard in her hand and began slicing at the wrist cuffs on the opposite hand. Nothing happened at first—just the sound of ceramic sliding on leather.

She fine-tuned the motion and slowed down to make sure she was hitting the same spot every time. After a few dozen passes, she put her finger to the area she was targeting and quickly began slicing again, her adrenaline pumping from the distinct feel of severed seams.

3

In downtown White River, Adrian was next in line to place his order for cheap hamburgers and Sprite. He watched with amusement as the driver of the minivan in front of him went between leaning out his window and craning his neck towards the passengers in the back seat. *How about a number three with extra diabetes?* When he finally got his own bag of nutrient-free food, he made sure there were straws in the bag, then received a tray of drinks.

"Extra ice in the Sprite, right?" he asked. After confirmation, he thanked the cashier and drove down the hill in the direction of the cemetery.

Upon arrival, he noticed that his usual parking space near the receiving vault was gone, and every other space beside the road was gone, too. *Should have known all of grandpa's friends were early birds,* he thought as he drove up the hill next to the vault and parked on the second level. He fixed his tie and prepared to be the face of Peace at Last's "world-famous graveside service," checking his hair in the mirror one final time before heading in the direction of his father.

"Jesus, Adrian, I thought you were right behind me," Scott said as he wiped the sweat from his brow. "What took you so long?"

"Relax, I stopped for a drink. This guy isn't going anywhere," Adrian said as he picked up and opened a tripod stand from the ground. He put a speaker on top and connected a small MP3 player, starting a playlist named "graveside piano."

"Why are there so many people here already?' Adrian asked. "Don't they know it doesn't start for another half hour?"

"I told Mary that," Scott replied, "but she wanted to have time to visit some of the other graves beforehand—the kids, I think—so she told everyone if they wanted to join, they could come too."

Adrian looked around at the almost two dozen faces standing in little groups around the cemetery. It wasn't unusual to have a handful of people watching as he and his father set up chairs and flowers, but this felt more like he was the star of the dead-man show, and they the mourning audience.

He was glad they hadn't showed that morning. His clothes hadn't been of the groundskeeper variety he usually donned when going in or out of the vault.

After completing setup and assuring his father that his tardiness was a "one-time thing," Adrian tapped the microphone and asked everyone to take their seats for the ceremony. He watched as two children began to cry in the back row, which would have been a saddening sight for anyone who hadn't seen the electronic devices that were taken from their hands seconds prior.

When everyone was finally seated, Adrian looked at his father, and, after receiving the nod, he slowly faded the piano music out. Though they'd had plenty of practice over the years, sometimes switching roles and having Adrian open the ceremony, Scott normally took the lead and did the talking. It was something Adrian knew his father could never get enough of.

Just as the music came to a stop, Adrian noticed a last-minute attendee walking up the hill behind everyone.

He soon realized it wasn't another family member coming to pay their last respects, but Officer David Demick Jr.

Adrian watched as David leaned against a tree behind the rows of family members. Some followed Adrian's stare and looked at David questioningly before turning back to give full attention to Scott's opening monologue.

What the fuck is he doing here? Adrian thought, then straightened up and faced his father again to retain professionalism.

"... but before I hand over the microphone to anyone wishing to speak, or to share a fond memory, I want to read a poem from Debbie Burton named 'Peddle.'" Scott opened the notebook in front of him to a page with a sticky note attached to the top. Adrian recognized it as their service book. It was filled with excerpts from the Bible, poems from various authors, and little bits of inspiring wisdom that his father had carefully curated from the internet over the years.

"'A loved one is a treasure of the heart, and losing a loved one is like losing a piece of yourself. But the love that person brought you did not leave, for the essence of the soul lingers. It cannot escape your heart, for it has been there forever. Cling to the memories and let them find their way to heal you. The love and laughter, the joy in the togetherness you shared, will make you strong. You come to realize that your time together, no matter how long, was meant to be, and you were blessed to have such a precious gift of love in your life. Keep your heart beating with the loving memories and trust in your faith to guide you through. Know that though life moves on, the beauty of love stays behind to embrace you. Your loved one has left you that to hold in your heart forever.'"

Scott thanked everyone for attending the service again and opened the floor to the crowd. As family and friends took turns speaking and placing items on the casket, he and Adrian walked towards David, who appeared to be getting as impatient as the children in the back row.

"Friend of yours?" Scott asked David when they reached the tree. He was no longer leaning on it, but had taken to kicking the roots.

"No, and sorry. I didn't know there was a service going on today. I just wanted to catch up with your son about something."

"Is it about Nicole?" Scott asked without hesitation. "Did you see her again?"

Again? Adrian thought, having been under the impression she hadn't seen anyone. *She saw him before the night she saw me? Fuck... And why is he here now? He can't have figured out what happened. There's no way!*

Adrian didn't show that that was running through his mind. "Nicole? What do you mean? She's BACK?"

"Well, actually," David started, "I thought maybe she came to see YOU, Adrian."

"No, I haven't seen her. I didn't even know she was considering coming home. Didn't think she ever *wanted* to."

David was surprised at that, not because he believed Adrian couldn't give two shits about anyone but himself, but because Scott had obviously never told him about their conversation outside the Petro Mart. *Why wouldn't he tell his own son that his estranged sister was back in town and hadn't been seen for days?*

70

"It's her birthday next week," Scott added. "It's her thirtieth birthday, and she came back to make things right, with me. I don't know if she got cold feet or what, but I know she'll come to her senses and find me—find US— when she's ready."

"Why didn't I know this?" Adrian asked Scott with more false concern. "Why didn't you tell me she was coming to town?"

"Well," Scott said, then stopped, looking at David and back again. "I didn't actually *know*, and you don't really do well with these things, son. You've been so busy lately, between the parlor and the mowing, and I didn't want to upset you without knowing for sure if she was going to stay. Why tell you she was here just to have to tell you she left and didn't say goodbye again?"

In the background, a man had taken a guitar out of its case and had begun singing a gut-wrenching, yet monotone version of "Hallelujah." It broke through the tense air as Adrian feigned understanding of his father's decisions and David assured the two that he would contact them if he heard anything.

As he was walking away, David couldn't help but think that Scott's concern for Adrian's "bad-news handling abilities" was a little suspicious. *This is Adrian we're talking about, the man who switches between burning bodies and whacking weeds like a damn robot. He was a mess when their mother died, but surely he can handle things much better now than when he was a teenager?*

He wasn't sure what it meant, if it meant anything at all, but he knew Nicole hadn't stopped to see her brother, either, which brought him to another dead end.

As he walked past the parked cars, he saw Adrian's car pulled off to the side, rather than in his normal space in front of the receiving vault-turned-lawn-maintenance tool shack. He looked back, and when he saw both the Emerson men talking to funeral guests, he peered in the window, eyeing a drink tray on the floor next to a brown paper bag.

Who's the unlucky lady who gets to eat lunch with YOU? he thought to himself with a snicker. He walked down the hill to his car, but before he pressed the button to unlock the door, he stopped and looked back up at Adrian's car with a new unsettling thought.

Maybe it IS an unlucky lady.

4

The service ended as it always did, with a handful of family members sharing final thoughts on their deceased love one and making shallow plans to get together more often now that the march of time was on their coattails.

Adrian listened to the familiar refrains of, "Wish it didn't take a funeral to get people together," and, "I know he'd want us to smile," pouring from their mouths like pre-recorded sentiments from the soundtrack for the grieving. He offered them tissues and little cards with a picture of their father—or grandfather, for a few—on the front and prayers on the back. They thanked him for a lovely service and asked that he tell his father the same. He agreed, and, at last, it was over.

Scott pulled up the hill in the company van just as the last few people walked away, parking it beside the fresh grave. Adrian helped him pack the chairs and arrangements in silence. It was part of the routine.

"You got it from here, son?" Scott asked through the window as he prepared to hit the road back to the parlor.

"Yeah, I think I can manage," Adrian replied. He remembered when his father used to insist on being part of the burial process, to make sure his company's work was done right from start to finish. Thankfully, time hadn't been very kind to his father's joints, so he was forced to trust his son's handiwork instead.

"Alright, well, if you want, I can take the burn off your plate tonight. No reason you can't take the night off if you need it."

Adrian sensed the guilt in his father's voice—most likely from hiding the fact that his sister was in town. *Well, you're not the only one with a secret there, so I suppose I can let it slide.*

"That's alright. YOU'RE the one who needs the time off, anyway, so don't worry about me. She's just a little old thing, so I'll be fine," he said to his father instead.

Scott nodded his head in agreement and got into the van. He gave one last wave and yelled, "I hear deep down, he was a good guy!" as he drove off. Adrian rolled his eyes. *Every. Single. Time.*

He watched his father drive away, then grabbed a set of coveralls from his car, changing into them in his backseat before stepping up onto the backhoe to fill the grave—his second-favorite part of the job.

He began dumping buckets of dirt onto the casket, thinking about Nicole and how things were more complicated than he'd thought now that David was aware of her arrival. *She really DOES know how to fuck things up.*

When he was satisfied with the filling portion of the burial, he jumped down from the tractor and grabbed the drink tray and bag from his car. *Hope the ice didn't melt.*

He brought them to a mausoleum with the family name "Bacon" etched in stone at the top, then unlocked the wrought-iron door and placed the food on a stone slab inside. Adrian had found the Bacon family weren't much for visiting dead relatives, which left him with a particularly useful space. He opened the Sprite and found that it was still in decent shape. *You were right about the ice, Mother.*

He walked back out and spent the next thirty minutes shoveling the last bit of dirt onto the grave, making sure that it was up to his father's standards. *Not too loose, not too tight, not too rounded, juuust right.* He found the last part was easier to do with a shovel. Plus, people assumed he did it ALL with a shovel, so he got a kick out of the reminder of their ignorance.

Once the great-grandfather of the whiny tablet-wielding brats was set in his forever home, Adrian drove the tractor up another hill and parked it behind a large shed on the top level of the cemetery. He began walking back to the mausoleum, and was beginning to think about how he was going to bring up the David subject to his sister when he saw David standing next to the freshly packed mound.

His first thought was to run, that he had somehow figured it out and was there to arrest him, but the lack of police cars blaring their sirens told him that probably wasn't the case.

"Sorry to bother you again," David started, "but I was just wondering if you could help me with something."

Shaking his head and raising his hands in a questioning stance, Adrian tried unsuccessfully to hide his annoyance as he had earlier. "What exactly do you need? I'm sorta in the middle of something."

"Yeah, I can see that. Nice job, by the way. It looks, um... nice. But I wanted to ask you something about your father."

"What about him?" Adrian asked as he wiped his dirt-covered hands on his coveralls.

"I wanted to know if you think he would ever hurt Nicole."

Adrian wasn't sure what to say, but he was reading David's eyes. He was sure this was just some sort of weird mind game, and that David didn't want to know anything about his father at all, but about him.

"Why on Earth would you even say something that stupid?"

David felt the heat in Adrian's words and wasn't sorry for it. In fact, he was counting on it.

When he was a boy, his father had taught him his favorite tactic for getting information from someone: "Just toss eggs at 'em." David had never understood what it meant until, one day, his father finally explained it.

"Son, if a farmer throws three eggs at you, you only have two hands to catch 'em, so the third is bound to break. Same thing goes for questions thrown at criminals. They don't have enough lies to catch 'em."

Adrian's answer about his father didn't matter. It was the first egg.

"Well, it's just that Nicole told me she was afraid of what might happen when she went to see him, that she had a bad feeling that he would freak out or do something terrible to her. I didn't tell him that, of course, out of respect, but you can see why that's alarming, can't you? I mean, she says she's going to see him, and a few days later, she's nowhere to be found? That's odd, don't you think?"

David watched as the red color on Adrian's face deepened a shade. *Egg number two.*

"Why are you asking *me* about this? Why aren't you asking *him,* or your cop buddies? You're not even on the clock, are you?" Adrian added after scanning David's civilian clothing. "Is this some sort of joke to you?"

"It's not a joke, Adrian," David said sternly, preparing his final toss. "Your sister called me on Friday, nobody's heard from her since, and you and Scott are the only family she has left in this town."

David watched as Adrian shoulders loosened a little and his eyes widened with an internal acknowledgement. *He's either legitimately upset, or calling my bluff.*

"I really wish I could help, David, but I don't know anything," Adrian said, picking up his shovel. "I know you have a thing for her, but she's not a fucking kid anymore. I'm sure she can take care of herself and doesn't need Officer Obsession up her ass the second she gets back in town. So, please, just leave us alone. I'm sure she's just sitting at the motel avoiding everyone, like she always does."

Adrian turned away at that and started hammering the dirt with the shovel again, unaware that what he thought had been a proper *go away* was instead a damning comment.

"I never said where she was staying, Adrian. How did you know she was at the motel?"

"Now wait, David, I thought I told you." Adrian turned around and raised the shovel as he spoke, kicking David's safety instincts into overdrive.

"I can explain," Adrian said through a half-barred jaw as the revolver reached chest height. "Just don't shoot."

"Where is she?" David asked, expecting Adrian to lie, but hoping the gun might force him to do the right thing. Rather than wait and see, David decided to up the ante, and reached into his pocket for the handcuffs he had brought in the event his instincts were right.

In an instant, Adrian stiffened his arms and twisted his body, connecting the side of the shovel directly onto David's face. The gun flew out of David's hand and crashed into glass behind him as he fell on the ground in agony. He saw stars shooting around in the corners of his vision and felt that some of his front teeth were gone. A second later, he heard something rushing through the air, and quickly rolled on his side.

The face of the shovel hit the ground next to his head. He kicked at Adrian and connected, knocking him off balance. As Adrian swayed in the air and raised the shovel again, David leapt forward and tackled him by the waist. They hit the ground, and David held Adrian's arms with one hand and punched him with the other, landing his blows on the cheek. After what seemed like a dozen thumps, Adrian lay unconscious on the ground and David rolled off him. He took the handcuffs out of his pocket and placed them on Adrian's wrists. Cuffed in front wasn't procedure, but safe enough for now.

With Adrian secured, he crawled to the nearest structure he could find and sat with his back against it as he closed his eyes and tried to catch his breath. He raised a hand to his face. It shook with pain as he felt that his nose was broken and his lips were busted in multiple places. He reached inside his pocket for his phone and remembered it was charging in his car. *Stupid. Fucking stupid.*

When he caught his breath a minute later, he put his hand on the wrought iron door of the structure he had crawled to and tried to stand. The door wasn't closed all the way, so when it moved, he lost his balance and fell to the ground again. After trying again and getting to his feet, David looked inside the structure through a jagged hole in its stained glass decoration. On the floor, he saw the revolver, and beside that, a drink tray. He looked up and read the word "Bacon" on the top before he opened the door and walked inside.

At first, he thought the worst—that Nicole was dead and that her brother had stuck her inside someone else's tomb, never to be found. He walked to the far side, expecting to see her body huddled in the corner, or at least what remained of it, but he got around the stone centerpiece and nothing was there. He sighed in relief.

Then he noticed that the concrete floor looked different on that side of the room, so he knelt and found it wasn't concrete at all, but a grey carpet square. He picked it up and revealed a trapdoor underneath.

He pulled the door open and saw that it lead to a staircase without any lighting, but with complimentary spider webs. *She's down here. I know she is,* he thought as he spat out another mouthful of blood.

He turned and walked back out the wrought iron gate, *but first.* He then knelt over Adrian and opened one of his eyelids, wanting to make sure he was down for the count and wouldn't be sneaking up to trap him inside. When he was doubly confident Adrian was in for a long nap he went back to the trapdoor and descended the stairs.

He reached his hands out on his way down, feeling the cold wet walls beside him and praying there were no boo-by traps lying in wait. His hand hit something hard as he reached the bottom.

He felt it and found it was a door. He wanted to yell her name before he opened it, to make sure he was right and that this wasn't the real booby trap waiting behind the door, but his face felt like it had been run over by the tractor, so he decid-ed to take the risk and hope that he'd made it in time. He felt the lock on the door and twisted, and when he didn't hear any clicks or other signs of traps loading up, he eased it open and walked inside.

Nicole screamed as she swung the shard of ceramic through the air, landing it directly in David's throat. She pulled it out and swung it two more times as David began to choke on his blood and fell to the floor. She heard a gasping sound as she threw the ceramic down and began to sob. She reached down for the lamp near her feet. She'd just turned it off to hide after hearing footsteps echoing down the stairway.

"ITS OVER," she yelled as she flicked on the light, intent on making this distorted version of her brother look her in the eyes as he bled out. She held the light up and was mortified when she saw David staring back at her.

"DAVID?" she screamed as the lamp dropped and shattered on the floor. She rushed to his side and felt where she had cut him with the ceramic blade. Hot, sticky blood covered her hands and flowed onto the ground like a sink being filled by an inattentive child.

"I didn't know," she choked out as she began to hyperventilate. She tried to apply pressure, but it was no use. The cuts were far too deep.

She screamed in pain as the attempts David's hands made to grab at her weakened. She didn't understand how David had found her, and wished that he hadn't.

"I'm sorry," she whispered and kissed him on the forehead. She felt the cuts and swelling on his face and understood he must have fought to find her.

She buried her head in his chest and cried, wishing he would just sit up and whisper something in that faux country voice. But there was nothing she could do. She was a killer just like her brother.

He's out there, she thought as she began running her trembling hands around David's body. She found his gun and picked it up. *He's either dead, or about to be.*

She stood, walked through the doorway, and made her way up the stairs, listening for the sound of footsteps at the top. The direction of the steps turned after she had gone up a flight, revealing a glow at the top of another, longer set of stairs. She began moving faster—it was the first real light she had seen in days, and every second, it seemed more likely that something was going to come out from the dark below her and drag her back down.

As she reached the light, she stuck the gun up first, aiming through the opening. Her arms made it through the hole and began to shake with the real possibility that she was going to be free.

As the thought raced through her mind, she heard a creak from behind the opening in the floor. She had started to turn when a shovel came crashing down on her gun hand. She screamed as her fingers radiated an intense pain. She turned to pick the gun up off the steps, but her smashed hand wouldn't close on the grip, giving Adrian enough time to jump down the trap door onto the step above her.

"Got somewhere to be, Sickole?" Adrian said as he raised his cuffed hands and wrapped his arms around her neck.

"I even got you extra ice, you bitch," he shouted as he pulled her close and began to squeeze. Nicole felt the chain digging deeper into her skin as her pulsating fingers made a weak attempt to pull them off. She thrashed her body around and tried to knock him off balance, but that too failed. *I'm sorry, David,* she thought to herself as the fight left her body. *All for nothing.*

As she accepted her fate, the tension around her neck released. "You figure out what to do with her, Mother," she heard Adrian say as he placed a hand on her lower back and pushed.

Nicole tried to catch herself on the way down the stairs, but heard an audible *pop* from her left ankle as she failed to grab ahold of the wall. She crashed down the first set of stairs and stopped on the landing, her head hitting the wall. She was immediately overtaken by a dizziness that felt like she was on a sinking ship.

An incredible amount of pain emanated from her ankle and fingers, rounded out by the sticky feeling of blood trickling down her face. With the sound of footsteps behind her, and David's corpse in front of her, she began to fade out of consciousness.

CHAPTER IV:
CHOCOLATE MILK & PERCOCET

David held Nicole's hand as she looked at him with a smile. He hadn't said anything particularly funny or given her any kind of gift, so he warmed at the thought that she was just happy to be there with him on the school bus.

It was the last day of the school year, and though being a high schooler next year scared her a little, David assured her that once fall came and she found herself in the middle of one of Mr. Rubinfeld's wacky science experiments, all that anxiety would fade away to nothing. He squeezed her hand a little tighter as she planted a kiss on his cheek and rested her head on his shoulder.

Adrian turned in his seat and rolled his eyes. *Get a room,* he thought, then yelled back at them. He knew that his parents didn't like them together, and that they had been secretly finding ways to smooch without their knowledge. He'd tried to tell them, but his sister had gotten too good at lying, and David too good at sneaking.

The bus stopped as a few kids way in the back grabbed their backpacks and slapped a few final high fives before summer break. David stood up and Nicole followed. Adrian looked at his sister with a "you've got to be kidding me" stare, then turned back in his seat. She sometimes got off the bus at David's stop and told her parents she'd gone to study with her friend Anna, and always roped Adrian into it somehow. Nicole stopped in front of his seat and reached out her hand. Inside was a package of Oreos and a dollar bill.

"I'm going to Anna's eighth-grade graduation party. Is that alright with you?"

"Whatever," Adrian said as he snatched the bribe from her hand and looked out the window. He didn't think it mattered if it was alright with him, anyway. This *was* Anna's stop, too, so even if she wasn't going there, he couldn't prove it.

"Just let Mom know I'll be home before Dad gets there, probably at seven."

"Yeah, yeah," Adrian said as he looked back at her with unamused, half-open eyes. "See ya later."

Nicole got off the bus, and Adrian watched as she gave Anna a hug, then proceeded to grab David's hand again and walk in the opposite direction of Anna's house. He opened the Oreos and grasped one in his fingers.

He was pretty sure this was what guilt felt like—that, and the fact that he didn't get a cool party for graduating sixth grade kinda sucked, so he stuffed the whole cookie in his mouth and squeezed the dollar into his pocket.

"Mom, I'm home," Adrian yelled as he threw his backpack onto the floor and kicked his shoes off. They landed askew on top of the rest of the shoes, which had been neatly paired and placed next to the door with care. He was going to leave them there, like he always did, but had a last second change of heart and fixed them. It was *his* fault his mother had a broken collarbone, after all.

He walked into the kitchen and began pouring himself a glass of milk. He also grabbed the chocolate syrup out of the refrigerator, intent on mixing a cup of chocolate milk big enough to wash away all his feelings of guilt. "MO-om," he yelled as he poured the chocolate, "I'm HO-ome."

He went to get a spoon out of the drawer and noticed it had been left open. He grabbed a spoon and thought about his mother struggling to complete simple tasks like fixing shoes or closing drawers. He grabbed a big spoon from the back, then squeezed the chocolate syrup container again until the bottle produced a *toot*. The sound made him feel better, so he laughed and began mixing the milk, closing the drawer with his best attempt at a ninja kick before he left the kitchen.

As he sat on the couch and began drinking his milk with one hand, he grabbed the remote and pressed the button to turn on the TV with the other. It roared to life with the sound of a news reporter talking about how oil prices were going to be affected by a plane that had been shot down in the Middle East.

"Ass, gas, or grass, no one rides for free," he heard his father say in his head. He flipped through the channels for a minute, and when the only things mildly interesting were the

knives that were being sold in an infomercial, he turned it off again.

"MOM," he yelled again, this time feeling a little upset that she didn't greet him at the door and congratulate him on his achievements in the world of middle school. When he didn't get a response, he gulped down the last of his milk and got to his feet. *Where are you?*

He had a good guess where she was—in the family room, the one where they talked about their feelings and their futures, and somehow got "closer as a family" by making cups and bowls out of clay. He knew his mother had struggled with the pottery process since the fall, but she still tried to make it work, and Adrian was sure she was just finishing up firing a squirrel figurine or something just as stupid.

He walked down the hallway and saw that the door to the family room was closed. Inside, he could hear the hum of the kiln firing, and on top of that, the smooth tone of Fleetwood Mac. His mother played their music almost religiously, and it relieved him to hear the singer ask him to, *"Tell me lies, tell me sweet little lies."*

"Hey, mom, I'm home," Adrian said again as he opened the door and saw nobody in the room. Puzzled, he took a step inside and looked behind the door, then over at the kiln, which was indeed doing its job.

What the hell? he thought when he didn't see his mother. *She never leaves the house while the kiln's firing, NEVER. She said she would be too afraid of something going wrong and the kiln catching on fire.*

His next thought was that he was wrong; that she must be in the bedroom, or in the backyard, or maybe even in the attic, grabbing one of those old photo albums she cherished and took out around the holidays. The idea had little time to ripen before he took another step toward the kiln and saw a foot behind the worktable.

"MOM?" Adrian shouted as he ran around the table and found his mother on the floor. She looked like she was sleeping, but one of her arms was stretched above her head, and her eyes were open. He dropped to his knees and grabbed her by the shoulders, one of his hands closing on the sling she had been wearing ever since she fell. It was a terrible reminder of what happened when teenage boys didn't get their way.

As he desperately tried shaking her awake, the arm inside the sling gently swayed back and forth. "WAKE UP!" he shouted. "WAKE UP!"

He shook her again and her body rolled to the side, her elbow hitting the floor with a *crack*. As her body shifted, something dropped out of her hand and rolled away on the floor. Adrian saw it and recognized it by its dark orange color.

It was his mother's medication bottle.

He jumped off her and crawled backwards on the floor until his head hit the table. He curled his arms around his legs and began to cry, looking up at his mother through tears, then burying his face in his knees. The CD player continued filling the air with its bittersweet reminder as the reality of what had happened sunk in.

"If I could turn the page, in time then I'd rearrange, just a day or two..."

Adrian got to his feet after what seemed like an hour, but was only five minutes. He ran to the phone and dialed 911, then sat on the porch as he waited for the police to arrive. A short time after they entered the house and closed it off, Scott arrived and found him there speaking with a detective.

"Oh my God, ADRIAN," Scott said as he knelt and hugged him.

"He's in shock," the detective said. "And you must be the father, Scott?"

"Yes," he said, then picked Adrian up and hugged him. "I'm so sorry, buddy. It's gunna be ok, though. I'm here now."

"Was anybody else in the house? Where's Nicole?" Scott asked, looking around. When he didn't see her anywhere, he added, "My daughter Nicole—where is she?"

"She wasn't here when we arrived, sir. Just your son."

Scott set Adrian back down and knelt to eye level with him. "Was your sister here?"

Adrian felt the guilt wash over him again, this time as strong as a hurricane inside his head. His face turned red with anger as he thought about her walking away from the bus stop, hand in hand with David, without a care in the world.

"No," he said, then began to shake. His mouth quivered as he finished telling his father the truth. "She's... she's with David."

Adrian watched his father close his eyes briefly and take a breath. It was the signal that he was angry, but trying not to show it. Scott stood up and put his hand on the side of Adrian's face, turning his head up to look at him.

"Thank you for telling me the truth. It's gunna be ok. I promise."

Adrian had drifted into a daze, thinking that maybe he was going to wake up soon, that maybe he was wrong, and that his mother really was just sleeping, and he was just a stupid kid who didn't know any better.

He watched as his father walked a few yards away with the detective and had a conversation just out of earshot. His heart sank as his father's body language seemed to confirm that what he had seen on the floor had been no dream.

Nicole returned home at 5:15, changing her stride from a casual stroll to a sprint after rounding the corner and seeing the police cars parked in the driveway. She ran to her father, who first hugged her, then took her aside to let her know what had happened to her mother. She screamed and tried to run to the door, to get inside and prove that it was all some sort of misunderstanding, but she was stopped by one of the police officers at the door, who informed her that she couldn't go inside, and that they were sorry for her loss.

She punched at the officer's chest and flailed her arms, trying to get past him. When she couldn't, she turned around and ran into the road, where she stood staring at the house she'd grown up in, the window where she'd watched cars passing by staring back at her as a pastime forever lost.

Then she saw her brother sitting in the grass on the side of the house. She thought about how her father should have still been at work, and was struck with grief as she realized her brother must have been the one to find her. She walked towards Adrian, who didn't appear to be crying anymore, but instead had a blank expression on his face. She sat down next to him and tried to give him a hug, but he pulled away.

"Don't," he said as his lip began to quiver again. "Don't touch me."

"Adrian, I'm… I'm so sorry. I should have been here."

"YEAH, YOU SHOULD HAVE!" Adrian yelled as he turned to his sister and looked into her eyes with resentment. "You SHOULD have been here, but no, you had to go be a stupid SLUT."

Nicole wanted to tell her brother off, to defend herself and say she wasn't being a slut, that she and David had never even thought about that stuff and were only taking a walk down by the river, but she knew it didn't matter. Instead, she just sat in silence and watched as the flashing lights faded into a blur.

After thirty minutes had passed, Scott strapped his children into his van and drove down the street to the park. The coroner was about to arrive, and Scott didn't want them to have to witness their mother being carted away in a black bag.

He hoped Adrian would eventually take up the family business and be on the receiving end of the coroner's deliveries, but this wasn't at all what he would consider a "professional development moment." He pulled into one of the parking spaces, then rolled down his window before turning off the engine.

"Dad?" Nicole asked as she looked out the window at the empty park. "What are we gunna do without mom?"

Scott took a deep breath and put his hand on Nicole's head, running his hand through her hair. He thought she looked a lot like her mother, and had certainly gotten her free spirit. "I don't know, hunny, but what I do know is that we're gunna be ok, the three of us."

He looked back at Adrian, who was staring at the floor with his arms crossed.

"Hey," he added, reaching back to tap Adrian on the leg. "Hey, we're gunna be ok, I promise."

"NO, WE'RE NOT," Adrian blurted out as he uncrossed his arms and smacked the window with his knuckles. He began to cry again, then unbuckled his seatbelt and made his way to the front of the van, where he hugged his father and let all his memories flow into his shoulder as a stream of tears. Nicole unbuckled her seatbelt and joined in the group hug, mimicking her father's pacifying strokes on Adrian's back.

After the funeral, the weeks passed with friends dropping by to make sure they had everything they needed and the few extended family members left in town reminding Scott he could call them any time. The r oom w here i t h ad happened was kept closed, and aside from Scott going in to make sure the kiln was unplugged, it stayed that way.

Adrian sometimes walked past the door and could swear he heard music coming from inside, but his father assured him that it must just be his mother swinging by to say hello in a memory.

The official cause of death had been overdose on prescription oxycodone. Scott assured his son that it wasn't his fault and that his mother must have made some sort of mistake.

"It was an accident," he repeated over and over. "She would never have left us on purpose. She loved you too much."

He told Adrian this, but knew that once he got older and understood the world a little better, he would have his doubts again.

Nicole spent more time at home initially, offering to wash dishes and take out the trash, along with taking up babysitting responsibilities if her father wanted to go out for anything except a date. Things with David had been very awkward since that day, and while she could tell he wanted to be there for her, she also sensed that he was distancing himself from her, so being present for her family seemed the most mature way forward.

"Dad, I'm a teenager now. I can watch him, really," Nicole had said, trying to convince her father that he could finally go back to work. He had been putting it off for weeks, saying, "I can't leave you guys alone," and, "What if something happens? He's not really stable yet."

Finally, after the electricity bill arrived in a red-lettered envelope, her father had accepted her help and decided to go back to work. Before leaving for his first day, he'd pulled Nicole aside at the door and given her a hug.

"Your mother would be proud of the woman you're turning into," Scott said to Nicole as he grabbed his keys and put on his boots. Nicole hadn't heard him talk about their mother in weeks, and while she first felt a tug of sadness, she was happy to think her mother was looking down at her with pride.

"Before I leave, though," Scott said as he straightened up and walked to Nicole, "I need your word that you're going to stay here all night, and that you're not going to leave your brother, or..."

He paused. "... have anyone else over here."

Nicole looked at her father. His face had gone from one of joy to one of authority. He had questioned her about the night their mother died a few days after it happened, allowing her to tell the "truth." She had lied, giving him the story about Anna's graduation party at first, but after seeing this same look, had copped to everything and promised it would never ever happen again.

"I'm not going anywhere," she replied, the feeling of pride leaking out of her smile as the impact that her lie had had on her brother sank in again.

"Good, that's Daddy's girl," Scott said as he saw the look on her face change. He knew she was trying to do the right thing, but part of him also knew that her free spirit was a wily beast that needed taming were it to ever prosper the way he intended.

"Dinner is in the refrigerator, and I'll have my phone on me. If anything happens, just give me a call or go across the street and knock on the door. The Moodys know I'm going back to work and said they can swing by if needed." She nodded that she understood, then made a fake disgusted face as he kissed her on the top of her head and went out the door.

The afternoon passed without incident. Adrian spent it looking at comic books in his room, while she watched TV and finished off a tube of cookie dough left over from their semi-successful family baking activity the night before. When the sunlight began to fade, she heated up dinner and served it to Adrian along with a glass of milk. She offered him chocolate, his favorite, but he said he didn't like it anymore.

They watched movies on the couch afterward. Nicole let Adrian choose the title and sat feeling accomplished when he fell asleep half-way through. She thought about calling David from the house phone, not to make any plans or try to sneak out, but just to hear his voice and maybe start working through the awkwardness.

She decided against it and woke her brother up to get him in bed. She helped him up the stairs and tried, but failed, to get him to brush his teeth first. "I'm not a baby, Nicole. You don't even need to watch me," he said through yawns.

Nicole sat back on the couch and hit play on the movie again. It was an older movie called "Home Alone," and while it wasn't quite Christmas time, she still laughed at the burglars' pain. The heartwarming family reunion at the end hit Nicole harder than it used to, so she turned it off, deciding she should go to bed before the temptation of grabbing the phone got to be too much.

She was getting ready to go to bed when she heard a sound coming from down the hallway. She got to her feet and moved toward it, unable to make out what it was. She thought maybe her father had left his cell phone there on accident and it was ringing, or maybe the kitchen window was open and the neighbors were being loud. She rounded the corner into the hallway and stopped in her tracks as she noticed the door to the family room was open.

She took a step closer and knew what the sound was. It was Fleetwood Mac playing softly on her mother's old CD player.

"Hello?" she called out down the hall. She took another step and listened for a response.

"Hello, is anyone there?" she asked again, with no reply.

She thought about running across the street and waking the neighbors, or running into the kitchen to get the phone, but her father's words poked at her.

"Your mother would be proud."

So she stepped up to the door and pushed it open.

She stared into the dark room, the music floating through the air like a ghastly opera. She felt an overwhelmingly strong connection to her mother in that moment, as if she were right there with her, sweeping her hair back and calming her trembling body.

"Mom?" she whispered at the shadows.

As the word left her lips, a loud *CRASH* rose from the side of the room. It sent a wave of terror down her body, and she jumped back.

Her arm flew up and scratched at the wall, searching for the light switch. As she fumbled around, she heard something moving and screamed. She felt the hair on her arms stick up.

It's moving toward me!

Her hands came across the light switch, and as she flicked it, she dropped to the floor screaming. The room flooded with light, and just as Nicole's hands came up in front of her, she saw what had made the noise.

"Adrian?" she said as she put her hands down and pushed up off the floor. She looked around and saw that one of her mother's vases was lying on the floor, shattered. She grabbed her brother by the arms. "What are you doing in here? I thought you were sleeping."

He didn't respond, so she shook him. Nothing.

She looked into his eyes and saw a blank expression. *He IS asleep,* she thought. *Sleepwalking.*

She brought him back to his bedroom and closed the door. Afterward, she went downstairs and turned off the music, then began cleaning up the broken ceramic. She picked up all the pieces and found a piece of unfired clay on the floor. She noticed that it had been slightly molded into the shape of a person.

After finishing cleaning, she went back to her brother's room and opened his door slowly. Not wanting to wake him again, she stood by the side of his bed and looked at him for a minute before pulling the clay figure out of her pocket and setting it on his nightstand.

The sleepwalking's new, she thought, and couldn't help but feel like that, too, was her fault. She hadn't been there when he had fought with their mother and shoved her down the stairs, and she hadn't been there when he'd found her dead.

But I shoulda been there for both.

She gently kissed him on the head, the same way her father had done just before leaving, then walked to the door. She heard her brother roll over behind her and turned to see his eyes were open.

"It's just me. You can go back to sleep. I brought up your little guy," she said, pointing to the crude figurine on the nightstand.

"It's not a guy," Adrian said, then closed his eyes and rolled over. "It's Mother's ghost."

CHAPTER V:
AIR DRIED

Back at Peace at Last, Adrian found himself staring at the big red button on the incinerator. He had just pushed another box inside, and was watching the light flicker off the sides as though it were a predator and the cardboard its prey. He pushed the button and stepped back as the door began to close, the sound of manufactured heat rolling out of the opening and filling the otherwise silent room.

He reached into his pocket and pulled out a set of keys, turning them over in his hands a few times before tossing them under the closing door and into the flames. He took a step back as the incineration process began and felt the bruising on his face. *What a prick,* he thought to himself and picked up his pen.

Adrian then heard footsteps on the stairs. For a split second, he thought it was Nicole again, his mind entertaining wild possibilities of her snapping her handcuff chains with superhuman force and coming to settle the score with her dear, dear brother.

As he positioned himself behind the door again, his shoulders tensed and he looked across the room at the metal pole he used to push boxes into the incinerator. He wished he would have put it back where it belonged. *Too late now,* he thought, taking the cap off the pen.

The door swung open and in walked his father Scott. Adrian watched as he walked up to the incinerator and looked inside the window. He stayed looking for a long moment, then turned around and saw Adrian staring at him from the corner.

"Jumping Jesus!" Scott said as he put one hand to his heart and raised the other in the air. "What are you doing hiding back there? And what happened to your *FACE*?"

"Damn grandkids," Adrian said as he took a step towards his father and felt the bruising on his face. David had gotten him pretty good in their little squabble.

"They came back after their grandpa's service—wasted, of course. Said something about 'Oh, that was all just for show, he was an asshole and didn't even deserve a funeral.' I asked them to leave, but they wouldn't. Said they were going to party now that the bastard was gone."

"Yeah, I guess some of them didn't seem all that sad," Scott admitted as he put his hands on his hips and looked over Adrian's face again. "But they HIT you?"

"They tried to get on the backhoe," Adrian lied. "Said they were gunna 'dig the fucker up' so they could spit in his face one last time."

"Jesus Christ," Scott said as he closed his eyes and rubbed his face. "Did you call the police?"

"I handled it," Adrian said, then walked over to the counter and set his pen down. *The cops DID come, but trust me, they weren't any help.*

"You could have called me too, you know. I told you I was willing to come take care of Mrs. Fletcher."

Adrian looked down at the cremation certificate in front of him. "Elizabeth Fletcher" was written on all the permissions lines except the signature on the bottom, which belonged to her daughter.

"I said I would be alright," Adrian replied as he began filling out the form.

"And I am," he said, nodding toward the incinerator.

"You'd tell me if you weren't, though, right?" Scott replied, putting his hand on Adrian's shoulder. After getting nothing but a blank stare in return, he took his hand back.

"If you do for some reason hear from Nicole, though," he said, walking toward the stairs, where he stopped and turned around again, "just make sure to call me."

"Ok, but I doubt I will," Adrian said, looking down again at the cremation certificate. He listened as his father's footsteps faded away, then continued his routine of checking state-mandated boxes and making labels for the bone pulverizer.

When he was sure his father was gone, he sat down and took the cremation form off the clipboard. Underneath was a set of police reports and documents from 1999. After driving David's SUV away from the cemetery and parking it by the river, he had gone through it to see if there was anything that could point in his direction. David *was a* sneaky bastard, after all.

When he reached the trunk, he found a binder filled with police reports and mugshots, all related to the unsolved murder of his father, David Demick Senior. He was intrigued and took it, unable to resist the juicy details surrounding the infamous murder, which had taken place when he was a kid, and still lived deep in the chatter of the townsfolk.

He scanned the doorway into the cremation room one more time before thumbing through a report found inside with a sticky note reading "LYING SCUMBAG."

Adrian knew the face in the mugshot attached to the report. It was good old lottery failure Cooper Austin. Inside the report, he read that Cooper had allegedly tried taking credit for David Sr.'s hit-and-run death, going around town trying to use it to gain street cred. Cooper had known the color of the car used, matching the description of the paint recovered from the clothing on the body, and was detained for questioning, where he refused to cooperate. *Yeah, then his partner beat you half to death, you idiot.*

Adrian had heard most of the information before—how David's partner, Brent Flurry, got kicked off the force for the beating, which had also resulted in Cooper being released on a "lack of substantial evidence." He read on and came across the interrogation interview from the following year, when a new state's attorney hell-bent on "protecting the boys in blue" had reopened the case.

Cooper had changed his story and stated that he'd found the car abandoned and driven it to the Shady Acre, where he'd planned to hand the keys off before realizing there was someone in the back seat.

"I thought he was dead!" the statement read. "They had a hoodie on and were facing down toward the seat with their hands behind their back, so I got the fuck outta there and ran inside. Shit, I was so scared, though, I went into the wrong fuckin' room, but the dude in there was passed out, so I just waited there. A few minutes later, I look out the window and the guy's in the front seat, hoodie and all! It spooked the shit outta me, so I bounced out the back. I know I shouldna lied, but you gotta believe me, I ain't no killer."

Adrian closed the folder and sat back in his chair, rubbing his face and thinking. He supposed he didn't really give two shits about David's father, but there was *something* there he could use to help with Nicole. He could feel it. The whole town believed it was Cooper, his rally for street cred fresh in the minds of gossipers, who had never really believed his cries for innocence were anything but the words of a desperate criminal. *But what if they weren't? What if the real killer was still out there? What would it mean?*

Adrian stood up and walked to the incinerator, then looked through the window at what used to be the body of an elderly woman, but had been reduced to a glowing red skeleton. *What am I supposed to do Mother?*

He took up the metal pole and opened the door, tamping down the bones with the flat end until some of them broke into smaller, more efficient fuel. He watched them crumble and closed the door again, this time returning the pole to where it belonged on the wall. As the flames engulfed the chunks of bone again, an idea began to surface.

Perhaps knowing the killer won't mean anything to me, but it could mean everything to the person who just killed his son.

2

Once the cremation was complete, Adrian labeled the box holding Mrs. Fletcher's ashes and placed them on a shelf. The planks surrounding her held around a dozen other boxes, all cremated family members and friends waiting to be picked up by their loved ones and set on mantles or scattered across whatever place they thought to be most befitting of their dusty last encounter.

After admiring his work, he thanked Mrs. Fletcher for the practice and shut off the lights.

He drove the five miles back to the cemetery, where he parked in front of the receiving vault and sat. He had grabbed the folder with the police reports inside, and, after one final glance at Cooper's mugshot, he stashed it under the passenger seat. *Lying scumbag,* he thought as the sticky note disappeared with the rest.

He reached the bottom of the stairs under the main entrance to the vault and unlocked the door, turning on the flashlight as he walked inside the chamber. The light bled across the floor and illuminated the broken table. It was surrounded by Ricky's ashes, mixed with broken ceramic and glass shards. He moved the light to Nicole and saw that she was awake, squinting and shading her eyes from the light.

"I thought you might be awake," Adrian said as he walked toward her. "If anyone knows how hard it is to sleep after killing someone, it's me."

Adrian shined the light on Nicole's wrists. They were now held together by the handcuffs he had worn earlier that day—David Junior's. He had pushed one end through the metal loop on the wall and placed her hands on either side. *A quick and effective fix.*

When he felt confident that the cuffs were still secure, he shined the light on her face again.

"What's gotcha down, sis?" he asked as he moved back and began picking up broken pieces of ceramic. "You feeling a little blue now that you're a murderer?"

"FUCK YOU!" Nicole yelled, then spat at Adrian's feet.

"Woah, hold on now, Nic. You don't blame ME, do you?" he said as he put a pile of glass on the top of the wooden shelf and returned to his sister's side. He grabbed her by the hair and pulled her head back as he shined the light on David's body.

"I didn't do THIS, Nicole. YOU were the one who couldn't wait for me to figure this all out. YOU were the one who slit his throat."

She closed her eyes. David had been moved away from the door and propped up against the wooded shelves, leaving behind a sickening streak of dark red blood. Adrian imagined she wasn't too used to seeing skin that pale, or the look of shock and confusion that remained on the faces of those who hadn't planned on a sudden departure.

"LOOK AT HIM," Adrian yelled as he yanked on her hair and twisted it behind her head. "I want you to *see* what you did, to *feel* what I felt after..."

He stopped, and after a second, let go of her hair. He knew what he wanted to say—that she should feel like he had when he killed their mother—but he couldn't get the words out, so he stood up and threw the flashlight at the wall, where it shattered with one final burst of light.

"ADRIAN!" Nicole screamed into the dark as his invisible pacing made her skin crawl with anticipation. She heard the footsteps stop and the room was quiet again.

She thought she heard a zipper, then a lighter brought the room back to life, and she saw that he was holding the brown pouch again. She twisted the handcuffs, not wanting to feel the needle's prick again.

"I know you didn't do it on purpose, Nicole," Adrian said as he prepared the shot. "I know you just wanted out of this place, and I can't blame you for that—it does come off a bit cynical to the untrained eye. But you have to remember that I didn't want you here; that it was your choice, not mine. See, YOU'RE a killer now, like me. And poor David here, well, he wasn't what I would call 'deserving of spiritual intervention.' But we can fix that, you and I. We can make it right... for Mother's sake."

"What do you mean, 'make it right?'" Nicole asked as she watched a drop of liquified heroin spill over the end of the needle and fall down the syringe. "He's already..."

Her words got stuck in her throat as she saw David's face through the dim light of the cigarette lighter. She dropped her head and couldn't say it out loud.

"Dead? Yes. Yes, he is, but more than that," Adrian said, walking to David's side, "he's lost."

Adrian then sat down next to David's body and placed the syringe on the shelf next to his head. He felt the bruises on his face, then put his arm around David's neck and lit the lighter next to his face.

"You are dead, aren't you?" he asked as he held up David's head with his other hand and pointed it at Nicole.

"He looks surprised, doesn't he? Like he wasn't expecting his teenage girlfriend to end his life while he tried to save her. It was a valiant effort, it truly was, and when I saw that it was just HER coming out of that hole, well, I couldn't believe my luck!"

Nicole sat in disgust as she watched Adrian ball up his fist and put it on the top of David's head, moving it back and forth rapidly in what they used to call a "noogie" as kids.

"AND YOU, you little rascal! I thought you had me; I really did. But let's be honest, it *was* kind of a sucker punch, you fucker." Adrian laughed and punched David on the arm as if he were playing around with an old friend. "But you didn't have to go that way, no. I mean, I probably would have had to kill you anyway—you *were* meddling around in *my* business, stopping the Lord's work, in a way. But maybe, just maybe, we could have helped each other first if it weren't for Mrs. Houdini over there."

Nicole closed her eyes and tried to drown out the sound of Adrian's one-man show with thoughts of her grandparents back in Arkansas. She could hear her grandmother asking her if she, "needed any laundry done while she was at work," and her grandfather using his mouth to emulate the theme song to the TV show *Matlock*. For a moment, she was transported back there, with nothing but what now seemed like a foolish, insignificant guilt for having been gone so many years. She took a breath, and as she blew it out, her grandmother's voice returned. *"Let me wash these for you, dear. I know the best trick for getting out blood stains."*

Adrian continued anyway, seemingly unphased by her attempts to ignore him. "I saw the papers, the ones you had in your car, FASCINATING stuff, David, FASCINATING. I especially liked the part where your Dad's partner beat that guy up and never got charged for it! What a delightful system we have in place! But what does that have to do with you, you're asking? Why do I care about a little old murder from twenty years ago? Well, to tell you the truth, David, I don't!"

He laughed and shook David's body to copy him. "But my sister here, well, our mother seems to think that the only way to keep her from going to hell is to make amends for killing you, and while I do feel a little selfish for satisfying my own curiosity, I can't think of a more fitting way to cleanse dear Nicole's soul than finding the person who killed your father and sending him to hell in her place!"

Nicole listened as Adrian got to his feet and then flicked the lighter to life. She opened her eyes as he walked toward her, the questions she had about his psychotic plans pushed out by the syringe in his hand. She winced as his foot landed next to her ankle, thinking for a second he was going to step right on it and send her into another world of pain.

"Oh, yes, I had almost forgotten. How's the leg holding up?"

Nicole sat in silence, still trying to think of her grand-parents, though they seemed to be just as curious about Adrian's plans as her. The truth was that her ankle was most likely broken—sprained at the very least—and without any medical treatment, it would be weeks before she could walk on it again.

Adrian put his hand on her leg, making her pull it back out of reflex. She thought about kicking him but knew it wouldn't do any good, since her hands weren't free to reach the keys even if she did somehow land a knockout blow.

"Easy, killer, I'm not going to saw it off. I'm not a maniac." He grabbed her leg and inspected her ankle, unphased by the cry she let out as he twisted her foot and set it back on the ground. "I think you'll live. And be less foolish this time around, I hope. When you wake again, we'll have work to do."

Adrian took the syringe and injected her. She felt the rush—it was just as powerful as the first time, except now a part of her embraced the pain relief. She thought about what Adrian had said about their mother wanting to keep her out of hell. It didn't make sense.

Her mother accepting a religion's role in their lives only happened shortly before she died, and was only to provide another tool for her children to decide for themselves what belonged in their heart. It was their father who had pushed the issue.

She realized that Adrian must have crossed wires at some point along his religious awakening and found himself left with a jumbled pile of scripture and pain, unable to separate one from the other. Every fiber of her heart wanted to be as unphased as Adrian was, but she couldn't help but wonder again if his transformation had been inevitable or only set in motion when she left.

She pushed the question out, but caught a glimpse of David before the drugs took full effect. The gruesome sight left a final impression in her mind that, in a faint and repulsive way, agreed with her brother: she needed to help find a resolution.

3

The following morning, Felix Robinson rolled over in his bed at 8:30 a.m. and picked up the cell phone that had been pestering him for the past hour and a half. He had received at least half a dozen calls that morning, which wasn't particularly out of the ordinary, seeing that he had a great deal of mentoring projects in town, but he wasn't used to ALL of them calling at the same time, and so he got up and put on his slippers and robe. As he walked to the bathroom, he opened his phone and saw that he had four voicemails. As he opened his robe again, he pressed play on the first message.

"Hey, Pastor, it's Mark. Don't mean to bother you or anything, but I, uh… was just over at the co-op and heard a chick at the register talking about a car that was abandoned by the river? Somebody walking their dog saw it and, yeah, they don't know what's up yet, but I was starting to get that feeling again, like I might want to go… pick up, so if you get this, please call me back. I'm good, I'm good, just, uh… call me."

Felix flushed the toilet as the message came to an end and pressed play on the second voicemail. "Hey, it's me again. I don't mean to bother you, but, um, now I hear they think it was foul play. That's kinda fucked up. It's not hunting season or anything, so where the hell did he go, you know? I told Aaron, and he thinks they went off the deep end and jumped into the river or something, but I don't know. It's weird. Call me, please."

Felix had been making his way to the kitchen and looked at his phone again to check the time. The message had come though almost an hour ago, and he hoped he wasn't too late to catch Mark before he used again. He dialed the number and asked Mark to meet him at the church in half an hour. He agreed and Felix hung up the phone to make a pot of coffee.

He wasn't overly surprised that people had taken a parked car as a sign of misdoing. They liked to gossip, and anything even slightly out of the ordinary would surely be hashed out over eggs and toast for weeks to come. Once the pot began brewing, he picked up the phone again and pressed play on the third message.

"We are trying to get in touch with you to discuss your vehicle's extended warranty."

Felix deleted the third message immediately; he had no extended warranty, and telemarketers did the devil's work. He poured cream into his mug and sat down, pressing play on the fourth message.

"Felix, my old friend, sorry to wake yuh." He knew the voice. It belonged to ex-cop Brent Fleurry. "I was gunna wait 'till the next lottery meeting to bring this up, but I heard there was some stuff going on at the park, and I wasn't sure if it had anything to do with it. That kid Morgan, the one we picked to win the lottery last week, well, he never got off the train down there in Connecticut. They still owed me a few favors at the station, so I asked 'em to keep tabs on him and his family down there, and nobody's seen or heard from the kid. I dunno if he went and got himself mixed up in something after we gave him those cards, but if Cooper got his dirty little hands involved trying to get him to go splitsies or whatever, well, stealing cars is Cooper's M-O, and who knows what kinda mess they got into. I'll be at the shop today if you want to stop in. I'll pray for 'em for now."

Felix downed the rest of his coffee in two gulps and got ready to leave, his head humming with the possibility that the lottery had once again failed and had only given another troubled soul the tools to feed their gluttony. He closed his eyes and prayed for Morgan as he put on his socks, praying that perhaps the police were wrong and Morgan had simply decided to start a brand new life elsewhere rather than risking another failure put on his family.

He put on his shoes and looked at his phone. He wanted to go to the hardware store and speak with Brent right that moment, but his duties to his mentees couldn't be set aside if he truly wanted his guidance to be his legacy.

When Felix arrived at the church, he found not only Mark waiting to speak with him, but also one of his female mentees and Scott Emerson. He got out of his car as Mark walked up and reached out his hand for a shake.

"Sorry to bug you so much this morning, Pastor. I just didn't have anyone else to call, and Aaron's kind of an asshole about those things. Jerk, I mean, JERK. Sorry!"

"It's ok, son. Have you been able to stay straight this morning?"

"Yes, yes, I have. Only an energy drink—well, two, actually—but that's it."

"Wonderful. Now, why don't you wait inside for me? I'll be there in a few minutes and I'm sure there's a chore or two that can help keep your mind occupied until then."

"Yeah, you got it. Thank you, Pastor."

Mark walked inside as Felix turned and greeted Scott, who had been standing a few yards away and had walked to him after the dismissal. Felix guessed that he was there to go over any funeral arrangements for that week, since the stricter religious families opted to have church services for their loved ones rather than services in a funeral parlor.

"Scott. What a pleasant... surprise."

"I'm not here for the show, Felix," Scott said as he looked over his shoulder at the second mentee, who was looking between them and her phone less than subtly. "I'm here about Adrian and Nicole."

Felix looked into Scott's eyes and saw that they appeared troubled, rather than filled with the usual confidence and borderline arrogance he had worn over the years. He thought about his conversation with David and felt his stomach drop when he realized Nicole must still be missing.

"Yes, I heard that she was back in town and looking for you. I take it she didn't find you?"

"No, she didn't, and how did you know that? Who told you?"

"David," Felix replied as he waved at the girl who had now put her phone away and was now fully focused on their conversation.

"Excuse me a moment." Felix said, striding toward the woman and ushering her inside to wait along with his other mentee. After she agreed and walked inside, Felix walked back to Scott and motioned him to walk away from the building. They got to the edge of the parking lot before Felix spoke again.

"Why are you coming to me, Scott? Do you think she's in some sort of danger? And, if so, what am I supposed to do?"

"I think she's still worried I'm going to blow my top or something. It's been over a decade, and she probably still thinks I'm some kind of monster, but you and I both know I only ever wanted what was best for her." Scott searched Felix's face for agreement, and when he found none, his expression began to sour.

"Don't play the saint card on me now, Pastor," Scott said, emphasizing Felix's title sarcastically.

"I just don't understand what you want from me, Scott. I prayed for Nicole, but aside from knocking on every door in town, I'm just not sure what else I can do."

"Adrian came back to the parlor with his face on backwards last night. He said it was some family members that came by after a funeral and gave him a run for his money, but I think he was asking for it, out of guilt. I think Nicole went to him when she first got back and he's keeping her away from me. I don't know why, but I can feel it. I know he looks up to you, and I was hoping you could talk to him and see if I'm right. He barely says anything to me if it's not about the lottery or the business, and if he's trying to keep her away from me because they can't let go of the past, then I deserve to know!"

Felix looked at Scott and shook his head. *She left because YOU were abusive, and HE probably figured out he wasn't responsible for his mother's death, you self-centered, egotistical...* He avoided the thought and looked up at the church steeple as the bell began to ring, signifying that it was time for his appointment with Mark.

113

"I'll do what I can, Scott—for their sake, not yours—but I can't promise you anything. I have to get inside now; I'll find you if I need to."

"Don't tell them I sent you. That would make it worse, I think." Scott watched Felix walk to the door, and when he looked back before going inside Scott yelled, "You have to help them see I'm not the bad guy in all this, you owe it to them."

4

Adrian returned to the vault that morning with two plastic bags and a new lantern. He turned the switch to the "on" position and set the bags on the table, then pulled a water bottle out of one and took a sip.

Nicole was already awake, and as the light came on, she rolled her head back and forth to lessen the pain she felt in her shoulders. Afterward, she rubbed her clammy fingers together to cope with the loss of blood from her hands hanging above her head. She watched Adrian take out another bottle and a granola bar, opening both and bringing them to her. She desperately wanted to say no, to tell him to go to hell, but she took a bite and accepted a swig of water. She couldn't imagine how she would be able to live after all this, but she wasn't sure she wanted to die, either.

After she took another few bites and washed them down, she expected Adrian to leave, but he didn't. Instead, he did the last thing she expected and took the keys out of his pocket, turning them over in his hand once before unlocking her handcuffs.

She pulled her arms down and furiously rubbed her palms together to warm them. She looked at Adrian's legs and didn't dare follow them up to his face. She could feel him watching and knew that the glow she sometimes saw in his eyes might send the granola bar on a reverse trip through her digestive system.

She looked around the room instead and saw that the everything was back in its original place. Adrian must have come back while she was drugged-out and cleaned up the glass and ceramic pieces. The table had duct tape around the leg, which seemed to be holding, and David was thankfully out of view in Adrian's shadow.

"You're going to need those," Adrian said as he walked to the table and pulled something heavy out of the other bag.

Nicole closed her eyes and blew hot air into her hands. She felt the blood starting to circulate, and along with it, a surge of pins and needles. She clenched her fists as the pain echoed through her extremities like a thousand tiny soldiers poking her with miniature swords, distracting her from her brother, who had moved to the opposite corner of the room.

"I know it's been a long time, but I'm certain you'll remember how to use one of these. It's like riding a bike." Adrian turned around and revealed the subject of his comment: the pottery wheel she'd eyed the first time she had seen the room lit up. He brought it to Nicole and placed it on the floor in front of her, letting out a breath as he placed it down. It stood just a few feet off the ground with a wooden wheel on the top and a larger wooden wheel on the bottom. Beside it was a rusted metal seat connected to the bottom with a curved piece of metal piping.

"I know Mother had a soft spot for old kick wheels like this one, and I do too. It really puts the art back into the work, unlike those electric ones that do it all for you."

Nicole looked at the wheel and had to stifle a laugh. She wasn't sure why, or where it had come from, but she couldn't help herself, and covered her mouth. She let herself fall on the floor and brought her hands to her face, closing her eyes and giggling to herself as she thought about her brother, the big, bad serial killer, sitting alone in the darkness, crafting coffee mugs and zoo animals. A clay zebra galloped past her and neighed, stopping to look at her and wink like some sort of cartoon.

Am I losing it now, too?

Beneath the chuckles, a tug of dread brought her back to reality. She knew what she was supposed to do: to follow Ricky's example and make herself a beautiful resting place for after she got acquainted with the machine lurking in the funeral parlor. She knew it was futile to run, and maybe she even deserved it after what she had done to David. She shooed the zebra away and sat up, wiping her face with her now red-hot hands, and looked at her brother.

"I don't think I've seen that before," Adrian said, appearing too shocked to be angry. "Usually, it's confusion, sadness, yes, and a whole lot of anger, but never laughter. I think you might need to drink a little more water. You and dehydration are both sneaky bitches."

He waited for her to take another sip of water before he placed a large square of clay on the table and sat down in the rusted seat, kicking the wheel to spin the top. His fingers caressed the clay and began to tear away at the edges, smoothing the block into a cylindrical shape. After it ceased looking at all square, he stopped the wheel and stood up.

"Your turn," he said as he walked to Nicole's side.

"I know it hurts," he said, looking at her leg, "but you won't be on it long."

Nicole got to her feet and hobbled to the chair. Her ankle rejected the idea of doing anything but resting and sent waves of disapproval through her body. She whimpered as she sat in the chair and got the weight off it.

As her brain flooded with childhood memories of time in the family room, she felt her brother's hand come down on her shoulder. She flinched and moved away slightly, her foot hitting the kick wheel at the bottom and highlighting her ankle's objections once again.

"It's exactly like you remember. Just spin the wheel at the bottom and let your hands do the rest. It's what he deserves."

He? Nicole thought. Surely he meant *she*, as in their mother. Or maybe "he" meant "God." The religion had clearly stuck to Adrian enough for the both of them.

"Oh, I see. You're *confused*," Adrian said, almost like he had read her mind. "You thought this was for YOU!"

Nicole shied away as Adrian took his hand from her shoulder suddenly and clapped in a brief applause.

"That's kinda messed up, sis. Kill a guy and steal his thunder too? I told you, Mother wants you cleaned up, so that's what we're going to do, the three of us."

Nicole understood what she was doing now as Adrian looked past her at the corpse in the corner. She was not making an urn for herself, but for David.

She turned slowly in the rusted seat. David had haunted her the night before as she sat wasted on heroin, dreaming of his southern accent. *"He's right, ya know. I do sort wanna be in one of them fancy jugs fer dead folks."*

She saw the vacant look on David's face and turned away again. Her mind tormented her with flashes of the moment the door had swung open and her failed attempt at an escape cost more than she could have ever imagined.

118

"I... I don't remember how," she said as she spun the wheel and felt the clay with her fingertips. It was cold and damp, reminding her of her first night in the hole, when she'd explored the walls in darkness.

"Just imagine David's ashes being poured into a dumpster and getting mixed with someone's half-eaten lunch, or maybe tossed over the bridge in West Hartford. It doesn't matter to *me* what happens with them, but I know you—well, I *did* know you—and I'm sure you wouldn't want that. I'm sure you would feel better knowing David's final resting place will have at least a little thought put into it."

She stared at the wheel, her hands hovering above the clay, unsure of how to start. He was right—she had never put much thought into what consisted of a suitable final resting place, but she was sure it wasn't anything Adrian could concoct or create.

Her hand rested against one side of the clay as she began moving the wheel at the bottom with her foot, the surface getting smoother as it spun. Then she took her other hand, pushed her fingers into the top, and began hollowing out the middle. It was morbid, and wrong, but also—compared to neck cramps and handcuffs—unnervingly relaxing.

"There, I knew you'd remember. I usually have to help them, like a fucking art teacher! It's not the easiest thing to do on drugs, I'm sure, but this, this is nice for a change."

Nicole felt her brother's eyes on her as she worked, and occasionally heard him move around the room behind her to watch from different sides. It reminded her once again of their childhood modeling exercises and how he'd always been roaming around the room, never sitting still through their mother's attempts at family time.

"There," she said as she stopped turning the wheel to present what she thought was a *good enough* vessel. She had used her fingernail to draw one coiled line around the body as the sole decorative mark, knowing any other techniques her mother had taught her would be lost on this project.

"Don't forget the lid, Nicole. You wouldn't want David to go flying off into the breeze every time someone opened that door unexpectedly—say, to save a damsel in distress?"

She felt her face get red-hot at the remark and closed her eyes, drawing in a deep breath and exhaling as she grabbed the pile of excess clay. She made a crude lid and placed it on the top, finishing as Adrian walked in front of the table and reviewed her work.

"What do you think, David? Will this do?" Adrian said mockingly, looking at David over Nicole's shoulder. "I agree, it's awful, but it'll do."

Nicole turned and matched her brother's gaze; she couldn't avoid looking at David anymore. She saw the same look on his face from the morning after, except his skin was turning a greyish-blue and the blood nearly black.

It was a silly thought, but she hoped that he *did* like it, that, in some way, he could recognize the hell she was going through and forgive her.

She thought of him looking down at her from heaven. She wasn't sure she even believed in such a place, but in that moment, it was as real as the pain in her leg. As she imagined him standing there with her mother, his arm around hers and both looking at her with acceptance and love, she noticed that the deceased David had something sticking out of his pants pocket.

"Can I sit with him?" she asked, wanting to get closer and see what David was hiding. "I just want to..."

She paused as she realized her next words were more than just a ruse. "... to say goodbye."

"I suppose that's a necessary part in all this. Make it quick." He motioned for her to go. She got to her feet, using the wheel to keep her balance through the pain, then hobbled over to the corner and sat down with her back against the wall, David on her side. She didn't want to look at him or use him as a pawn, but somehow, she knew David *wanted* her to see what was in his pocket. She could sense it was for her.

"I'm sorry it isn't nicer. It's not what you deserve at all," she said without thinking. "If I would have known, I might have just stayed home, and then you'd still be here."

She wrapped her arms around David and began to cry. She amped up the performance, wailing the word "sorry" and moving her hands around his body, taking a second to feel the outside of his pocket. She felt a sharp point jutting out and, after a second, knew what it was: a badge.

After taking a few labored breaths, she looked at her brother. He had a solemn look on his face, as though he felt sorry for her. She turned and kissed David on the forehead.

Nicole turned back again and saw that Adrian was no longer looking at her, but had begun carefully moving her urn onto the wooden shelves, probably disgusted at the sight of the kiss, just like always. She took advantage of the moment and slid the badge out of David's pocket. It wasn't a real badge, she decided as she felt the points against her palm, and when she glanced down at the inscription, an overwhelming urge to wail and ask for forgiveness struck her: it read "Detective Demik."

She couldn't believe he had kept it all these years—a stupid gift that had gotten messed up in the making. And why was it in his pocket? She hugged him again, knowing he must have been planning to show it to her when they met up, not knowing their next encounter would have lethal consequences.

"Alright, you two. I think you've had enough."

Nicole panicked as her brother began walking towards her. The badge was still on the ground between her and David's legs.

"NO," she shouted as her hand dropped between their legs. She pulled David closer with the other arm and hugged him, feeling his crusty blood against the side of her face. "I haven't said goodbye yet."

"Go on, then. Say it," Adrian said as he crossed his arms and stared.

While shouting, Nicole had used the side of the badge to dig into the dirt. It wasn't much, but she hoped it was enough to conceal it from Adrian. She wished she would have thought to put it between her legs, where she could have penguin-walked back with it, blaming her awkward movements on her leg pain.

But she didn't, and so she turned to David one last time as she covered the badge with loose dirt and pressed down on it with her palm.

"I don't have the words to say goodbye the way I should. You meant so much to me, and I thought about you every day I was gone. I'm sorry I didn't keep in touch. I thought I was selfish for wanting to be alone, but after a while, I knew you were probably better off without me anyway. I don't know if you're up there or not, but if you are, just know I never meant to hurt you, and that..." Nicole closed her eyes and kissed David on the forehead, then leaned in to whisper so Adrian couldn't hear. "*I love you.*"

She refused her brother's help getting to her feet. She looked down and saw that the badge had disappeared. The thought of David's delight upon first receiving the gift played in her mind as she made her way back to the other side of the room.

She sat back down and raised her arms for Adrian to cuff. She knew it was coming and had no energy to fight it. The handcuffs closed, and she felt her fingertips begin to cool as the blood left them again.

Adrian moved the wheel back to the corner and cleaned up the room in silence. When everything was back to what he considered normal, he looked at Nicole and smiled.

"You did good," he said as he turned off the light and opened the door. "You'll be with Mother in no time."

CHAPTER VI:
FRIENDS IN LOW PLACES

On Tuesday morning, Adrian walked into the small kitchen space of his house and fixed himself a neat plate of eggs benedict, then sat to eat them with the Valley News. He only opened the paper to make sure obituaries were submitted with correct information. The grieving were not always sticklers for grammar.

This morning, though, the front page read, "Abandoned Car Sparks Search For Missing Hartford Police Officer."

Adrian studied the caption below the image of a car parked in the woods: "A vehicle belonging to a Hartford resident was found early Monday morning near the Watson Upper Valley Dog Park. While the search continues for the missing officer, David Demick Jr., anybody with information is being urged to contact HPD."

Adrian flipped to the continuation page on B7 and read the two accompanying paragraphs. It seemed they didn't have any more information than he wanted them to, and that was a beautiful thing.

He had thought about driving David's car deep into the backwoods of the neighboring town of West Hartford, but decided the drive would be too risky and that a semi-public place would leave authorities questioning the severity of the find long enough for him to get the rest of his predicament sorted out.

Excellent, he thought as he slit his eggs open and watched the yolk bleed onto his English muffin. *Time is on my side.*

He moved to the living room and sat down on the seldom-occupied sofa, staring at the TV without turning it on. His head hurt from mulling over the Nicole riddle.

Does a path exist that saves her soul AND her life? He had asked himself the question a hundred times, and could never come to a satisfying conclusion. He knew she was guilty; the blood caking onto the floor told him that.

She'll never recover from the damage she's done. She's doomed to walk the earth with that guilt. He repeated the sentences to himself, hoping they would tear down the obvious mental hurdle that she was family, his own flesh and blood. He hated her for tossing him into this chaos again and forcing him to consider doing something that, after causing their mother's death, he'd vowed he would never do again: kill a woman.

After a while, he walked back into the kitchen and took a cell phone out of a drawer. He wasn't a fan of carrying it around and depending on electricity to stoke his serotonin glands for pleasure. He saw it as a weakness and refused to

126

give into society's lust for vanity, so it sat in the drawer, barring the occasional night of charging.

Now, he flipped it open and navigated to the contacts. It was a short list—less than half a dozen names illuminated by the LED backlight. He found one listed as "H" and pressed the call button. It rang a few times, then went to voicemail. He closed the phone without leaving a message and placed it down on the seat next to him. He knew the routine: *call, wait, answer.*

While waiting, he reached for the Bible sitting on the stand next to the sofa and opened it to a passage from Isaiah: "If you pour yourself out for the hungry and satisfy the desire of the afflicted, then shall your light rise in the darkness and your gloom be as the noonday."

He read the lines twice and closed the book again, allowing the words time to shower him in their glory and remind him of his own journey beneath that of his sister and the others he had helped along the way. He felt complacent again, and when the phone began to ring next to him, he sat up straight with confidence and flipped the screen open.

"Hello," he said as he put the phone to his ear. It wasn't a jovial salutation, but a dry, business-transaction monotone. He heard a woman cough on the other end of the line before responding.

"Hey, *you* again?

"Yeah, me again. I was hoping to see you sometime today if you can... get away."

After a brief pause, the woman replied "Hold on," then went silent again. He heard the faint sound of a door opening and closing, then passing traffic and what he assumed was a lighter sparking up a cigarette or, more likely, a joint.

"He's not here right now, if you're wondering why I didn't bring up the Army. You lookin'?"

Adrian thought about it and said, "Yes, for three." It was more heroin than he usually bought at once, but he thought it would probably be necessary. He sometimes got it for free when the gentlemen he assisted into the afterlife were holding—often, actually—but sometimes, like now, he had to take matters into his own hands, and so he had carefully found his own source: Jamie Austin.

Aside from being whom Cooper Austin lovingly referred to as his "mouthy wife," Jamie was a small-time dealer who had been around long enough to know how to do things with discretion. He knew his name was listed under "Salvation Army" in her phone in the event Cooper was around when Adrian called, allowing him to simply pretend to be a volunteer when he needed to pick up. Then, once he met up with her, he would give her a small box of assorted foods to keep up the façade and leave with his instrument of obedience. It was a simple system, and it worked. He only needed to call one or two times a year if his angels had particularly dirty wings.

"Holy shit, you havin' a party or something? I don't know if I can do that all at once without Coop askin'. That's halfa what we got left."

"No, no party. I'm just sort of paranoid these days—you know how it is. I just want to get more all at once and limit the times I have to call. I'll make it worth your while, I promise." This time, he added a fraction of sauciness to his words. He had gotten the impression that she would toss in a free *favor* at no extra charge if he had ever asked, and her schoolgirl crush on him was another reason he knew she would never give his name up.

"Well, I suppose I can figure somethin' out. When are you thinkin'? He'll be back in a little bit, but he's going out later tonight around six."

"Is he going out of town?" Adrian asked, knowing that the answer was more crucial than the others.

"No, nothing like that, but should be a couple hours at least. Stupid fucker thinks he's gunna get rich on guns, but ain't shit for buyers around here."

"Six is perfect. Send me..." He loathed the next words he had to say and released them more slowly. "... a text when he leaves. I'll call."

"Okey doke, see you later... handsome."

He closed the phone and placed it on the stand next to the sofa, picking up the Bible and reading the passage from Isaiah one more time before standing up to get ready for work.

The day passed by quickly. No cremations were slated for the afternoon, and there were no families to help with arrangements, so he spent most of the morning going over records and double-checking his previous work. No mistakes, as usual, and everything was in its place. On his lunch break, he brought some food to Nicole and did a sweep of the graveyard, making mental notes about which stones needed to be fixed before he mowed on Friday.

He felt slightly annoyed that Nicole hadn't even looked at him while he dropped off supplies. He was trying to save her, after all. The least she could do was muster up a "thank you."

He stopped at the bank and made a withdrawal before going back to the parlor, deciding it was smarter than having to rush around at the end of the day. He stuffed the envelope into the glove box and returned to work feeling prepared.

A little while after he'd resumed the mundane task of vacuuming the viewing area, his father stopped by with a reminder that he was attending a funeral conference and wouldn't be in town until the following Friday. "The things they do with superglue would amaze you" he said, mentioning the "setting the features" segment that kept him wanting to return every year. He also mentioned that Pastor Robinson would be stopping by at some point the next day with some newer items for the prayer book, and that Adrian needed to be available.

Being tethered in one place had always made Adrian feel like a prisoner—like he was powerless over the schedule of those with no respect for his time—so he decided he would just call later that night and set a meeting time rather than sit around twiddling his thumbs. He appreciated Felix for everything he had taught him, but now wasn't really the best time to be locked into a situation akin to waiting for the cable guy.

"And if you hear anything from Nicole," Scott added while walking out the door, "pick up your phone and call me. I'll come right back. Unless you think I should just skip the conference?"

He shot Adrian a look that said he would take advice either way, but would prefer if it leaned toward disagreement. "They'll have another one at the end of the year, but who knows when your sister's gunna show up again?"

"Who knows if she'll even show up at all?" Adrian replied, needing to convince his father to leave. "You can't stop what you're doing just for her. That doesn't show her your priorities are in the right place at all. You go, and I'll hold down the fort and let you know if I hear anything. Like you said, you can always jet back if she comes around, but your jaw setting has gotten a bit sloppy lately, so you definitely shouldn't miss it."

"Sloppy," Scott said, shaking his head, but simultaneously surprised Adrian had said a real joke. "Alright, alright, but call me any time; I'll have my phone on me. Should be pretty quiet here next week. I went ahead and let Harvey over in Lebanon know I was leaving, so they're gunna take our clients until I get back. You've been a little... on edge lately yourself, and I figured you could use a break, so finish up here and take some time off. I mean it."

"You didn't have to do that," Adrian said, feeling a little annoyed his father still didn't trust him to take care of the business in his stead. He stifled the urge to ask his father why as the idea of extra time to deal with Nicole sank in. "I'm sure I can find something to help me relax, I suppose. Have a good trip. Pay attention to the wiring segment."

The workday came to an end with just as much excitement as the start. Adrian locked up the parlor at 6:00 p.m. and took the phone out of his pocket as he walked to his car. The feeling of being a slave to electricity washed over him again as the screen opened and relayed that he had one new message that simply read, "Gone." He scrolled to the contacts again and pressed the small green phone icon after finding "H."

"Where are you?" he said.

"Still at the motel. You?"

"Getting in my car now. I was thinking the Leb spot, if you can get the bus?"

"Yeah, sure, I gotta run outside if I'm gunna catch it, though. I'll see ya there." She hung up the line and Adrian got into his car. He drove over the bridge connecting White River, Vermont to West Lebanon, New Hampshire, and after driving through a few lights, eventually turned into a shopping outlet containing a few smaller box stores.

He parked in a half-full lot between two buildings, with one side of the space fronted by a footwear store brandishing a "Going out of Business" sale and the other side the employee entrance of the pet and aquarium center. The parking lot was usually only occupied when people couldn't find a spot in front of the other stores, which made it the perfect place to disappear into the tree line behind the loading docks.

Adrian got out of his car and walked to the end of the lot, taking the phone out of his pocket and putting it to his ear to give the illusion that he was making an important call or waiting for someone to show up and shop for discount shoes with him. He didn't see anyone around, so he walked to the end of the lot and into the trees. After scanning his surroundings one last time, he took a few more steps into the woods and heard the brook bubbling down the bank.

No doubt some shady shit has gone on here, he thought, staring at the empty liquor bottles thrown precariously into the bushes. But the coast was clear.

A few minutes passed before he heard leaves rustling from the same direction from which he had come. He put the phone to his ear to make another fake phone call, but closed it again when Jamie's face appeared through the tree branches.

She was wearing pants that had holes ripped in the knee—probably sold that way, Adrian guessed—and a black sweatshirt. She looked a little old to be wearing distressed jeans, but the deep lines and crow's feet under her eyes mixed with the lack of color in her skin told anyone who looked at her that attire was probably the least of her concerns. Adrian thought she had probably been considered beautiful when she was younger, before the popularity faded and the onset of real-world responsibilities got to be unmanageable without a mind-altering chemical escape route.

"Anyone behind you?" he asked as he looked past the place where she had entered.

"Nope, just me. Here ya go." She pulled two bags out of her pocket, each filled with smaller bags banded together, or—as Jamie had informed him—"two bundles."

He had taken the envelope out of his car on the ride over, and now produced it from his pocket, trading it with her and quickly stashing the heroin where the envelope had been.

"So," she said after counting the money and putting it into her bra, "was I right or what? You havin' some sort of party?"

"No, no. Like I said before, I don't think it's going to be easy to meet up with all this stuff happening around town, so it makes sense to buy in quantity."

"Yeah, I s'pose that's true. OH, HEY," she added, turning to make direct eye contact, "did they figure out where your sister is yet?"

Adrian looked back at her in disbelief. *How does EVERY-ONE know she's in town?*

"Nicole?" he said calmly instead. "She's been at my father's house. Why? I wasn't aware that you knew her."

"I don't—not really, anyway. Double D stopped by the motel looking for her a few days ago and I told him she was in the room next to me and Coop. Said he hadn't heard from her in a few days and her car was still there—saw it walkin' to the bus, actually. Figured she was missing or something, and Coop told me she was one of you Emersons."

Adrian knew "Double D" meant "David Demick." He listened to Jamie's story, absentmindedly twisting the plastic baggies in his pocket and trying his best to conceal the anger building up inside as the Nicole chaos continued to unravel.

"Ahh, ok. I don't know if you knew this, but she was gone for over a decade, so there's quite a bit to catch up on. She's been reliving her glory days, mostly, catching up with the old gang and such. I'm sure she'll be back in a day or two so she can get home to Arkansas—she lives there now, and it sounds like it's a bit nicer. Warmer, too, she said, which I could be persuaded by."

He recognized he was babbling and took a breath. "What's your husband up to tonight anyway? You said he was off buying guns or something?"

He had laid out enough of a cover story, and wanted to press forward with the other portion of his plan. "I might," he said, taking a step closer to Jamie and looking from her eyes to her chest, "feel a bit like partying after all."

"Is that right?" she said as she took her own step in and ran a finger down his arm.

"Well, I know you're a married woman and all," he said, grabbing her hand and kissing it, "but I think maybe I'm going to miss having to call you."

He read the desire in her eyes, then pulled her body against his, kissing her on the lips. She reached down and unpinned his belt buckle.

"Not now," he said and stepped back, running his hand through her graying, dirty-blonde hair. "You said Cooper was going to be out a while?"

"Yeah," she said as she came back to her senses. "He said he'd probably be back at ten or eleven, but I wouldn't be surprised if he stayed out all night. The bastard never comes home when he says he's gunna."

"Meet me here," he said, then kissed her on the hand again. "At nine."

She looked at him, her eyes searching for proof that he was serious. He put his hand on her hip and pulled her in, kissing her on the lips again to make sure she knew he was.

After a minute of barely surviving the smell of cigarettes and vodka, he pulled away from her and said goodbye, then made his way back through the trees, pulling out his phone and preparing for the old trick named, "I just checked the woods by the store, are you sure they left the bike there?"

He got in his car and watched Jamie come out of the woods before exiting the parking lot and driving in the direction of White River, feeling the high he had gotten addicted to over the years, one that didn't take any drugs to achieve—just prey and a plan.

When the mouthy wife is away, the naughty husband can play.

2

While waiting for his date, Adrian returned to the parlor and swapped out his car for the company van. In the front, he put his phone in a cup holder, and in the back, he placed a short strand of rope, a tarp, a box of nitrile gloves, and a zippered black body bag.

He turned the key and was met with hesitation from the engine. *Come on, you piece of shit,* he thought, hitting the steering wheel and listening to a clicking sound mock him. The van was old, and probably should have been replaced years ago, but Adrian suspected his father would keep it on the road until the odometer maxed out or the wheels fell off.

It started at last, and he thanked the heavens before getting back on the road and making his way to the vault, where he backed up to the front entrance, a ritual he had performed dozens of times with only a rake to distract the prying eyes of townsfolk, rendering him beautifully harmless and boring. He got out and eyed his parking job, and when he decided it was good enough, he reluctantly turned off the engine.

He unlocked the door and swung it open, then made his way to the lamp and turned it on. He could have probably done everything he needed to in the dark, his time spent in that place having mapped out every corner in his mind, but he was curious whether his sister would continue sulking, and wanted the light to read her face.

She winced as the brightness caught her face without warning, and kept her eyes closed as he unlocked the handcuffs. "Only for a minute. Don't do anything stupid."

He watched her rub her hands together and blow hot air onto them again, knowing she couldn't actually do anything even if she wanted to.

"I'll be right back," he said, swinging the door open again. "Leave the urns alone, please. Show some respect for the dead."

He returned a minute later with gloves on his hands and holding—to Nicole's premature dismay—a body bag.

"Don't worry, it's not for you," he said as he laid the bag on the ground and unzipped it. "It's for him."

"What can I do to help?" she asked, surprising him.

"Help? Well, you could go back to Arkansas, I guess!" he replied sarcastically, then opened the bag and used the bottom of his boot to nudge David's body into a prone position.

"Please, just… just let me help," she begged. "I did this to him, not you. I NEED to help."

Adrian felt suspicious of her sudden change in demeanor, but ultimately decided it didn't matter. If she tried anything fishy, he could just kick her over too. "Legs or shoulders?"

He could tell she was holding back the pain from standing on her busted leg. She barely squeaked out her reply. "Shoulders."

After a three count and a heave, David's body flopped over onto the body bag, causing Nicole to lose her balance and fall on top of the corpse. She let out a shriek and pushed herself off, sitting with her back against the wall almost exactly where David had sat before. She rubbed her leg and scanned the ground out of the corner of her eye before taking a deep breath and looking back at Adrian.

"What?" she asked as he stared back.

"Nothing," he said, then took his own curious glance at the place she had looked. "I wasn't sure you'd have the stomach for this part."

He adjusted David's body so he could pull the bag up around him, pulling the zipper closed to finish the job.

"I appreciate your willingness to do your part," he said, offering his hand to help Nicole to her feet. "You're full of surprises."

She took his hand, and just as she got to her feet, he pulled her in close, his face almost touching hers.

"But make no mistake," he said, the faint glow returning to his eyes, "Mother would hate to see her son made a fool of, so if you've anything but repentance in your head, you better get it out now, before it starts a fire."

Adrian locked the handcuffs again and dragged the bag to the door, positioning it on the side of the stairs before connecting a large metal hook to the bag's handles. The hook was connected to an old pulley system that made it easier to raise or lower things between floors.

Adrian turned off the light and walked to the door. "I'll be back in a while. Hopefully with a friend."

The pulley came to life with a squeal and a moan, paired with the muscle-clenching sound of plastic scraping wood. The load reached the top of the stairs and disappeared, leaving Nicole alone with her thoughts once again.

The van was easy to hear firing up on the surface, and when the engine's noise faded away, Nicole let out a sigh of relief. *It's buried,* she thought as she replayed the moment Adrian had almost noticed her looking for the badge on the ground. *Who knows what he would have done with it, or done to me?*

She had thought she was starting to read Adrian pretty well, but now he seemed to be pinballing hard between being outright awful, and deceptively collaborative.

The loneliness sat with her in the vault, waiting for what she assumed would be a horrific answer to the question: *What did he mean by 'friend'?*

And while it was silly and downright disgusting to think she hadn't been alone before seeing that David's body was cold and lifeless, it struck her that now she wasn't just alone in the present, but most likely would be alone in the future too.

If I have a future, she thought as the teenage version of David wandered into her mind and flopped himself down next to her on the school bus.

"You do," he said as he raised up his hand and caressed her cheek. "I promise."

3

Adrian fired up the incinerator and pushed David's body inside.

He looked at the clock on the wall as he closed the door. *Perfect*, he thought. It was only 8 p.m.

Once the first step was complete, he shut down the machine and used the pole to move David's ashes into a container to be pulverized. *I never said she was staying at the motel, Adrian. How did you know?*

"If you're so smart, David," Adrian said to the ashes as he started the pulverizer, "why are your bones in such small pieces?"

He listened for a response that didn't come, then continued. "Nothing to say?"

"Your mother's never going to take her back, Adrian. She killed me, yes, but she'll kill you, too. You have no idea how resilient she is."

"What would you know? She ran away from you as fast as anyone else, and you don't know anything about her—or ME, for that matter."

"I know you killed your mother. Hell, the whole town knows! Little Adrian Emerson had a temper tantrum and knocked mommy down the stairs. Do you really think this is going to save her? Do you think..."

"SHUT UP," Adrian yelled at the empty room.

He stopped the pulverizer and emptied the ashes into a bag. He thought they might melt the plastic, having been moved through the steps much faster than a normal cremation, but they had cooled just enough for the bag to hold its shape, so he threw them into a box. Before he closed the lid, he closed his eyes and offered one final retort to his imagination: *She'll be too dirty to live, or clean enough to die, if not a little bit of both.*

Adrian looked at the clock. It was 8:50 p.m.

He picked up the box and put it under his arm, where it stayed until he deposited it into the trunk of his car. He thought about using the van, but decided it was too risky to put that much pressure on a failing starter. He could also get a two-for-one if his plan worked the way he wanted.

He felt the rush returning as he started his car and set off.

He drove to the next stop and got out. The sign at the co-op grocery store illuminated the mostly empty parking lot. It was general knowledge that that particular lot doubled as a park-and-ride after hours, and anybody seen coming or going was either down at the bar or walking their dog somewhere along the grassy roadside.

He locked the door and took off on foot, wanting to keep a low profile by subtracting a vehicle's approach from the equation. He reached the front entrance of the Shady Acre at 9:15 p.m. and threw up the hood on his jacket to keep a low profile, knowing the absence of vehicles didn't mean the rooms were empty. More likely, the rooms were just full of people with DUIs who didn't fully appreciate the benefits of free after-hours parking.

He moved onto the property, his mission guiding him like water seeking its level. He walked in the shadows and narrowly avoided being hit by a beer can that came flying

141

down from the second-floor balcony. He heard a woman laughing, followed by a man assuring her that littering was mandatory at the Shady. *Cleanliness is next to godliness, however, asshole.*

He pulled Nicole's keys out of his pocket and followed the numbers until he reached the door of the room she must have only gotten to see once. *"She was in the room next to me and Coop,"* he remembered Jamie saying, and quickly determined the one to the left must be theirs due to the full coffee can of cigarette butts.

He had never actually met Jamie there before—the gossiping pack of filthy motel rats surely would have destroyed any semblance of discretion he had enjoyed the moment he stepped foot on the property in daylight.

He opened Nicole's door and walked inside, turning on the light and ensuring the blinds were closed before sitting on the bed and taking out his phone.

"Running late. Hope you didn't change your mind," he typed out, then sent the text to Jamie, praying she hadn't. He looked around the room at the outdated furniture and painfully dull artwork on the walls and figured the owners hadn't made any changes to the place since the early 90s. *You get what you pay for,* he thought as he reached for Nicole's luggage, which had been hastily thrown open at the end of the bed. He pulled out a shirt as his phone began to vibrate.

He picked it up and read the text. "Here handsome, don't be 2 late."

Perfect, he thought. *Now where's that devious husband of yours?*

He opened a text message chain and typed a new number into the recipient box. He had taken it from the most recent lottery application for Cooper Austin and hoped, as the previous few applications had suggested, that he hadn't gotten yet another new phone.

"Is this Cooper?"

The response was almost immediate, which didn't surprise Adrian. Most people were chained to their phones these days like a bad dog in an electrical storm. "Who this?"

"I'm at the Shady, I think someone broke into your room."

"Who are u? How u know it's mine?"

Adrian decided he didn't need to respond to the last message. The idea was planted in Cooper's head, and that was all he needed. Men like Cooper didn't operate on the same wavelength as him; they didn't see the lining of every situation unfold before them to reveal what lay in wait beneath the crust of existence.

He waited exactly one minute and messaged Jamie again, "On my way." He knew people shortened it to "OMW", but he wouldn't allow himself to stoop to that level. He would trade places with David Demick Junior first.

"Gotta go. Coop called, said sum1 broke into r place."

Adrian read the message and stood, closing the phone with a *SNAP*. He knew the buses didn't run that late, and even if Jamie were a brisk walker, it would take her at least thirty minutes to get there from West Lebanon.

He walked out of the room and leaned on the door to the Austin suite, then, after a quick look around, raised his leg and mule-kicked the door. He expected it to take three or four tries, but felt the door break after only two. He walked inside and turned on the lights, then went over the room and picked up anything that looked like it was valuable.

If I were truly a thief, he thought as he pocketed only a knife, pot pipe, and 18 dollars cash, *I would regret trying to rob these people.*

He grabbed a spoon out of the drawer and took out his brown leather pouch and plastic bags. He loaded the syringe and placed it on the table next to the spoon. *Too neat,* he thought, and used his arm to sweep everything off the table onto the floor.

The room looked trashed—more than it already had, anyway—so he walked back out to the balcony and took the phone out of his pocket, feeling slightly intoxicated again by a rising tide of excitement.

Ten minutes passed with nothing but the sound of bass thumping from one of the rooms at the end of the row. Adrian watched as a few cars passed by the motel, but none of them stopped, so he opened the phone and looked to see if maybe Cooper had sent any last-minute "I don't believe you," or, more likely, "fuck off," texts. He found none and closed the phone as a car turned into the Motel parking lot without a signal. He watched it hastily pull into a spot below him, depositing Cooper out of the passenger seat and another man Adrian didn't recognize out of the driver's seat.

He thought about going back inside Nicole's room. He wasn't prepared for extra muscle. *I'm committed. Find a way,* he thought, then instead leaned over the balcony to yell at the pair. "HEY, one of you guys the one who lives in that room?"

He gestured at the broken door. "I think someone just broke in; they took off that way a few minutes ago." Then he pointed at the road, hoping the muscle would take the bait.

He watched the men look at each other for a second. "You go, I bet it's that's bitch Dizzy. Find him before the cops do."

The stranger got back into the car and peeled out of the parking lot in the direction Adrian had pointed while Cooper ascended the staircase and approached. Adrian opened Nicole's door and stood in the threshold, wanting to at least give the illusion that he belonged there.

Cooper walked up to his room and saw the broken door. "FUCKING CHRIST," he shouted, walking inside to inspect the damage.

Adrian heard him moving around inside, spouting off profanities while finding his treasures amongst the missing. Then, the thunderous footsteps stopped, and Adrian listened as Cooper started talking to someone he hoped was on the phone, and not in the bathroom.

"Someone broke into our place. Where the hell are you?" Adrian was relieved. Jamie was on the other end of the line, probably a little less than halfway between West Lebanon and the Motel, and desperately trying to figure out a lie that could cover up the fact that she had been out to cheat on him in the bushes behind a footwear store.

"Well, it had to be Dizzy, the fucker left a NEEDLE behind! Jay's out looking for him now, but hurry the fuck up. They didn't find your stash, but the cops might come, so we gotta get rid of it."

Of course there was a secret stash, Adrian thought. *These people could hide a skunk's asshole in a candy store if they thought they'd make a dollar doing it.* He heard the talking stop and knew it was showtime. He walked back out onto the balcony and opened his phone, joined a minute later by Cooper.

"Hey what did the guy look like—the one you saw?"

"I didn't really see him, to tell you the truth. He had a hood on and was moving pretty fast."

"Shit." Cooper looked out at the parking lot for a second, then turned to him again. "You're Adrian, right? The lottery guy? Well... the funeral guy. Why are you here, anyway?"

Adrian opened his mouth to respond, but Cooper figured it out first.

"Your sister, right. Did she see the guy? Pretty sure I know who it was, but can I talk to her?"

"Yeah, of course. Anything we can do to help."

They walked into Nicole's room, Cooper first and Adrian two steps behind him. He reached inside his pocket and closed his fingers around a strand of rope, closing the door behind him and assuring Cooper she was probably in the bathroom. *This is it,* he thought as his veins worked double overtime to ensure his blood didn't burst out of his skin. *The man who can answer your sister's prayers is right here in the flesh.*

"If it's who I think it was, he has a—"

Adrian threw the rope around Coopers neck and pulled it back, knocking him off balance and onto the floor. Cooper kicked his legs and flailed his arms, but Adrian shielded himself by lowering his face into his back and listened as Cooper gasped for air, his lips belting out short choking

146

bursts. He felt Cooper's skin get hot beneath his arms, and the acceptance of what he thought was death sink in one pulse at a time.

It's not your time quite yet, he thought as he removed the rope and got to his knees. He checked Cooper's pulse to make sure he was still alive, then, after confirmation, tied his hands together with the rope. He took a shirt out of Nicole's luggage, and after being momentarily distracted by how slutty the shirt was, tore it in half and made a gag.

Once Cooper was tied up and against the wall, Adrian took the phone out of his pocket and turned the ringer off, knowing Jamie would soon be back and most likely wondering where her husband had run off to after giving her the business over the phone. *She'll assume a hunt has ensued and probably won't miss him for hours, maybe days.*

He thought about the other man outside and bet he wouldn't be back either. That type was good for a show of strength, but crumbled under the threat of getting busted on someone else's dime.

He opened the brown pouch and concocted another dose of heroin, this time injecting it into Cooper's arm. He knew a higher drug tolerance was likely and he might have to give him another dose before the night was over; the bass-bumping neighbors could be at it for hours, and Adrian couldn't risk moving Cooper until he was sure the only ones left awake were too drugged-out to remember anything.

He turned out the lights and sat down on the bed, pulling his phone out and holding it up next to Cooper's. He marveled at the thought of someone living in a motel room for $250 a week on state assistance and still being able to afford a brand new phone. Surely it was the drug money that made it possible, and not taxpayer dollars, but still, he wondered how some people could ignore the obvious pain brought on by their greed, prioritizing electronic devices over things like transportation and—thinking about his kiss with Jamie—dental care.

Close to ten minutes after he thought about her, Jamie arrived back at the motel and walked through the broken doorframe into her room. Adrian pulled up Cooper's phone and felt the vibrations as the screen read she was calling. *He's a little busy at the moment, but leave your name and a number, and he'll call back when he isn't tied up.*

He sat in the hotel room until the bass music faded to nothing and the number of cars passing on the road had dwindled to one or two per hour. He looked at the clock. It was 12:30 a.m. Cooper had partially woken at one point, but the heavy dose of heroin running through his veins ensured he would be useless for hours to come.

The last thing Adrian was waiting on was Jamie; he had no idea when or if she'd gone to bed, and, having essentially been robbed, might not get a wink. He had peered through the curtains each time she went outside for a smoke every thirty minutes or so, and now watched her as she typed elaborate messages on her phone and tapped her foot anxiously on the floor. Cooper had said something about a stash, and since it wasn't in his pocket, Adrian knew it was still in its hiding place, and was likely the sole reason the police hadn't been called about the break-in.

At 1:00 a.m., an hour since the last time Jamie had been outside, Adrian decided it was time to move. He cracked the door open slowly and walked outside, greeted only by the cool night air. He waited again, listening for any stirring in Jamie's room.

When he heard none, he walked back inside and tapped his hand against the side of Cooper's face. He removed the gag from his mouth and untied his hands, making sure to keep the gag close in case Cooper suddenly developed a higher level of tolerance.

"Hey, wake up," he whispered, hitting him again on the other side of the face. "We found the guy who robbed you and choked you out."

"WHERT," Cooper blubbered, coming to slightly. Adrian had never used heroin personally, but after administering it as many times as he had at the vault, he knew the euphoric state his victims found themselves in was more like a dream than reality—a malleable, manipulatable, magical little dream.

"We have to go get him. Come on," Adrian said, trying to coax Cooper off the floor. It was a slow process, but once he got under Cooper's arm, he was able to lift him up and ferry him out the door. Cooper stumbled as they got onto the balcony and nearly fell over the edge. Adrian managed to grab the back of his shirt and pull him back, placing his arm around his waist to correct for the weight difference. They made it down the stairs after a few more wobbles, and, after navigating the parking lot, they arrived at Nicole's car.

"Whu...where is it...he?" Cooper said as Adrian clicked the unlock button and flopped him into the passenger seat.

"Not far, Cooper. Not far."

Adrian closed the door and ran back to the stairs. The near-fall had forced him to leave the motel room open, which would be a normal *oopsie-daisy* moment in most other circumstances, but this one seemed like the kind that would raise questions he didn't want to answer later. He made it to the top of the stairs as quickly as he could without making any unnecessary noise, but less than ten feet from the door, he found himself looking at a sliver of light stretching across the balcony from Jamie's open door.

He wasn't sure what to do at first. *Should I back against the wall and hope she doesn't look to her left for five straight minutes? Jump over the rail and run to the car? Strangle her and throw her in the trunk?* He knew he couldn't do any of those things, so instead, he took a breath and resumed his stride toward Nicole's door.

"Adrian?" she asked, squinting her eyes to get a better look through the darkness.

"Hey, sorry I missed you tonight," he said as he walked to the front of Nicole's door. "You said someone broke into your place?"

"Yeah, look," she said as she turned and pointed at the wood splinters jutting out from the door frame.

He eyed them with curiosity. "Oh, wow. That's a bit scary. Who was it?"

"Not sure," she said as she flicked her lighter and lit up a cigarette. "Coop's out looking for the guy now, I think. Probably just some asshole. What are you doin' here though? He could fly back any minute, but if you're quick I suppose..."

"Oh no I'm just grabbing some things for Nicole," he said hastily as he stepped on the threshold of Nicole's room and turned on the light. "She met up with some friends at the pub and got herself a little too tipsy to drive."

Adrian watched as Jamie's eyes then moved from him to Nicole's running car. He clenched his fist in his pocket as she did so, preparing to go with the trunk plan if that didn't work.

"At least she's got you to take care of her," Jamie said to Adrian's relief. He loosened his fingers and nodded in agreement. It was probably too dark for her to make out anything other than the shape of someone's head in the passenger seat, and any moving Cooper may have done would have resembled that of a drunk pub patron anyway.

"Is she coming up?"

"No, no, she's going to stay at our father's place one more night. It's not a mansion or anything, but he's gone for a few days, and at least the beds were made in this century!" They both laughed as Jamie put out her cigarette and threw it into the coffee can.

"Well, if the mood strikes again, you know how to reach me, handsome."

"Count on it," Adrian said with a smile. He watched her close the door, and a minute later the lights were out.

"Thank you," he said, looking up at the sky. He didn't necessarily feel good that things had almost gone sideways, but it did seem like God had his back on that one.

He had another moment of clarity and went inside Nicole's room to grab her luggage. *Good thing I grabbed these now, or I may have had to buy new ones.* He closed the door behind him and walked back to the car, placing the luggage next to David's box before entering the driver's seat.

Cooper was sleeping, stone-cold wasted. Adrian marveled at his luck. At any moment, he could have jolted awake and opened the door, forcing Adrian to double the amount of luggage in the trunk in a less-than-discreet way. *I knew you were going to be a big help, Cooper.*

He drove to the receiving vault and dragged Cooper out of the car. He didn't need him to be awake for this part either, since there was no talking his way out of walking a semi-coherent man into a cemetery in the middle of the night.

He got Cooper into the hatch door as fast as he could and connected the pulley hook to his belt, letting him slide down the stairs slowly. *Like a sack of potatoes*, he thought. He pulled back on the hook's rope as Cooper landed at the bottom, his feet hitting the ground first and eliciting a faint disoriented grunt.

Adrian turned on the light and found Nicole was awake and looking at him with bewildered eyes. He figured she'd heard the pulley at work, though she appeared to be under the impression a dead body would be returning.

"I know I'm not usually here this early, but I told you I was bringing you a friend. Look who it is!"

Adrian walked through the doorway and dragged Cooper into the room, sitting him against the wall where David had been earlier that day. He pulled the rope out of his pocket and tied Cooper's ankles, then placed the gag back over his mouth and put his hand on Cooper's head, ruffling up his hair. "I may be many things, but seldom is a liar one of them."

"Who is he?" Nicole asked, unable to look away from the poor man Adrian had literally roped into his delusion.

"His name is Cooper Austin, and he's the local legend I was telling you about. You may remember him as the criminal who took credit for killing David Demick Senior. I know, what a guy! Now, I'm not sure if it's true—in fact, I'm almost certain it is not—but the real truth is in there somewhere. It has to be. We're going to solve the Demicks' unfinished business, and, with any luck, make Mother proud of you again."

"Then what? I get to just leave?" she asked with zero expectation of a warm response.

"Then," Adrian said as he collected himself and stood up straight, ironing out the last few wrinkled cells of excess energy floating around in his bloodstream, "Mother decides from there."

CHAPTER VII: SCREWDRIVER BLUES & PURPLE HUES

Around the time David's skeleton was burning red-hot in the incinerator, Pastor Robinson opened the front door of Fleurry Hardware in White River. A small bell hanging from the doorframe chimed with his entrance and alerted the employees they had a dreaded "last-minute shopper." The girl behind the counter had been counting her drawer and stopped to offer help to Felix as he passed.

"We're closing in fifteen minutes, so if there's anything I can help you find, give me a holler."

"Actually," Felix said, placing his hands on the counter, "I was just coming by to see Brent. Is he still around?"

He saw relief wash across the girl's face as she realized she wouldn't have to help an aging gentlemen sort through boxes of screws to find the exact one needed for a dusty old coo-coo clock—or something else as painfully annoying—at closing time. He also remembered a time when Brent Fleurry's name evoked an uneasy response from people in town, back when he still wore a badge and rode shotgun with David Demick Sr.

"He's on the phone in the back. Should be up to help me close in a minute, or I can go get him if you want?"

"No, that's quite alright. He's expecting me, and I believe I know the way. Thank you..." He looked down at her nametag. "Halie."

After walking to the back of the store and finding the manager's office, Felix looked through the wire-covered window and saw that Brent, a man who had recently left his silver-fox years behind him and was easing his way into retirement, was no longer on the phone, but was rifling through papers on his desk.

"Gimme a minute. I'll be right out. Make sure the checks get put in the deposit bag this time, please," Brent said when Felix tapped on the door.

"And what about the pastor? Do you think he'll fit inside the bag too?" Felix said, feeling amused that he had been mistaken for a teenage girl.

Brent turned in his chair and got up. "Sorry, didn't know it was you," he said as he rushed to the door. "Come on in."

Brent looked out the window again, then closed the door behind Felix, pulling down the window shade before sitting. "Wish you woulda called first. Got six million things to do and only time for five."

"Yes, I know," Felix said as he sat in a chair next to Brent's desk, "but I thought perhaps an in-person conversation may bear more fruit."

Brent eyed Felix suspiciously for a moment, then picked up a pen from the table and began rolling it between his hands. "What's on your mind?"

"Well," Felix started, taking a look at the door himself before jumping into it, "I think that abandoned car you mentioned on the phone wasn't a fishing mishap, or something as easily explained. I get the feeling there are OLDER roots than meet the eye."

He watched as Brent's expression changed from inquisitive to ashamed. It was subtle, but the dropping of the eyebrows and slight pursing of the lips was a look he'd seen a thousand times on the faces of those he mentored and, not infrequently, in the mirror. Felix knew that Brent could sell a million hammers and a pound of nails with each, but would never be able to escape the memory of losing his partner in that hit-and-run all those years ago.

Brent looked down at the pen in his hand and rolled it a couple times. "And what makes you think that?"

"The vehicle belongs to David Demick Jr. Am I correct?" Felix asked quickly, afraid that if the question lingered too long, he may say something he didn't intend, incriminating himself.

Brent confirmed with a nod of his head, then added, "Whole force is on edge about it. Hushed up the details tryna catch someone with information they shouldn't have."

Felix understood the reasoning behind it; the blood from David Sr.'s death didn't even seem dry yet, and that was twenty years ago.

"Well, I saw David a day or so before he went missing," he added as Brent's pen-rolling slowed with suspicion. "He was looking for Nicole Emerson."

"Nicole? I didn't even know she was around," Brent said, his fidgeting speeding up again. "You're talkin' 'bout Scott's kid, right?"

"Yes, and nobody knew she was coming back, not even her father. That's the part I haven't quite figured out. Apparently, nobody has seen her for days except David, Cooper, and Jamie."

He shared his interaction with David outside the motel, citing David's quick getaway as the last time he had seen him before the discovery of his vehicle at the river.

"I guess I don't quite understand what you're sayin' here. You think she's got something to do with David's disappearance, and, what, his own father's murder on top of that?"

"I'm not sure what to think," Felix said to buy time. His intention wasn't to poke the beehive and get himself stung—not yet, anyway. He had spent years waiting for the right time to tell Brent the truth about David Senior's murder, but this wasn't it. For now, he only wanted to find out what the police knew about David Junior.

"I know David was infatuated with solving his father's murder, maybe even a bit more than you in those last years of polishing the badge, and I can't imagine all of this being a coincidence."

"No such thing as a coincidence," Brent said, his demeanor sinking along with his weight in his swivel chair. "I'm not privy to all the facts like I used to be, but the few sources I got left say they haven't found any evidence another person, male or female, was in the vehicle. They seem to think he's either bein' held captive somewhere, and a ransom note is gunna pop up, or they're gunna find him in the river."

Brent threw the pen down on the desk and put his fingers to his head to massage his temple. "Now what the hell happened to this town to deserve all this, anyway? Some freak kills a cop in cold blood, runs him down like a dog and goes back to his hidey hole. Then, comes back all these years later lookin' for his son? What the hell are we s'posed to do?"

As Felix opened his mouth to offer some form of calming reassurance, there was a knock on the door, followed by the muffled voice of a young girl. "Sorry to interrupt you, Mr. Fleurry, but I have the bank deposit for you."

Brent opened the door and took the bag, thanking her afterward and assuring her he would be out to help close the store momentarily. He sat with the maroon bank deposit bag in his hands, a token of the extreme metamorphosis he had gone through since retiring from the force, and trading a gun for a discount screwdriver.

Felix knew Brent had been a crooked cop of sorts, making money flipping shorted drug-bust hauls to him and a short list of others. He knew Brent had been shaken by the murder, and the town whispers had implied he'd been off making some side money when it happened and not "chasing down a robbery suspect" like he had claimed.

"The night of your partner's murder," Felix started again, "Cooper said he was in someone else's room."

"He never named the guy," Brent hurled back quickly, having been over the information hundreds of times. "Said it was just some junkie he'd never met before. We looked at that every which way AND sideways. There's only so much someone like that's gunna remember after a year, and you know as well as I do that Bev doesn't keep the cleanest books down there."

Felix almost slipped and asked how someone like Cooper could be the judge of what a junkie was, being so far from reality himself, but he internalized the urge and accepted that it was actually true—he had been.

"What if it didn't matter who was in the room?" he said, moving the conversation in the direction he needed. "But, rather, what he did with the car keys?"

He pulled a small set of keys out of his pocket and threw them on the desk in front of Brent.

"How did you—" Brent said as he carefully scooped them off the desk. He saw there were two small golden keys, a General Motors car key, and a key fob with a Chevy symbol at the bottom. "Where did you get these?"

"One of the young men I mentor gave them to me. Said they'd been through more than a few different hands over the years as some sort of 'vigilante criminal artifact' from the man who stood up to justice and won. Now, before you call in the big guns, just know I can't give you a name, and he's much too young to have had any part in what happened to your partner. But I think with a little more time at the church, I can get some more information, maybe even trace the keys back to who he got it from, and then, with any luck, the person Cooper stole them from that night."

Brent rolled the keys over in his hands and admired them as though they really were treasure. "I'm guessin' there's a reason you put these in my hands instead of turning them in?"

"Involving the police," Felix started, having expected the question, "may tip off the perpetrator and send them into the wind again, maybe forever. The best course of action would be looking into this ourselves. There's too much at stake to let some hotheaded freshman destroy our opportunity to finally have answers."

Brent rolled the keys over one last time before nodding his head in agreement and tucking them safely into his pocket. "I'll see what I can turn up on the fob," Brent said while standing and opening the door, "you squeeze that kid."

Felix left Brent to close the shop with his employee, knowing she would be doing most of the work now that Brent had the lead of a lifetime, a redemption route for the murder that shook the town to its core and cost Brent his career.

Before he left, he asked Brent to call him if his sources turned up anything else on Morgan, the winner of the hobo lottery and original subject of their concerns. The front door chimed again as Felix walked back out into the street, offering the girl a thin smile through the window before walking away.

His steps felt heavy on the way back to his car, as though they had expected to have a little more weight taken off them. He prayed Brent would keep his word about the keys, and, if so, the answers he sought would probably arrive sooner than he'd thought.

Not before I figure out what to do with you, he thought as he put his hand in his pocket and closed it on the small black key he'd kept for himself.

2

Adrian pulled open the hatch inside the Bacon Mausoleum on Wednesday morning and walked down the stairs with a small black bag under his arm. He opened the door at the bottom half-expecting to see Cooper rolling around at the entrance, trying to get free. Instead, he found him still slumped over on his side when he turned on the lamp.

He checked the restraints, proudly finding the knots in good order. He grinned as he opened the black bag and reached inside.

Nicole watched as he worked, fearing the next part in Adrian's master plan must be getting information out of Cooper with force. She saw also that Adrian seemed to be in a good mood, walking with a chilling bounce in his step. *This isn't just for me. He likes this.*

Out of the satchel came a small fat-handled screwdriver, a pair of pruning shears, a shaker of salt, and a handgun. She watched him place each item on the table in a neat line before pulling out the brown leather pouch from his back pocket, placing it at the end of the line with a small tap.

"Please have a seat," he said after unlocking her cuffs and motioning toward one of the wooden chairs. "And, before your mind wanders too far, know there aren't any bullets in that gun."

He reached into the front pocket of his pants and produced a bullet, holding it in his fingertips and moving slightly to allow the lamplight to bounce off its shiny surface. "David only left me three, so we can't waste them."

Nicole looked again at the gun on the table. It had been a tempting thought—surely firepower outweighed her handicap in the present situation—but she also knew nothing about guns, and the likelihood of her first attempt at shooting one being successful was laughably unrealistic. Instead, she sat in the chair and began the process of warming her body with her hands, a process sped up by the torture-implement display's energizing effect on her heart rate.

"How did you sleep?" Adrian asked as he returned the bullet to his pocket and stepped toward the table. He took two water bottles out of the bag and tossed one to her. He opened the other and began drinking.

"He kept talking in his sleep," she said after taking her own sip, the rush of water calming the scratchy feeling in her throat. "Something about a deal. I couldn't really understand him, but it kept me awake most of the night."

"I'm sure he's had plenty of deals gone sour. Nightmares are a side effect of scandal, and he's the self-proclaimed king."

"Adrian, I don't know what you're planning to do," she said, imagining salt being poured into wounds and Cooper's reality becoming more extreme than any nightmare, "but there has to be another way. He probably won't remember anything. Just drug him and bring him back to where you found him. Please. He'll think it was all a dream. Besides, I NEED to see a doctor. My leg isn't getting any better, and the longer we spend down here, the higher my chances of getting an infection."

She rubbed her swollen ankle and grimaced as if to prove her point, knowing the opposite was true, and that her ankle was less swollen today than it had been the day before. While the pain was still there, it had certainly felt less excruciating when she had gotten to her feet.

"That would be neat, wouldn't it? If things just worked out that way? But," he said as he used his foot to lightly tap at Cooper's side, "I've found that people don't accept the Lord's brand of equality with open arms."

Adrian then kicked Cooper in the side, jolting him awake and into a coughing fit. "I think you'll live."

Cooper came to and began violently squirming on the ground after turning to see where the blow had come from. "HRMM MRNNN," he mumbled through the gag over his mouth.

Adrian sidestepped a weak attempt at a headbutt, then put his foot down on Cooper's back, digging into his spine to stop the struggling.

"Hello, Coop. Glad you could finally make it to my humble abode. I'm going to take the gag off you now, but only if you promise not to bite. What do you say? Are you going to be a good dog?" Cooper nodded his head in agreement, and when the gag was removed, he kept his mouth closed, aside from a whimper escaping his trembling jaw.

"Good. Now, Cooper, meet Nicole, my sister." Cooper looked up from the ground at her momentarily, then rested his head back in the dirt.

"Now, you may not remember her very well, so let me catch you up. She moved away about fourteen years ago, after deciding she didn't care about her family anymore. She spent those years in Arkansas, where she became a nurse—a clumsy one, as you can no doubt tell by the size of her ankle.

She decided after all that time that the need to have her decisions validated was more important than what anyone else had going on, so she returned to our cozy little town and, wouldn't you know it, she was right! She wasn't here even a week and she went off and killed a cop. I'm sure you must find that at least a *little* impressive. After all, *you* have quite the reputation for menacing the police yourself."

"I didn't kill that cop," Cooper said, his demeanor changing to anger as the demon he'd created came back to bite him again.

"Careful, now. I know this situation isn't ideal, but if you tell me the truth, I won't have to hurt you."

"I DIDN'T KILL ANYBODY! LET ME GO, YOU FUCKING PSYCHOPATH!" Cooper began thrashing his head back and forth again. This time, his fingers joined the fight and stretched over the side of the rope, reaching for the knot.

"Oh, but you did. At least, you *said* you did, don't you remember? So, which is it? Are you a liar, or a killer? I know which one I'd rather be," he said as he let out a laugh and picked up the fat little screwdriver from the table, "but my sister thinks it's both."

Adrian twisted Cooper's face upward and plunged the screwdriver into his right eye socket, leaving only a quarter of its two-inch shaft exposed. Nicole let out a shrill scream as Cooper's body jolted from the blow. Her ankle gave way and sent her falling onto the floor, where she began panting and crawling back to her space on the wall. She sat back and looked at her brother, observing Cooper with a look of fascination on his face. *Or satisfaction,* she thought.

Cooper let out a long, agonized howl. Blood and tears ran down his face, mixing with the dirt on the ground to form a thin layer of mud on his cheek. "Get it out, GET IT OUT!" he shrieked, his fingers stretching for the knot more desperately than before.

"Shhhh," Adrian whispered as he put a finger to Cooper's mouth.

"How the FUCK do you expect me to be quiet? You stabbed me in the fucking eye!"

Adrian turned to Nicole, who had begun to shiver in the corner. "Hey, sis, what would you recommend for an abrasion to the eye? Tylenol? Aspirin? I can never remember."

When she did nothing but shake her head, he turned back and grabbed the end of the screwdriver still protruding from Cooper's face. "Oh, I remember now. It's Visine," he said as he twisted the handle, sending Cooper into another fit of pain. "Oh, shoot, it's a little crooked now, let me fix it..."

"OK," Cooper cried out as Adrian's hand neared the handle of the screwdriver again. "Ok."

"Excellent. Now I'm going to ask you what happened to that police officer again, and this time, I expect a little honesty." Adrian put his hand on the end of the screwdriver and pulled it out of the socket, causing Nicole to wince as it exited his body and revealed the mangled eye beneath.

"I already told you, I didn't kill him!" Cooper said between labored moans of pain. "I wasn't lying, I swear!"

"I think I believe you," Adrian said, to Nicole's amazement, "but you do know *something*. I can smell it on you. My sister here needs to know what it is, or she'll never be free, so tell me: who killed David Demick Sr?"

"I don't know. Like I told the feds, I just took the car and split when I saw the guy in the back seat, that's it! I don't know who the guy was. Maybe he got into a fight with the cop and was just sleeping it off in the back. I DON'T KNOW!"

Nicole watched as Adrian's face began to contort with anger again. *I can smell it on you,* she repeated in her mind as the lines on his forehead deepened. She was certain that being *free* also didn't mean free to leave, but rather free to die, but she didn't want to see another display of Adrian's interrogation skills, so she closed her eyes and tried to think of anything that might help Cooper remember.

"What about the keys?" she said at last, hoping it was enough.

"The keys?" Adrian asked. "What keys?"

"To the car," she said, thankful her distraction had worked, at least momentarily. "You said you saw someone in the back, then went inside, but what did you do with the keys?"

"Stupid question," Adrian said when she had finished. He shook his head and looked at her again. "The cops never found the car, so he must have left them in the ignition."

"No, I didn't," Cooper said as he rolled onto his side and looked at Nicole with his good eye. "I threw them in the trash at the motel. I remember wipin' 'em off and tossing 'em in there. I'm pretty sure the maids must have emptied the trash and never seen 'em."

"And who *was* the other guy?" Adrian asked. " You said you didn't know him in your interview, but that's not true, is it? You said he was just some junkie, and I'm not sure there's a needle in this town that doesn't have you or Jamie's name on it."

Cooper dropped his head and closed his eye again. "I didn't actually know him at the time. That part was true. And you know how it is out there—snitches get stitches. Besides, he didn't do it. He was passed out on the couch. Whoever owned that car killed that cop, not him."

"Who was the man at the hotel, Coop?" Nicole asked, knowing Adrian's version of that question would have been phrased the same, but been delivered fundamentally differently.

"It was… Pastor Robinson."

"Felix?" Adrian said in disbelief. Nicole watched the information wash over him like a hot iron to a plastic raincoat.

"You're lying," he said, pulling Cooper's hair back again and aiming the screwdriver at his face.

"I SWEAR IM NOT, PLEASE YOU GOTTA BELIEVE ME."

"He's not lying!" Nicole screamed. Adrian looked between her and Cooper with frustration, unable to accept what he was hearing.

"And how on earth would you know anything about it, you stupid bitch?"

She could sense the accusation was devastating to Adrian and the self-righteous persona he must have developed through his relationship with the pastor in the years after she'd left the state.

"I remember seeing him around town, hanging out on the street corners, before he turned all… godly. You were too young to pay attention to things like that, but I did. After David's dad was killed, I couldn't help but picture EVERY person on the street as the secret killer. I remember thinking it was strange that people like him could be hanging out under the bridge one day and going to church the next, but Dad said that's what church was for—for turning your life around. He's telling the truth. He has to be."

Adrian's hands tensed at Nicole's words. Then, after a second, he let go of Cooper's hair and got to his feet.

"So," he said, beginning to tap the screwdriver against his hand and pacing around the table, "you leave the keys, and either Felix takes them, or the maid finds them, but that doesn't explain what happened to the car. How did it just disappear?"

"A spare," Cooper added as Adrian rounded the table near him again. "I was inside the hotel for a while, if the driver lived close by, they coulda ran to get a spare key and came back. Maybe they weren't done with the guy in the back."

"Why wouldn't Pastor Robinson turn himself in if he knew they were looking for the person in that room?" Adrian asked. Nicole could sense Felix's potential involvement was eating at him, blinding him to everything else Cooper had said.

"Felix must have known who owned the car, or..." He stopped pacing and closed his hand around the shaft of the screwdriver. "... he knew something about the cop. Something that made him deserving of the fate he received."

Or the cop wasn't dead yet and Felix used the car after Cooper left, Nicole thought. It didn't account for the man in the back seat, who may or may not have existed, and she didn't dare say it out loud anyway. She could tell Adrian liked his own version of the events—the one that let him keep his pride.

She watched with relief as Adrian dropped the screwdriver into the black bag, but sucked in a quick burst of air as he instead picked up the pruning shears.

"What are you doing? He told you the TRUTH!" she shouted as the glow of the lamp streaked across the metal blades.

"I'm not very good at untying knots," Adrian said as he brought the shears to Cooper's side. "Now roll over."

Cooper kicked his feet out and got enough momentum to roll onto his stomach. He looked at Nicole and mouthed the words, "thank you," to acknowledge the fact that her last-second interruption had saved his eye, and probably his life.

"Wow, that sure is a tight knot. I'm not sure I could have ever untied it," Adrian said as he lowered the shears. "And I really don't want YOU to, either."

Adrian pulled the shears closed and cut off Cooper's pointer finger. Blood began gushing onto his back as he screamed in agony.

"Don't think I didn't notice your little hands squirming back there, Coop. We're not finished here. Not yet. So, if I were you, I would quit while I was ahead," he said. Then, after thinking about it for a moment, he added, "Or while you still HAVE one."

Adrian retrieved a syringe from the table and injected Cooper with another dose of heroin. After a few minutes, Cooper's screams began to quiet and his body went limp.

Adrian picked up the lamp and walked to Nicole's side. "We'll have to fix that. Unless we want him to die, of course."

What's the point? she thought as the lamplight spread across the pool of blood on the floor. She knew now the chances he was going to let either of them out alive were as slim as Cooper getting a pilot's license. "What am I supposed to do? I'm just a nurse, not a doctor."

She expected him to belittle her, to laugh at her and remind her how poor her decisions in life had been, but he didn't. Instead, he held up the lamp and stared.

"No, you don't mean…" she said, looking at the flame. *He wants me to cauterize the wound.*

"Yes," he said, hovering his hand above the flame. "It has to be you."

She hoped to find any small implication that he was joking, that this was one of his sick mind games. She found none. "Why? I didn't cut it off. YOU did. And that wouldn't kill him anyway!"

Adrian smirked at Nicole and removed the glass that surrounded the lamp's core. "Wouldn't it though?" He said with a matching grin, implying if one finger didn't do the trick, there were nine more to try. "This is for YOU, sister, remember? I can't do ALL the work. Otherwise, Mother may think you cheated her somehow, and that's not fair to her, is it?"

Nicole closed her eyes and took a deep breath through her nose. She opened them again and looked at Cooper, who was mumbling on the floor as the blood continued to drip out of the wound where his finger used to be. She decided he was right about it needing to be done, at least. The thought of her mother wanting her to do it was sickening, but jumping headfirst into Adrian's delusions was the only way out.

"Ok," she said, looking back at her brother. "I did this. I need to make it right."

She reached out her hand and used Adrian's shoulder as a support to get to her feet, then made her way to Cooper. She knelt and brought the flame to his hand. "Mother, I don't know if you can hear me or not, but I want to say I'm sorry for letting you down. I'm sorry I couldn't control myself and strayed so far from your lessons. I hope this pleases you, and that soon, you can accept me back into your heart."

Adrian stepped on Cooper's back to keep him from moving, and Nicole moved the flame to his hand and placed his finger into the fire.

Cooper let out a low, guttural cry as the blood began to evaporate and the flesh began to burn. A sizzling sound emanated from the wound that reminded Nicole of grilling hamburgers. The room filled with the stench of burnt flesh and blood, and when at last the wound was sealed, she moved the flame away from his hand and wept.

Adrian took his foot off Cooper's back, then sat him up against the wall to inspect the size of his pupils. "I'm sure that wasn't easy," he said, seemingly convinced Cooper was down for the count, "but how did it feel?"

"I... I don't know," she said, wiping her eyes and straightening up, "but it needed to be done. What I feel doesn't matter anymore."

She swallowed hard after the words left her lips. It wasn't just a ploy—it was the truth.

"I told you we were in this together now. I know you would probably say just about anything to get out of this place, but I can see in your eyes that you WANT to make this right."

Nicole nodded, then stood up and walked back to her side of the room, ready to reclaim her space on the floor and have this whole encounter be over.

"Now is not the time to rest. We've still got so much to do," Adrian said as he looked into the flame of the lamp and replaced its cover. "And I think the next step is to get you out of this place and cleaned up."

3

Adrian cuffed Nicole momentarily, then left the vault. He returned a few minutes later through the other door, then placed the rest of the items from the table back into his bag and zipped it closed, leaving out only the handgun, which he chambered with a bullet and held out at arm's length.

Nicole thought she would have felt the urge to take her chances trying to wrestle it from his hands, but instead, an overwhelming sense of sadness struck her at the sight of the white pearly grip, fortifying her doubts about her ability to fight without more innocent people getting hurt.

"What are you going to do with that?" she asked, knowing it would be irrational, but not implausible, for Adrian to drug Cooper and then immediately shoot him.

"Well, this gun belonged to David, and his father before him," Adrian said as he held it in front of him and turned it over to show her the sides.

"Each of them met an untimely demise while brandishing it, but I believe that had more to do with their foolish nature than anything else. Now," he said as he placed it into the waistband of his pants and covered it with his shirt, "it's my insurance policy, an objective participant in tonight's activities that will decide if you've followed my directions and done what I've asked or have strayed beyond redemption. If you try to run and fail, it finds our good friend Cooper here and escorts him to the afterlife. If you try to run and succeed, it does the same. If you call any kind of attention to yourself or me, it makes up its own mind on what happens. Get it?"

Nicole nodded. It wasn't unlike what she had seen dozens of times before on true crime shows and movies. Except those were just things that people made up in Hollywood, not secret cemetery vaults in the backwoods of Vermont.

"I know you're still in pain, but unfortunately, we have to take the long way out." He moved to the door guarding the entrance to the mausoleum and opened it, motioning for her to begin ascending the stairs. She made her way up slowly, feeling the sides and taking in every detail she could, like the roots and rocks jutting out from the wall and the creaking of the steps. The light went out behind her and she heard the door close again, leaving the stairway in total darkness.

Nicole felt the pain in her ankle flare as she reached the top of the stairs. It certainly wasn't completely healed, but she knew if this had been a few days prior, the journey may have been impossible.

The faint outline of the hatch glowed red at the edges with sunlight trying to break through the sides. She pushed, and after a moment, it popped open and showered her with a dozen different-colored lights. She squinted at first, having been in the dark for so long her eyes felt as if *they* were being attacked with a screwdriver. After a moment, she could see that the room was filled with the colors of the stained-glass artwork making up the mausoleum windows.

"Hold on," she heard from behind her. Adrian poked his head out of the hatch and pulled himself up first, turning around after and offering his hand.

"Wait here," he said as she stood up and began looking around the room, spying a table covered in dusty picture frames and a statue of Jesus hanging on the wall. The casket in the center of the room was also covered in a thick layer of dust that spoke to the march of time but didn't detract from the exquisite craftsmanship beneath. She was reminded of having almost reached this room once before and felt a phantom pain ripple through her still sore fingers.

Adrian opened the door and stepped outside. After deciding the coast was clear of any visitors, he returned. "Time to shine."

They left the mausoleum and made their way to Adrian's car. He opened the door for her and got in the other side, removing the gun from his belt and placing it between his legs. As they drove down the hill and approached the exit sign—one she couldn't have imagined ever seeing again—another vehicle slowed on the road and signaled their intention to turn into the cemetery.

"Remember our friend," Adrian said, forcing a slight smile and waving his hand at the vehicle, allowing him to make his turn first.

Nicole avoided eye contact with the other driver and looked down at the floor, knowing that the only real way out was to dig even deeper. She also didn't know of a look that could say, "Pardon me, but this guy is insane. He's going to chuck me into a fire if you don't jump out and save me—at the risk of your own safety, of course."

Adrian turned on the radio as they drove down the road, the sound of NPR filling the air with an aging senator talking about why he thought unemployment rates were at an all-time high.

She had a strange feeling then that if things had worked out just slightly differently, she may have been on this car ride anyway. She could have been riding around town and catching up with her little brother, talking about things they'd never had the chance to, like how awful it was to pay taxes, and how senators always seemed to say one thing and do another.

She had always had a picture of Adrian in the back of her mind that she subconsciously dusted off and promised to take better care of in the future. In that moment, the smiling face inside the picture seemed to be of a stranger, not the wicked man sitting beside her.

A few minutes later, Nicole's heart rate sped up again as they pulled into the funeral parlor and the radio went silent again. *It was all a lie. He just wanted to get me here quietly.*

"Don't worry your pretty little head," Adrian said, reading her mind again. "We're not here for that."

They walked into the building through a side entrance that was mostly used for people who needed to get in a quick smoke between depressing speeches or to occasionally take a swig off a bottle in salute. Once inside, Nicole's suspicions were temporarily benched as she was hit with nostalgia; they were in the viewing room.

The walls were festooned with extravagant flower arrangements—probably fake, but still impressive—and wooden chairs that had been cleaned, polished, and placed in perfect rows before a podium and casket bier. She remembered running up and down the aisle when she was a child, the carpet absorbing her footsteps and the walls making her voice echo like magic. It was only on sparing occasions that she and Adrian had needed to accompany their father to work, and while they were only fleeting memories, she recalled a time when she had been shielded from the realities of what that room meant, and not thrust inside them at full speed.

As the ghost of her childhood ran between the rows and screamed "READY OR NOT, HERE I COME," a shiver ran down her spine as a second reality hit her—heat.

The daytime in the vault was filled with hopeless thoughts of lost love and the threat of imminent danger, but the night brought with it a mild and persistent chill. It was summer, so it wasn't the worst she had ever felt—the brutal February freezes of her childhood carried their own set of apparitions—but it was enough to invoke a restlessness inside her that was amplified by her inability to rub her shoulders or tamp down her gooseflesh. She crossed her arms at the thought, allowing herself to appreciate the moment, as foreboding as it seemed to feel something good.

"It's much nicer than you remember, I'm sure," Adrian said, watching Nicole take in the beauty, "and while I'd love to watch you marvel at my contributions to this place, now is not the time."

He began walking toward the opposite side of the room and motioned for her to follow him through the next set of doors.

The hallway they entered connected the viewing room to the front of the building on the left and the stairs to the basement on the right. Nicole's mind insisted they were going down the stairs—*to the incinerator*, she thought—but

Adrian instead opened the door opposite the viewing room, which was simply labeled "Office."

"Have a seat," he said, sitting in the chair behind the desk. She sat on a small couch beneath a large pane of glass that looked out over the funeral planning room, where people decided which casket or urn was appropriate for their dearly departed, then signed the funeral book at the very same table the day of services.

"What are we doing here?" she asked, her hands still sliding up and down her forearms in mild disbelief about their current state of warmth. "What if Dad shows up?"

Adrian sized her up for a second, then took up the landline phone into his hand, dialing a number as he spoke.

"He's out of town at a conference. But I suppose if he *did* return early for some reason, you would have to put on two shows."

She didn't like the sound of that, mostly because she didn't know what the *first* show entailed to begin with. As the question reached her mouth, it was muted by Adrian's finger in the air. The other end of the phone line had connected.

"Hello there, Pastor. It's Adrian, Adrian Emerson." The faint sound of another man's voice filled the silence with inaudible chatter.

"Yeah, my father said you were planning on stopping by at some point?" He listened for a moment. "I don't think that's going to work, I actually got in touch with Nicole, and we're supposed to be going out to catch up!"

The gooseflesh returned to Nicole's arms at the sound of her name. *Someone else knows I'm here. Maybe there IS a way.*

"It sounds like she broke her ankle at the motel the day she got here and had to have surgery." He listened again as Felix spoke on the other end of the line. "You would have thought so, but she didn't have our numbers yet. I picked her up from the hospital last night, though, and she seems to be doing much better."

He looked over the end of the phone at Nicole with a glance that said, "You'd better be paying attention."

"I was thinking the three of us could have dinner tonight. You can bring along the additions, and we'll supply the pasta? Oh, and one more thing: Nicole's going to be staying at our father's place for the last few days she's in town, so we'll have to meet over there."

Another line of mumbled syllables floated out from the speaker end of the phone. "No, he's still out of town, but I have his blessing to use the place if I need to. Maybe when he gets back, we can all sit down together."

Adrian produced a mechanical laugh that probably would have fooled most people, but made Nicole shrink in her seat. "She still hasn't seen him yet, though, and I figured tonight you could share some advice on the issue. So, if you wouldn't mind keeping it between us, I would appreciate it. We were planning on figuring out that part when he gets back."

After what seemed like an agreement on the issue, Adrian thanked Felix and ended the call with a tentative plan to meet at the Emerson residence on South Main Street at seven o'clock.

"Did you get all that?" he asked as he placed the phone back on its cradle.

"I broke my ankle and had to get surgery." She searched his face and decided to go a step further. "It was a displaced lateral malleolus fracture. The surgery went extremely well, and I should be back on my feet and headed home to Arkansas in no time."

"That's the spirit," he said. "Now we just need to clean you up and find some pasta."

They exited the office and, to Nicole's dismay, began heading in the direction of the bottom floor. They made their way down the stairs and through the door to the cremation room.

Nicole paused as she reached the swinging door at the bottom, reflecting on the man in the box pleading for his life. *"Please, let me go,"* she heard him say as the memory rushed back at full speed. *"Just let me go."*

Before the thought could manifest into a panic attack, Adrian ushered her through the door, past the incinerator, and into the next room. Inside was a metal table positioned in the middle, surrounded by glass-fronted cabinets and shelving units. Stored on the racks and shelves were neatly organized bottles, gadgets, and tools, each with its own bold-font label marking its home. She vaguely remembered the space—it was the area she'd spent the least amount of time in when she was a child, as the more gruesome work was completed in its walls.

Adrian stepped to the front of one of the cabinets and opened the doors, then pulled out a wooden box from within. He carefully swung the door closed and brought the box to the table in the center of the room. "Here."

She approached the table, biting her lip anxiously as the lid flipped open, expecting either a device with which to torture information out of the pastor, or another menacing insurance policy. Adrian stared inside the box for a moment before turning the front towards her.

Inside was a set of brushes and sponges of varying sizes, and nestled beside them were multiple palettes of colors and skin tones. It wasn't a torture device—at least, not by most people's standards. It was makeup.

"Have a look," he said, grabbing a small maroon-colored case and handing it to her. She took it in her hand and pressed the button on the side, popping open the mirrored top.

What she saw looking back in the mirror caused her eyes to well with tears. She was hideous. Beneath her sunken eyes were deep-purple bags that stretched lower than she had ever seen, even after the grueling hours she'd put in to get her nursing license. On top of the skin were the remnants of her last makeup job—eyeliner that had been diluted with sorrow and scattered across her face in faded marks of black. She put a trembling hand to her face and touched it with her fingers, needing its confirmation that she was indeed looking at herself.

"That's the same face I see dozens of times a year, though they aren't generally amongst the living," he said, his face conveying a bit of concern for her looks—although, Nicole sensed, for wildly different reasons. "We can't have you eating dinner with the pastor looking like the corpse bride."

"I... I can't," she said, placing the makeup container back on the table and closing the lid.

"You *have* to. Felix will..."

"No," she interrupted. "I just mean... shouldn't I shower first? My hair is a mess, and," she said, looking down at the table, ashamed, "there isn't really a bathroom down there."

She assumed he hadn't kept anyone down there long enough to need a lavatory solution, and the lack of consideration showed now as a slightly red embarrassed cheek hue. *He's probably smell-blind to bodily fluids and the stench of decay by now.*

"Yes," he said, scooping the maroon case from the table and tossing it back into the box, "of course you have to shower first! I just wanted to know if you could use these to fix yourself up afterwards, or if I would have to do *that* for you, too. So, can you handle it?"

"I think…"

"I don't care what you THINK, Nicole. Are you capable of covering the bags under your eyes with the same brush that caressed the skin of a nine-year-old cancer patient a month ago? I know, probably more than anyone else, how weak your thoughts can be, so save them and tell me either yes or no."

"Yes," she blurted out, "I'm sorry."

"That," he said as he put the box under his arm and stood, "is an understatement."

They made their way back to the car and headed in the direction of South Main street, Adrian gripping the wheel tighter this ride and not bothering to turn the radio on to ease the discomforting silence. Nicole saw through him in that moment—that even though he was methodical and precise, he was still capable of leaving the door open for error to creak in her favor.

They pulled into the driveway of their childhood home and got out, Nicole's shoes hitting the crushed stone with a *crunch* that brought the ghost of her adolescence back to life once again. Adrian retrieved the makeup and her luggage from the trunk while she thought about her brief stop there when she arrived in town. She wished the ghost would have appeared then to do what they did in movies: warn her she needed to go away.

I would have listened, I swear.

They went inside, leaving the ghost alone to play with her toys.

Once she crossed the threshold, she saw just how little the place had changed over the years. The furniture seemed to be the same old, slightly uncomfortable couches they had grown up jumping on, and the pictures and knickknacks scattered around the living room looked untouched, apart from scant dusting.

She picked up a small sculpture of a lion and ran her hand down its clay mane. Made by her mother, it sported the smile of a friendly cat, rather than the expression of a dominant predator. She placed it back in its spot and began running her hands up and down her arms again. The rushing back of time felt as cold as the vault.

"It's just like it used to be," she said out loud. "He hasn't changed a thing."

Adrian dropped the luggage bag onto the couch and began unzipping the front. "Yes, our father is a bit nostalgic that way, though I can't say I agree with it. The unpleasant memories have a way of soiling the good ones if you do nothing to change the way you think of them. Here," he said, motioning for her to look through her clothing. "Find something nice."

She thumbed through her clothing and thought about the day she had packed it. She'd tossed in a handful of stretchy pants and her favorite shirts to help her relax on what she'd known was going to be a stressful journey. It all seemed so trivial now, and there wasn't a fabric in existence that could hold up to the stress of baiting a man of God into eating what would likely be his own last supper. She also wasn't sure if she would have another wardrobe change anytime soon, so she chose the warm clothes she had packed and set them aside.

"Really?" Adrian said, picking up the sweatshirt she had chosen and spreading it out in front of him. "You're visiting with a pastor you haven't seen in over a decade, and you're going to wear a 'City of Greenwood EMS' sweatshirt? Are you repenting or bragging?"

"I think..." She paused, remembering the reaction she had gotten the last time she started a sentence that way. "I would be wearing comfortable clothes if I had just gotten out of the hospital. It would sell the story a little better, and the pants make it easier to hide the fact that I have no scarring there from surgery. I wasn't sure, though; what do YOU think I should wear?" She hoped he didn't have a varying opinion on the matter, and that simply giving the semblance of choice would make him agree.

"You'll still need some sort of brace, I'm sure," he said to her relief. She had a few items in her luggage that were hard to wear for an hour at a restaurant, let alone an unending stay in a hole.

She gathered up her clothes and walked down the hallway toward the bathroom, her feet knowing the way without having to think. As she did, she passed more familiar pictures in the hallway—shots of her and Adrian's marve-

185

lous elementary-school sporting achievements hung next to those of dead relatives and bygone family vacations. They had faded into the background like bland wallpaper when she'd still called this house a home, but now, they seemed to flash like warning signs in her mind, the pretext to a manifesto. She moved beyond them, and just before she reached the bathroom, she passed the door to the old family room. She looked back down the hallway, and when she didn't see Adrian, she placed the clothes in a neat pile on the floor and grabbed the door handle.

As she turned on the light, she was flooded with the memory of finding young Adrian alone in the dark. *I should have known then,* she thought as her eyes darted to the place he'd stood that night. *And I should have never left.*

She looked around the room and saw that it too had remained relatively the same, apart from the windows being perpetually winterized and the absence of gentle music. She wondered why her father had kept it this way, why he hadn't just sold the kiln and turned the room into a storage space. She knew that people kept things in place after people died, but surely their bedroom would have been enough. Surely keeping the room their mother died in would be more painful than the memories were worth.

"Care to make a piece?" Adrian said from the doorway behind her, startling her and nearly prompting a scream. "It still works. The kiln, that is."

"No, I just... wanted to see," she said as she turned, not sure how to end the sentence. It felt inaccurate—she didn't want to *see,* but to *feel.* To feel that the roots that tugged at her waist and whispered to her on lonely nights in Arkansas were still planted in something real, and not rotting away beneath the surface.

"What DO you see?" Adrian asked curiously, rather than out of the anger she had expected.

"I see... you," she replied as she began walking into the room. "I see you standing there, that night dad left us alone for the first time after..."

She watched as he closed his eyes, finishing the sentence in his head. "And I see me, too. What a foolish little girl she was. Foolish, and selfish."

Adrian walked into the room and squatted down in the middle, staring blankly at the floor. He stayed in that position for a long time, not speaking, and, Nicole thought briefly, *not breathing*.

"Right here," he said finally, getting down on his knees and putting his hand on the floor. He moved them as though he were touching something that wasn't there.

"Right here is where she took her last breath." His hands moved through the air with long, gentle strokes, then bent over and pursed his lips before making the sound of a kiss. Afterward, he picked up an imaginary item from the floor and held it in his hand. He looked at it for a moment, then moved as if he were opening a jar, with one hand stationary and the other twisting. Finally, he fixed one palm flat and shook the other hand over the top.

The pills, she thought as he put the flat hand to his mouth and tipped his head back, swaying on his feet before dropping to his knees. *He's acting out her suicide.*

She closed her eyes. Adrian had never told her any of the details from that day, let alone given her a reenactment. She took another breath and began walking backwards toward the door. She didn't want to see any more.

"Why did you have to hurt me like this?" he asked from the floor, his eyes closed and his hands sprawled out beside him. "Why couldn't you be a good boy?"

She wasn't sure if she was supposed to answer, so she didn't. She took another few steps back and reached the doorway.

"WHY?" he screamed from the floor, opening his eyes and sitting up. He turned to her. "Why did you leave me to die?"

Nicole stumbled out of the room and hastily picked up her clothes. A wild thought of slamming the door shut crossed her mind, but she could swear the glow in Adrian's eyes was real this time, not just a reflection. She walked down the hall and into the bathroom, swinging the door shut behind her.

From outside, she heard nothing, and couldn't decide if that was better, or worse. She put her ear to the door and listened, hoping the sound of her mother's dying words didn't begin echoing through the hallway in her direction. When she didn't hear anything, she began taking off her clothes, disgusted at the way they peeled off like stickers from an overripe apple. She twisted the knob in the shower and the water burst from the pipes and hit her hand with icy drops. It slowly began to warm, sending another appreciative shiver through her bones.

A loud rapping sound filled the little bathroom and sent her off her balance and onto the floor. "Don't think about climbing out that window. I'm watching," Adrian said from outside the door, the sound of his approach muted by the water.

She watched as the doorknob began to twist. She felt the pulse in her body pound at the sickening thought of him seeing her without clothes on. She covered her chest with her hands and crossed her legs. It was ugly, and perverted, but she knew there was nothing she could do to stop it.

"Don't go in there. She's *naked*," Nicole heard from outside the door. The voice belonged to Adrian, but—*was he talking to himself?*

"I'm not. I just wanted her to know that I would if she tried anything stupid, that's all." Nicole watched the handle flip back to the closed position. She let out her breath and loosened the arm pressed against her breasts as it turned. "You don't have to worry; I can take care of her."

She listened as the conversation made its way back down the hall, Adrian's voice getting softer as he walked away. Once she was sure he was gone, she got off the floor and sat down on the toilet. As she tried to force her body to do something, anything at all, she stared at the wallpaper, which had been peeling since the days when she'd first learned what a period was, and thought about her mother. She knew Adrian was just displaying a manifestation of his psychosis, but she also couldn't help but wonder what her mother would be saying if the delusions *were* real and she could see her daughter now, desperately trying to avoid having to roll over on the ground and pee in the corner of a musky receiving-vault prison.

All at once, the wallpaper swirled into action and began taking on a three-dimensional form in front of her eyes. "He's not going to hurt you. Not as long as he has *me* in his heart."

She saw her mother's face speaking, her smooth skin wrapped in long, beautiful locks of hair that danced and flowed with her words. A smile formed on her face as she finished her sentence, and Nicole, accepting that this was also a delusion, spoke back.

"But what if he does? You know better than anyone that when he's angry, he loses control."

"Perhaps that's when he needs your help most," the floating bust replied.

"What would you know? You left us high and dry, so this is really all *your* fault!" she said, much louder than she intended. She turned her head to the door and listened again, afraid that maybe Adrian had heard her and would come back to open the door to check on her for real. When she didn't hear anything, she turned back and tried to conjure her mother again. She stared at the wallpaper and tried crossing her eyes to lose focus, like she was looking at a stereogram, but it didn't work—the only thing that swirled was her brain as her eyes regained focus and left her slightly dizzied and perplexed.

She felt partially offended by her mind's interpretation of her mother. *Why would I help him after this? Why wouldn't she—I—save myself?*

To make matters worse, she couldn't pee. She knew her body was storing up energy and trying not to lose any precious liquid it didn't have to, but she also knew that wouldn't continue forever, and if—*when*—she ended up back underground, she may have to cross another unfortunate item off her bucket list and go in front of Cooper.

She pressed the thought out of her mind and stood up, getting into the shower and feeling the hot water on her back and shoulders. She had heard that moving water released tension and charged the air around you to make you feel more relaxed, and while she did feel slightly better watching the muddy water wash down the drain, the water also had a slight pink hue that reminded her of what couldn't be un-done—the blood drying on the vault floor.

As the river of soil and regret flowed past her toes, she stared at her ankle. It looked better than she had thought it would, which, she decided, wasn't a good thing. She knew that keeping the façade going was going to benefit her in some way, and that being fully mobile seemed like it would set a clock for her that could chime her demise at any hour.

She finished washing up and got out to dry off, staring at the wallpaper for a last bit of advice that didn't come. When she finished, she put on her clothes and made her way back to the living room, where Adrian sat, holding a small gray item in his hand.

"That's much better," he said, turning over what Nicole realized was the figurine he had referred to as "Mother's ghost" the night she'd found him sleepwalking.

"The makeup is right there," he said, lifting the hand that held the ghost and pointing his finger at the box, which had been placed on the TV stand. "I trust you don't need my help with that?"

"No, I don't think so," she said, taking an exaggerated hobble towards the stand and grabbing it by the edges. She picked it up and began walking to the bathroom, then stopped and turned around again.

"What does she say about me?" she asked, hoping for some insight into the subconscious thoughts he had about her, and if they might show his intentions.

Adrian stopped twirling the figurine in his hand. Instead, he opened his palm and looked at it. "She doesn't talk about you all that much. She doesn't even know you, but she wants to. She wants to see you make amends for all this. To see you the way she used to."

"Does she know how?"

"I think so," Adrian said as he closed his hand around the figurine again, "but I'm not sure we agree on that yet."

Nicole walked away at that and closed herself into the bathroom again. She took out the brushes and palette and began putting on what felt like a hideous mask. When she felt the job was adequate, she dug through the box and found a container marked with only a small golden dove on the top. She opened it, and next to the skin tones were colors of deep purple and red.

She pulled up her pant leg and took another look at the door before dipping a brush into the purple. She began furiously swabbing the color onto her ankle, pushing the color into her skin. She added splotches of the dark red and mixed them together, and after a minute, she judged her work. It looked downright disgusting, and convincingly bruised.

She finished, then walked down the hallway and found Adrian in the kitchen, rifling through cupboards and speaking to himself. This time, it wasn't a mumbled call and response, but an attempt to make a recipe out of the items he had found. "Maybe some sort of casserole?"

He noticed her walk into the room and looked her over briefly before returning to his task. He moved the long-preserved canned items around one final time, then closed the cupboard doors. "It appears we have some shopping to do."

CHAPTER VIII:
THE DINNER PARTY

The time was three p.m. when Adrian and Nicole opened their car doors at the shopping square, just late enough to miss the lunch crowds, but early enough to miss the hoard of workers punching their time cards and scrambling for last-minute groceries to bring home. The square, aside from the parking benefits Adrian had enjoyed the night before, contained only a couple of stores and a fitness center that, over the years, had housed many different attempts as keeping the townspeople from getting obese, including a Jazzercise, a boxing gym, and now a martial arts dojo.

Adrian had spent the ride reminding Nicole of the consequences lying beneath the surface at the cemetery, letting the flashy nature of the pistol's appearance do most of the talking and adding only that the police station was three times the distance as the vault. He watched as the small circle of children inside the dojo kicked invisible objects in the air, then uttered one final warning. "It would sure be a shame if they didn't get their belts."

They stepped out and made their way to the curb in front of the Kinney drugstore, another relic Nicole imagined would be there at the end of the apocalypse, still selling ibuprofen and cheap toys. They walked inside, and, after assuring the elderly woman at the counter they needed no help, found the leg braces.

"Which one?" Adrian asked, pointing at three different options.

Instead of trying to decide which would make the most sense with the story she was supposed to tell, she thought about which one may have the best advantages for her after this meal from hell was over. She thought maybe a smaller one might be easier to move around with and provide a speed boost if and when an exit opened up, but decided that the large plastic boot may hold a little more power when she kicked. Or, if broken, it might have sharp edges.

"That one," she said, pointing at the boot. "If I hadn't been put into a cast, I definitely would have been put into one of those."

Satisfied with her answer, Adrian grabbed the box, brought it to the register, and made the purchase. Once in the parking lot again, Adrian opened the box and pulled out the boot, tossing the box into the trash between the drug and grocery stores. "I would say that practice makes perfect, but I think we both know there's no such thing," he said as he knelt and prepared the straps.

She winced as he pulled up her pant leg and looked at her ankle, praying her makeup job would fool him. *All he needs to do is touch it and he'll know...*

"Ouch," he said, to her relief. "I'm surprised you're not in more pain." He lowered her pant leg and took her shoe off, replacing it with the brace and marrying the Velcro strips.

"I think there's still some drugs in my system. They take the edge off," she replied, knowing there was probably some truth to it.

"I suppose there's a lesson in each step you take now," he said as he stood. "That's quite beautiful, actually, and you might even think by some kind of design."

She watched as Adrian briefly looked at the sky, then took her shoe and threw it in the trash. For a moment, the question, "Why?" rose to her lips. But she didn't ask it. Instead, she just followed him to the front of the grocery store and walked inside, making sure to exaggerate her limp.

As they journeyed around the store, Nicole thought maybe he had thrown her shoe away to be an asshole, but she couldn't shake the thought that he had tossed it because she would never need it again.

The thought persisted as they made their way to the checkout counter and then the car again. She wanted to let it go, but as Adrian took the car out of park, she spoke up. "My shoe," she blurted out. "I was focused on practicing, like you said, but I need my other shoe."

Adrian looked at her and smiled, placing the car back into park and taking the keys out of the ignition.

"Do you believe, deep in your heart, that you really need it?" he asked, looking her in the eyes. She searched his face for the answer to her question and realized there really was no right answer. *He doesn't know either.*

"Yes," she said boldly, "once I've finished." This time she stared at her brother with confidence, asserting her commitment to his will.

"You may be right," Adrian said, then got out of the car and walked to the trash can, pulling out the shoe and dusting it off with his hand. He brought it back to the car and handed it to her, holding onto the heel as she pulled on the toe. "But time will tell."

They returned to their father's house and began cooking, their seven o'clock deadline still a few hours away. Nicole was surprised by Adrian's culinary abilities, though she knew too that living the single life either made you a personal chef or a master microwave user. As she watched him measure spices, she wondered again why Adrian would go through all the trouble of making an elaborate meal if his intentions were for it to go to waste.

Instead of speculating, she asked, "What is the plan, anyway? The only thing we know is that Felix was in the motel room that night."

"The plan," Adrian replied in a condescending tone, "is to find out what Pastor Robison knows about the hit-and-run. If he knew who did the deed and didn't involve the police, then there must be something else at play, something righteous enough to surpass the judgement of the deeply flawed judicial system man created."

"But what if it *was* him?" she asked, not following his logic on ruling out the pastor so easily. She knew Adrian had been a lot closer to Felix than she was as a child, but the idea of a religious figure being unable to sin seemed grossly naïve, given the situation.

"I don't think you quite understand what Felix has done for this town—for ME. The sacrifices he's made to get the trash off the street and keep the filth from flowing over the gutters are more than you'll EVER be able to accomplish with your little nursing badge. As you might remember, our father was less than qualified to give healthy life lessons, and after you left, Felix was the only one who made an effort to teach me how to survive through the pain. He showed me how to find the light and, without knowing it, share that light with the ones who need it. So watch what you say, and don't ask any questions I haven't told you to. Is that clear?"

She nodded her head in agreement, knowing any further attempt to open his eyes to the facts would be a lost cause. *What if it is true, though? What if your saint is really a sinner?*

The afternoon slipped into evening faster than Nicole anticipated. She thought the hours would draw on, like the last day of school before summer vacation, but her anxiety seemed to loosen as she sat on the couch and waited with the pictures of her mother smiling back at her from the walls.

They had gone over the story of her injury a half-dozen times, each marked by some new minute detail that Adrian questioned and forced her to produce a satisfying answer to. *"What if he asks you why you didn't call the police department to speak to David? Why didn't you just drive yourself to the hospital? Which doctor did you see?"*

She had answered them all and left Adrian feeling prepared as he set the table and pulled last-minute items out of the oven.

Just past seven, a vehicle pulled into the driveway. They both watched as Felix got out and walked to the passenger side of the car, retrieving a black folio and a bottle of wine. "You're on," Adrian said as Felix walked up the path and knocked on the door.

"Welcome, welcome," Adrian said as the door swung open and Felix entered the house.

"Let me take that for you," he added, taking the bottle of wine from his hand and setting it on the counter.

"Thank you, son," Felix said as he wiped his feet on the floor mat. "It's not the most exquisite wine you're likely to taste, but it did come with a nice price tag. And, Nicole Emerson," he said, turning his attention to her as she made her way around the couch to greet him.

"My, oh my, is it wonderful to see you. What's it been, fourteen years?"

"I think that's about right, though it feels like it could have been a thousand," Nicole said, forcing a laugh and a smile.

"Yes, indeed," he laughed, looking her up and down. "Time has a funny way of tricking us like that, you know. We make believe we can tell time, but seeing you now, all grown up, I'm CERTAIN that time tells *us!*"

"Come on in and have a seat, Pastor," Adrian said, chuckling at Felix's turn of phrase. "I'm sure you've had quite a long day."

"When you get past the halfway point in life, they're the only kind that exist. Now am I supposed to take my shoes off in here or not?" He posed the question to Nicole and waited for a response.

"Uh," she said, confused by the curveball and realizing she wasn't sure. If she had been staying here, she *should be.*

"We have plenty to clean up already, Pastor, so you can take them off or leave them on. It's your choice," Adrian interjected, tossing Nicole a short angry glance as Felix took his shoes off and left them next to the door.

They walked to the table together and sat. Adrian placed himself across the table from the other two so he could see both their faces without effort. He opened the bottle of wine and poured glasses for each of them, making sure to fill the Pastor's a little more than the others.

"Should we begin with a toast or a prayer?" Adrian asked, raising his glass in the air.

"A toast is in order, I believe," Felix replied, raising his own glass. "To strength and courage. It brings me an overwhelming amount of joy to see you two together again. My, how I longed for this day! To you, Nicole, for making your way back home, and you, Adrian, for keeping the Lord's message of forgiveness in your heart."

"To Nicole," Adrian added, looking at her and smiling as he took a swig of wine. "But I'd also like to make a toast to you Pastor, if I may. Over the years, you've done a great service to this family, and me especially. You took the time to sit with me on countless occasions, most of which you spent pacifying a less-than-level-headed young man and helping him see the road to peace and salvation. And before that, you offered your time to both of us when we were lost in the thicket of despair. Through all of it, all the services, the speeches, and the check-ins, you stood by your convic-

201

tions. I always admired that, and hoped to mirror it through my own work. The persona you developed was built on faith, but beneath that was another layer—one that the common man so easily manipulates and destroys, yet YOU managed to polish and turn into a central piece of architecture: the truth. So, here's to you, Pastor, for always reminding us that we had more strength than we knew, and that honesty is more than the best policy. It's the foundation of a good life."

They all drank. Nicole swallowed more than the other two. Aside from the fact that Adrian having "found forgiveness" was especially heinous, she couldn't decipher where the line between admiration and setup was.

She remembered when Pastor Robinson began taking special notice of Adrian and offering his time to him when the loss of their mother grappled their family. He hadn't been officially part of the church yet; just some guy who had "seen the light." Back then, she'd been more aligned with her mother's convictions, and hadn't really seen the point in going down the road of angels and commandments. She'd had a sneaking suspicion that Felix was probably one of those pedophile people she heard about in the news.

As those thoughts came crawling back into her mind, a switch went off that connected the dots: *What could open a man's heart to the light as swiftly and radically as taking the life of another?*

She stared at Felix, taking a gulp of wine that went down like a sideways hammer. She was having dinner with not one, but two killers.

"So," Adrian began again, beginning to dish out salad onto plates, "you've brought some new material for us, I hear? Anything particularly fascinating, or was my father just trying to keep tabs on me like usual?"

"Well I suppose it's both," Felix replied, the smile on his face straightening out slightly. "He actually, come to think of it, thought perhaps the two of you may have been in contact before now, that you were conspiring against him. You know how he gets."

"That's our father—a comic on the road and a paranoid soldier at home."

"I'm not sure I've heard it said quite like that before," Felix replied, "but it's accurate, I suppose. He got himself all worked up thinking you—" He turned and looked at Nicole. "—were still too upset to talk and might skip town again, with *his* help."

He aimed his fork at Adrian, circling it in the air and returning it to his salad.

"Well, isn't that something," Adrian said, turning his attention to Nicole and nodding slightly for her to chime in.

"It's not that I didn't want to see him; I'm just apparently too clumsy to go anywhere without hurting myself." She reached her hand below the table and scratched at the outside of her plastic boot. "I didn't drive all the way up here just to take in the views at the Shady!"

"I believe it's on the top 100 places to visit in New England now," Felix joked. "And yes, I heard you had a slight mishap when you arrived. Are you healing alright?"

"Well," she said, glancing at Adrian before she spoke, "it was a displaced lateral malleolus fracture. The surgery went well, and I should be able to head home before too long." She dropped her head and began scooping up lettuce again, hoping she didn't need to dive any deeper.

"Oh, you poor, poor girl. That sounds painful. I'm glad you were able to get it taken care of so swiftly. I would have thought something as serious as that may have taken weeks to recover from."

"Oh, it will," she added, this time trying to convince Adrian. "They gave me this boot so I can at least make small trips, but it still hurts, and probably will for a while. It's alright, though— I've got plenty of vacation time saved up, so I suppose I can take a few days to relax after this trip instead of rushing back into things."

"That's good to hear. I'm sure this must be painful in more ways than physical." She knew he was referring to the eventual Emerson family reunion, and blinked a slow acknowledgement.

"I'm sure you spent years deciding what you would say when you came back. Are you feeling prepared?"

"Yes. I mean… I think so," she said, taking a moment to think about it and deciding that, no matter how hard it seemed to her when role-playing that scenario in her mind, no matter how much she hated her father for stealing the early years of her adolescence with his overbearing and abusive parenting, it couldn't be any more difficult than what she had endured thus far on her journey home.

"Well, as long as you speak from the heart, I'm sure you'll get out what you need to. It's the bits that come from the mind that tend to sully our intentions. I know it pained us all to see you leave, but I was rooting for you all the same. I can't speak for your father, but I think your mother would be proud of you. Of both of you," he said, looking from Nicole to Adrian and back again.

The pastor's words nearly brought tears to Nicole's eyes. Beneath the pain and anger she felt at her mother for the mess she'd left behind, there was still an annoying, tiny little insignificant need for acceptance—the same one that must have been amplified, warped, and disfigured in the mind of her brother.

Though she didn't subscribe to most of the holy sentiments, she sometimes looked to the sky and wondered if she was in her mother's graces. "Thank you, Pastor," she said, looking up at him and smiling her first genuine smile since her conversation with David at the Petro Mart.

"Don't go thanking me now, child. Lord knows it was all you that found the strength to get back on your feet and make something of yourself."

"Truly inspirational," Adrian added, tipping the bottle of wine into his own glass again. Nicole could sense he was becoming uncomfortable and partly wished that it could continue, but knew that it wasn't the headspace she wanted Adrian in before the salad had even gone.

"Speaking of the hospital," Nicole said when another look from Adrian urged her to move on, "while I was in it, I read in the paper they found an abandoned car in town. Did they ever find out who it belonged to?"

"I heard it was a hiker from upstate," Adrian lied. "There's a lot of wild animal trails that look like beaten paths over there—easy for someone to get lost. I'm sure she'll find her way back, though, unless, god bless her, she came across a catamount."

"I don't quite know how to say this," Felix chimed in, "but I think you're wrong about that."

"Oh?" Adrian said with more manufactured surprise. "Well, who do they think it belongs to, then? Is it someone from White River?"

Felix looked between the two of them again before setting his fork down on his plate and joining his hands together beneath the table. "I believe it belongs to Officer Demick, and..." He paused. "I'm not under the belief that he's coming back."

"What do you mean?" Nicole asked, this time with her own bit of acting. "What happened?"

"I have a few theories, none of which I could possibly prove, but I could be wrong. Lord knows I have been in the past. In fact, I *hope* I am."

"Do you think it has anything to do with his father?" Adrian asked as he began plating the main course for the trio. He had recognized the window for his plan was opening, and, as he handed a plate to Felix, added, "I know he was obsessed with finding out what happened to him, maybe he was getting close and..."

Adrian frowned and widened his eyes to punctuate the thought.

"Thank you, son," Felix said as he accepted a plate. "And that's one of my theories."

He returned his attention to Nicole. "I'm sorry you had to hear it this way. I know you two were close, and this could all be one big misunderstanding. Who's to say?"

"Who would do such a thing?" she asked. "He's done nothing his whole life but try to help this town. Why on earth would anyone want to hurt him?" Nicole could feel her blood pressure rising as she posed the question. She felt as if she already had the answers to a bloody and terrible test.

"The last I heard, he was looking for you," Felix said, once again turning in his seat to make eye contact. "Whatever happened between then and now, God only knows."

"Oh no," Adrian said, as if to himself. "I actually think I know something."

He looked at his sister, then back to Felix again. "I saw Cooper the other day. He was looking for you, Pastor. Said he went to the church, but you weren't there. He looked a little out of it and kept mumbling about the old case—you know, the one with David's father—and how he was going to 'set things right once and for all.' I wasn't sure what he was going on about, but I assumed he needed confession time and, to be honest, time to sleep off whatever was in his system. I didn't think much of it until now, but perhaps Cooper knows something? He was part of the whole thing, wasn't he?"

Felix stared at Adrian for a long time, seemingly shocked and trying to sort out a response. "I, too, had a feeling that history has its hand in this, but I don't see Cooper taking things to that extreme. You know as well as I do that his bark is worse than his bite."

"What about the 'ministry of lies' thing?" Nicole said to Adrian—another planned line. "Didn't he say something like that?"

"Nicole," Adrian said in a faux *"I thought I asked you not to mention that"* tone.

"Ministry of lies?" Felix said, taking the bait.

"I asked her not to say anything, but yes, Cooper said he was looking for you and..." He paused to heighten the suspense. "... that your whole career was a 'ministry of lies.' I was truly offended. Like I said, I appreciate all you've done for us, so whatever it was must have been the drugs talking."

Felix closed his eyes briefly and brought his hands to the top of the table. As he did, Adrian looked at Nicole and nodded, signifying she had done well.

"I believe it's time for a confession of my own, but you have to know," Felix said, looking back up from his lap, "I never knew how bad things were going to get."

Just as Felix finished up his sentence, a loud banging sound came from outside, near the garage. Adrian jumped to his feet and anxiously looked at Felix, wanting him to continue his story, but unable to let the noise go uninvestigated.

"Hold that thought, Pastor. I'm going to see what that was. Are you going to be alright for a minute, Nicole?"

Adrian threatened her with a look that said, "*You better be alright. Don't be foolish and get someone killed.*"

"I think I can manage," she replied, knowing the silver-plated pistol was still much closer than the police station.

"Is it your father?" Felix asked. "I thought you weren't expecting him back?"

"We're not," Adrian replied, looking out the front window at the parked cars. "Just in case," he said, grabbing the house phone from its cradle as he left the room.

As Nicole sat with Felix in silence, she pondered her options. She could spill the beans, let him know what Adrian was up to, and take a chance on family values winning over homicidal tendencies, but that seemed unlikely, given the sporadic nature of Adrian's behavior.

She looked at Felix and saw that a troubled expression had taken hold of him—one that had etched the lines on his face from consistent use over the years and now held with it a seemingly crushing weight. She supposed she could tell the truth and beg Felix to play along, but that, too, seemed like she would be battling against history, some of which may end up buried again anyway, rendering the entirety of her plight useless.

Her body vibrated with energy as the thought of sharing her dilemma tugged at her, begging to be set free.

"You seem troubled, child. Are you in pain?" Felix asked.

"I, uh...yeah. The ankle, you know," she said, the thoughts continuing to swirl enough to give tightness to her stomach muscles. "You don't look too good yourself. What were you going to say, you know, before?"

"I should probably wait until your brother returns for that; it's for both of you to hear. I've spent a lot of time imagining what this day would look like, when I could sit down with the two of you as adults. I suppose I kept telling myself the timing wasn't right, but I think that was selfish of me, looking back. You deserve to know the truth."

"He's got a gun," she blurted out, the energy exploding through her veins as the words exited her lips. She put a hand to her mouth and covered it. She had yelled unintentionally, and wanted desperately to take the words back. "He's got a gun and he's going to kill me. US. YOU HAVE TO HELP!"

Felix's eyes widened in shock as her words washed over him. "What do you mean, he has a gun?" he asked, turning fast in his chair toward her and twisting his head violently to look around for any signs Adrian had returned without notice. "Did he do this to you?"

"Yes," she whimpered, "and he has Cooper, too. He said he would kill him if anything went wrong tonight." She let out a series harsh coughs as the reality of what she had done squirmed through her body like a demon being exorcised. There was no going back from here.

"Went wrong with what? Where is he?" Felix asked as he cupped her hands inside his own. "Where is Cooper?"

Another loud noise came from outside. "He's going to be back any minute. You have to tell me what's going on so I can help you." When she didn't respond, he reached inside his pocket and produced his cell phone, dialing 911 and putting the phone to his head.

"NO!" she screamed and lunged at him, grabbing the phone and hitting the red button to end the call before it connected with the dispatcher. "You don't understand. He's NOT STABLE! If you call the police, he's going to kill us!"

"It's ok, it's ok. I'm here now; I can help," Felix said, pulling her in and wrapping his arms around her. She buried her head in his shoulder and wept, feeling an immense relief wash over her as the feeling of being alone left her body.

Nicole wiped the tears from her face and began breathing hard again. "I have to fix my makeup, or he'll know I talked," she said as she stood up.

"He wants to find out what happened to David's father because..."

"Because SHE killed his son."

Nicole froze. The words had come from behind her.
Adrian was back inside the house.

CHAPTER IX:
COPS & ROBBERS

Brent Fleurry stood outside the Chevy dealership in West Lebanon just after four p.m., watching as a salesman inside got to his feet and made his way toward the door. He reached into his pocket and rolled the keys Felix had given him between his fingers, trying to imagine the ignition they'd once called home. His fingers found the buttons on the key fob and pressed one.

The clicking sound was accompanied by the thought of someone jumping into what would eventually become a death machine.

He had spent some time trying to research the keys himself that morning and afternoon, gaining a newfound respect for the cybercrimes division, which had been growing in the department during his final years on the force. He was able to find exactly zero pieces of useful information and half a dozen hazardous computer viruses.

The keys were the first tangible lead he had ever had in his partner's murder, and while turning them in may have been the right thing to do, the opportunity to single-handedly solve the case that had ruined his career was too much to pass up.

"Goooood morning, sir. Is there anything I can help you find today?" The salesman who came out of the building was a younger man—mid-twenties, Brent guessed by the way he parted his gelled hair to the side—and carried himself with confidence. He remembered his partner had used to say, *"You can tell someone's age just by how weighed-down by life they've gotten."*

It wasn't particularly true, and, of course, by that estimation, the crackheads downtown would be hitting supernatural age ranges, but Brent enjoyed the thought all the same.

He reached his hand out. "Detective Brent Fleurry, retired," he said as he grasped the young man's hand.

"Oh, well, good morning, officer. My name is Alex. What can I do for you?"

"Mornin', son. I just had a few questions 'bout a set of keys and thought maybe you folks could help me out." He pulled the keys out of his pocket and handed them to Alex with a bit of reluctance.

"I see," Alex said, taking the keys and inspecting them front to back. "What do you want to know?"

"Mind if we step in? I'm not sure this convo is really public knowledge. It's sorta like a police matter." He looked around the empty lot and back to Alex again. Nobody was likely to hear them, but he knew if anything came from this, it would be from a data bank, rather than from someone still in the womb when murder took place.

"Sure thing, officer. Follow me."

They walked inside. Brent could sense that a fascination was quietly growing inside Alex; his steps hit the shined showroom floor with the bounce of someone eager to be an undercover crime fighter and not of someone irritated about missing a sale. They sat down at his desk.

"So, you said this is a police matter... of sorts?"

"Yes, a very old one. The keys you're holdin' went to a vehicle I believe was used to kill a police officer, wayyy back in '99."

"Holy cow," Alex said as the keys slipped out of his hand and hit his desk with a twang. "The prints—I messed up the..."

"No, no, don't worry bout' that. The prints are long gone. I was hopin' you could tell me what kinda vehicle it was. You know, make and model. And, if so, maybe get me a printout of the folks who mighta bought one from you."

"Whew!" Alex said with a chuckle. "I thought I tampered with evidence or something! Let me bring it out back and see if the mechanics know anything about it. I can tell you everything you could possibly want to know about that new Silverado out there, but as far as the older models go, they're the ones to ask."

"Sounds good, thank you, but if you could keep the significance of this between us for now, I'd appreciate it. Might be evidence, after all, and too many folks knowin' about it could spell trouble for us both."

"Absolutely. I will be right back." Alex walked the rest of the way down the showroom floor and opened a swinging door, behind which Brent saw a truck on a lift and realized it was the service bay. This time, Alex's steps seemed a little more spaced-out as he walked, like the superhero cape had been replaced with a bomb.

As Brent waited for the keys to return, he took out a small notepad from his pocket. The cover had ripped off years ago and left a dirty, chicken-scratch-covered page as the new one. He flipped through the entries, pausing on each one to read the inscriptions. He got to a page with the words "dark-colored car" scribbled at the top and read the notes he had taken.

"Cooper—I don't remember the make, maybe Chevy, Cadillac?"

He remembered putting in overtime going around to different dealerships and trying to figure out who the car may have belonged to, but without a definitive make, model, or year, he came up with a not-so-short list of around twelve thousand names. He had combed over them a few coffee-fueled nights and chased down dozens of dead-end leads, plagued by the fact that the nearby interstate system inflated the possible number of "dark-colored car" owners to an astronomically high amount.

I don't think I have it in me to chase down a thousand anymore, he thought to himself. *A hundred, maybe, and that's if I eat some Wheaties first.*

When Alex didn't return in the following ten minutes, Brent became concerned that the temptation to blab about the case may have been too much for the young man to handle, so he got to his feet, walked to the back of the showroom, and looked inside the round window encased in the service bay door. Inside, he saw Alex standing with two mechanics who looked, to Brent's satisfaction, impatient.

He decided that if they HAD been informed the key in question was the principal piece of evidence in a murder investigation, they would probably be taking pictures with it, *selfies*, and chattering like school kids. One of the mechanics shrugged and reached for the towel on his shoulder to wipe the grease from his hands, taking a step backward and giving one last remark before returning to work.

Brent understood their conversation was over and returned to his seat. Alex joined him a minute later.

"Whadidya find out?" Brent asked eagerly.

"Well, my mechanics seem to think it goes to a mid-nineties model, going by the shape of the fob. They said it's a little hard to tell, since you can buy knockoff replacement ones so easily and they don't always look like the original, but if this WAS an original key fob, it probably went to either a Caprice or an Impala."

"Now, are you able to hop on that thing and figure out who you sold those to back then?" Brent asked, pointing at the computer on Alex's desk and praying the technological advances of the modern car dealership were akin to those of the police department.

"Maybe. What else do you know about it?"

"It was a dark-colored car," Brent said, his attention remaining on the computer screen as it booted up with a flashing logo. "That's really 'bout it. Between '90 and '99, I would say."

"Alright, I'll see what I can do," Alex replied, his fingers getting to work and making Brent feel like a goat that had traded its jumping days for those of long naps in the pasture.

"Says here that we sold about eight thousand vehicles in the nineties. BUT," Alex added, seeing the disheartened look on Brent's face, "about a third of those were pickup trucks, so I'll take those out, bringing us down to five thousand. Now I can narrow it down to just Caprice and Impala sales, if you think they're right."

"If I had a better guess, I would have made it long ago," Brent joked.

"True," Alex said as he used the mouse to navigate to a side menu on the screen and check the boxes for his search criteria. "Here we go!"

The screen refreshed when he hit the button and a new list of buyers popped up on the screen. Brent read the number as Alex said it out loud. "Three hundred forty-two."

"Jeez, that still seems like an awful lot," Brent said, hoping the number would have been a little more manageable for an old goat to track down.

"Well, I can't search for the specific color, but it does list it, along with the rest of the information here," he said, pointing to a line that read, "WA/ 9753. 1994 Caprice Classic LS- '94 Banks, Meredith."

"Am I missing something?" Brent asked, rereading the line and not seeing any indication of color.

"This right here," Alex said, pointing to the numbers at the beginning. "The paint has its own codes. Here, I can get you a list of the color codes of the darker models and we can go through the list and narrow it down even further."

"Could you possibly just give me a copy of the codes and tell me which ones are dark? No offense—you've been a big help, but I think if you can get me that, I can handle the rest."

Can't risking you blabbing about this to your buddies. One Tweeter could ruin the whole thing for me. Brent watched as the spark went out in Alex like he'd just had his favorite toy taken away at his own birthday party.

"Yeah, I can do that, not a problem." He printed out the list of names and another shorter list of color codes, circling two codes with a highlighter before handing them over.

"Thank you, son. You've been most helpful. Hope you get a sale today after all of this!"

"Well, if you find what you're looking for soon enough, maybe YOU could use a new ride! The new Silverado has more than nice looks—it has heated seats!"

"Perhaps I will," he said, laughing as he folded the papers. He tucked them in his pocket and shook Alex's hand again before walking out the door and standing in the lot.

He took the papers out again and quickly scanned through the names. A few of them he recognized, but most he didn't.

"Sir," he heard from behind him, startling him until he realized it was just Alex again. "You don't want to forget these."

Alex held out the keys and dropped them into Brent's hand.

"No, I do not," he said as his hand closed around the fob. He put the list and the keys back in his pocket and got into his truck, still shaking his head and kicking himself for being so careless. *Jeepers creepers, I AM getting old.*

He thought about calling Felix and letting him know he had made some progress, but decided he had better wait until he had an actual lead, rather than getting anyone riled up for nothing. *But how am I gunna track down all these people myself?*

Then he had an idea. There *was* someone who might be able to help sort through the list—someone who had their own stake in finding the true owner of that vehicle.

Cooper Austin.

2

Brent drove across town and parked in an empty space at the Shady Acre, slamming the vehicle into park and thinking he probably DID deserve something better than the crapbox he was currently driving. He made his way to the front counter and found the co-owner-slash-receptionist, Bev Carter.

"Hello, dear. Is your mother around?" he asked jokingly.

"Well, I'll be damned. Look what the cat dragged in," she replied, turning from the TV and winking at Brent as she leaned forward.

"How's the old man?" he asked, teeing up the catty reply she always gave to that question.

"That old bastard? Still alive, I think." Brent laughed. He had heard that one probably a dozen times when he was in uniform and at least half a dozen since. "You still the guy a gal looks for when she needs a screw?"

"Oh, boy, that's a new one," he lied. Hardware-store ownership came with its own set of recurring puns, and the neighborhood kids seemed to think they were timeless classics.

"It's good to see you're still holdin' down the fort, Bev, but I'm actually lookin' for Coop, if he's around?"

"I see how it is—all work and no play. I remember the days when that was the opposite, you know," she said with another wink. "He trying to enter the lottery again or something? Lord knows it would be a heavenly day when that man finally got his life together. I don't know why he even tries anymore. He ain't ever gunna win."

Brent knew a good cover story when he saw one, so he played along. "Well, he still has the right to apply, like everyone else in his... *unfortunate* position."

He didn't really believe the unfortunate part. Cooper may not have been the one who killed his partner, but he was still a liar, a thief, and a drug dealer.

"Well, I haven't seen him around, tell ya the truth, but that's nothing new."

"Shoot," Brent said, imagining Cooper was probably out making rent money in a way that was less than legal.

"What about Jamie?" he asked, figuring she may have a better idea about his whereabouts.

"Yeah, she's up there," she said, rolling her eyes and leaning back in her chair to take a sip from a cup of soda before she spoke again.

"Been up there smoking like a damn chimney and throwing her butts down here in the lot. Don't tell me you like 'em blonde now?" She took another sip, this time tossing her hair over her shoulder and batting her eyes.

"No, no, nothing like that," he said, feeling embarrassed. "Which room they stayin' at these days?"

"She's up on the balcony. Just follow your nose."

He would have preferred an actual door number, but as he walked out of the office, he spotted Jamie sitting on the balcony in a quad chair halfway down the row of doors, smoking.

He decided to make his way towards her before Mrs. Carter decided she wanted to chat him up any further.

He walked up the stairs and she looked at him as she took a drag off her cigarette, then returned her attention to the phone in her hand.

"Well, hello there, stranger," he said as he walked up beside her and put his hand in his pocket to feel the keys.

"If you're looking for Coop, he's not here," she said, to his surprise. Surely he could have been there to see either of them, he thought, but he supposed his past dealings with Cooper outweighed the good he had tried to do through the lottery.

"Mrs. Carter told me he hasn't been around. Any idea where he made off to? I just wanted his help with somethin'."

"That lyin' bastard ain't been here all day," she said with a huff. "Someone came through and trashed our place and he just up and disappeared. Sure, he's out getting drunk and fuckin' someone. No good, lyin' mother-"

"Whoa, now, that's quite the language, young lady. I know as well as anyone that Cooper can be a dirty dog from time to time, but it ain't like him to just up and leave, is it?"

"Sure it is. He never tells me where he's going or what he's doin', says, 'the less I know the better,' like that's supposed to help or somethin'. Well, it doesn't, and it usually ends with him crawlin' back with some sorry-ass excuse."

"But he always comes back, doesn't he? Comes back for you in the end?" Brent recognized that Jamie would probably be less inclined to help him if her hopeless mentality persisted. "I've known you two a long time. He may not be the sharpest crayon in the box, but he knows where home is. Ya think he got himself into some trouble?"

"I don't know shit anymore," she said, defeated. "All I know is, he left me to deal with the mess some asshole left behind, and I ain't heard a word from him since."

"I haven't heard anything about him being arrested, or…" He kicked his foot out and tapped it on the floor as he lowered his voice. "… or *found.*"

She took a long and deep pull off her cigarette before tossing it over the railing of the balcony and lighting another.

"Thank you for that," she said. "Now, what did you say you needed him for again?"

"I think I got a lead in the old case," he said as he carefully slumped down in the quad chair next to her and pulled the keys out of his pocket. "A friend gave this to me. Says it goes to the vehicle Cooper stole that night—the one that ran my partner down."

Jamie's eyes looked like they were going to bug out of her skull, matching the nervous tick that coalesced as a twitch in her left eye. "Like he said a thousand times—HE NEVER KILLED ANYONE! HE JUST STOLE THE CAR!" She leaned forward as she spoke, little droplets of spit flying with her words.

"Shh." He moved his hands in a quieting motion, then produced the lists. "I know, I know; that's partly why I'm here. These are the people that owned cars matching the description he gave, and I was hopin' he could help me rule out a few. Find out who was driving the car that night *before* he stole it."

Jamie leaned back in her chair again, wiping her mouth and looking down at the sheet of paper. "Why the hell didn't you say that? Give it here."

She looked through the list and tapped her foot on the floor. "Definitely not a Caprice; had to be the Impala—but wait, you're retired, aren't you? Why didn't you give this stuff over to the real cops?"

Brent was slightly offended. Being retired didn't mean he wasn't a *real cop*. But rather than squabble over semantics, he decided to move on. "I'm not here in an official capacity, but it's still my duty to find my partner some justice. How do you know that thing about the car?" he asked, leaning forward and trying to see if he had missed something on the list.

"He told me the engine was loud when he got in it, and not loud like busted—loud like powerful. Guy who dated my friend back in the day had a Caprice. Everyone called it the bitch mobile cuz' the engine had no balls."

"Well, that narrows it down, I guess. Anything else?"

"I don't think so. He doesn't like talking about it all that much. You assholes pretty nearly ruined his life over this, you know."

"My partner lost his life that night, so if us takin' the necessary steps to find his killer inconvenienced your husband, you'll have to find pity elsewhere. He threw himself into that arena when he decided to take advantage of the whole thing."

"Yeah, right. Kinda like how it was *necessary* for you to hide the fact that you were out selling coke when it went down. Right, officer?"

Brent stood up and ripped the list out of her hands. *How can she sit there in her dollar-store tank top with less than half a mouth full of teeth and judge me?* "I have my faults, like everyone else, and I paid for 'em, too. Keep watching Coop circle the drain—be my guest. I'm gunna find out who really caused all this."

"Wait," she called when Brent had made it back to the top of the stairs.

"Let me look again, please," she begged. Brent took a deep breath of his own, coughing slightly as he inhaled the menthol smoke wafting in the air. He walked back and sat down, tossing the papers into her lap.

"Here—right here," she said, grabbing the color-coded sheet and comparing it to the list. "A '94 Impala, all black, and look at the name."

Brent leaned forward and read the line. "I already went there. Already had a new vehicle made in 2000. Woulda stuck out like a sore thumb if they woulda tried driving the old one around town for a whole year."

"No wonder you were such a shitty cop," Jamie said, offending Brent again as he waited for the punch line. "Jesus Christ. You ever bought a car that was actually MADE the year the model says? If they had a brand new '2000 vehicle, they BOUGHT it in '99, the same year your partner got killed."

Brent felt another wave of embarrassment wash over his face, this time running deeper than the one evoked by Bev's saucy flirting. *How the hell did I miss that?*

"My Uncle Rich always said the easiest place to hide is in plain sight."

"I have to go," Brent said, getting to his feet and reaching for the list.

"I'm comin' with you," she replied and stood up with him, pulling the paper away before he could grasp it.

"You can't. I don't want anybody gettin' hurt over this. It's my burden to bear."

"Look," she said as she dropped her palm down on the table, "you came here for my help, told me some bullshit lie about helping get Cooper, when we both know this is about clearing your own conscience. Now, I'm comin' with you, whether you like it or not. That," she said, cocking her eyebrows, "or Bev down there is gunna have a whoooole new set of gossip for the girls at bridge night."

Brent read her face to see if she was joking and decided she wasn't. "Shit. But we ain't storming the house like SEAL team six. Just gotta find more proof than a vehicle-sale receipt so I can hand this in."

He looked at her and rolled his eyes. "To the REAL cops."

3

Jamie got inside the passenger seat of Brent's truck and rolled down the window to light a cigarette. They were making their way to potentially absolve her boyfriend of a crime he had once been wrongly accused of, and though it felt liberating and adventurous, it also wracked her nerves.

"Whoa, now, I don't smoke in here. Sorry," Brent said, holding up his hand. "You can wait five minutes, I'm sure."

"Fine," she said, shoving the smoke back in her pack and spinning the lighter in her hand to pass the time.

They crossed town and made their way toward the address listed on the paper—the one Brent ignored, since he knew exactly where he was going anyway. They turned onto the road and passed the house.

"Shoot, get down," he said as he noticed the cars in the driveway.

They drove a few hundred yards further and turned around, passing by again with a little more speed than the first time and turning onto a side road.

"I know those cars," Jamie said as they pulled up to a sign that read "Ratcliff Public Park" and exited the truck. "I think the white one's the fuckin' pastor's."

"Yeah, I suppose it is. What about the black one, though? Not sure I've seen it before."

"His daughter," she replied, looking at the name on the list. "I thought she would have left town by now. Her brother was at the motel picking up her stuff the other night. Said she didn't need her room anymore."

"What night was that?" he asked, the idea of shared family secrets filling his head like a thick October fog.

"Same night Cooper left," she said, lighting up a smoke. "Wait, you don't think they had anything to do with him leaving, do you? I saw them get in her car and leave. Couldn't have been."

"Well," he said, the fog clearing up a bit, but still leaving him with questions, "I think we're just gunna have to wait here til' they're gone. I didn't see Scott's rig in the driveway; I think I heard he was outta town." He looked at the clock on his dash. "They must be having dinner or somethin'. Been a long time since Felix saw her."

"What, are you crazy? Now's the PERFECT time to go in there, before it gets all quiet."

Brent looked at her, puzzled, not quite understanding what she meant.

She rolled her eyes. "You know how if you lay there perfectly still and listen to the world for a while, you can hear the little sounds you might not have noticed before? The sound of cars, trees tapping against your house and shit. There's a hum, kinda like when you're standing under those really tall power lines or somethin'. You can listen to it come to life in the morning, like the roar of a crowd, and it's the same at night, except in reverse. The cars stop going by, and everything just gets, well, quiet. I don't know if the girl is staying there or not, but if she is, then we'll never be able to find anything out without her hearing us."

"Why do most robbers rob at night, then?" Brent wondered, seeing the flaw in her logic.

"Most of em' are stupid and get caught, and the good ones rob people who ain't home. Besides, we don't need to go inside the house, do we? Just the garage. We can slip in there unnoticed while they break bread and praise Jesus or whatever. I know it."

Brent didn't like it, but he figured she was right. Even if she wasn't, he had no idea when Scott would be back in town, if he was indeed gone at all, so taking the risk now seemed like the best shot he would get. "Alright, but if things go sideways, just let me do the talkin'."

They walked out of the park and back onto the road, opting to walk onto one of the side trails the local teenagers had made to avoid been seen. They followed it back to South Main Street and crossed onto the side of the street the house was on, approaching it with caution a few minutes later. After watching the house for close to ten minutes and one "no smoking" warning, Brent signaled that it was time to move past the driveway. He put his arm around her and began walking briskly.

"What are you—" she began.

"Just keep walking. Just a happy couple out for a stroll," he said, mostly to convince himself. Once they were on the opposite side and had determined the coast was clear, they worked their way through the thicketed woods next to the garage and waited just outside the fence line.

Brent closed his eyes and listened, remembering Jamie's words about the quiet. The wind swept by his face and he heard it—the hum of the town. Inside it were the sounds of children playing somewhere off in the distance, a lawn mower making its final cuts of the day, and a faint buzz from the electricity lines in front of them. He could smell something savory in the air. *I was right. Dinner.*

They made their way over the fence and around to the back door of the garage. *Moment of truth,* he thought as he grabbed the side of a garage window and pulled it up. Thankfully, he found it unlocked.

"You," Brent mouthed to Jamie when the window reached the top of its track.

"What?" she mouthed back.

He then used his hands to frame the size of his midsection and raised them to the window to show her the obvious disparity.

"What?"

"I'm too fat," he whispered when she didn't get the hint. "Hurry!"

"Fine," she whispered back before climbing through the window and unlocking the door.

Brent winced as the door opened and hit the trash can behind it. He got inside and shut the door behind him, then crouched with Jamie behind a project motorcycle in the middle of the room. He listened for the sound of someone approaching from the house, and after hearing nothing, decided Jamie's knowledge on the buzzing sound of life was good intel after all.

"There," he whispered softly while pointing towards the tools. They crept over to the tool bench and began looking around.

"What am I looking for?" Jamie asked, knowing the time for that question was probably somewhere between the truck and the empty beer bottles in the woods, and certainly not here.

Brent produced the keys from his pocket and flipped down the fob and General Motors keys, leaving only the small golden keys in view. "A padlock."

"Like that one?" she said, pointing to a standing metal chest on the other side of the room. They tiptoed across and each held their breath as Brent slid the key into the lock.

"Nope. Probably would have cut it off by now." They looked around the room and saw there were no other items with padlocks.

"Now what?" she asked.

"Keep lookin'. Quietly."

"No shit, Sherlock," she mouthed, turning to a workbench and opening one of its eight drawers.

Brent opened another and began thumbing through the contents. He found a box of deck screws, pliers, a manual for a washing machine, and what looked like a stash of acorns from an unwelcome guest—*of the chipmunk variety,* he guessed. He closed the drawer and opened another, again finding nothing but the remnants of a do-it-yourself dad and his critter pals.

"Found one!" Jamie whispered excitedly, pulling her arm out of a drawer in which she had been elbow deep. She held it out with the key entry point toward Brent. His hands shook as he put the key inside and twisted. It opened.

The owner of the car was Scott Emerson.

Brent stared at the lock as it twisted open and released the latch. Part of him was overwhelmed with joy, and another part with anger. *Maybe if I hadn't been so foolish, I woulda figured it out sooner.*

The idea of changing the past faded as the wind picked up outside and ushered him back into reality. "We gotta go."

Brent took the key out of the lock and carefully placed both inside the pocket of his jacket. He knew there probably weren't going to be prints on the lock anymore, but he thought it would at least be enough for a warrant. Criminals were not unlike squirrels and chipmunks—both in their stupidity and their tendency to hide things rather than dispose of them. If the lock was this easy to find, there HAD to be more evidence stashed somewhere. *You drove that backhoe long before your son did. Did you bury a car with it too?*

They carefully closed the drawers they had opened and began tiptoeing back toward the door, being mindful of the trash cans as Jamie grabbed the doorknob and turned it. Jamie poked her head out the door to check if the coast was still clear and jumped back with a gasp.

Brent had no time to wonder what had startled her before he saw the barrel of a pistol round the doorway. He recognized the man behind the trigger.

It was Adrian Emerson.

"Shh," Adrian said as he slowly moved closer and herded them back inside the garage. He put his finger to his lips as he did, holding the pistol outright and moving his aim toward Brent's head. He entered the garage with them and closed the door.

Jamie spoke first. "Adrian, we can explain."

"Shut your mouth, whore," Adrian replied, pointing the gun at her again.

"Please, you gotta—" Adrian reared his arm back and smashed the pistol against the side of Jamie's head. The blow knocked her off her feet and sent her crashing into the trash cans and onto the floor, where she laid unconscious.

Brent jumped forward as the gun connected with Jamie's head. He managed to grab the barrel of the gun and was now in what he knew was a life-or-death tug of war. As he fought for control, his eye caught the silver plating on the side of the gun. *David?*

The small window of time that Brent spent marveling at the gun was all Adrian needed to swing his other arm around and connect with Brent's ribs. As his knuckles crunched against the bone, he felt Brent's grasp on the gun weaken, enabling him to twist the pistol sideways and tear it from his hold. Brent took a step back and doubled over, holding his side with one hand and putting the other in front of him.

"Wait, don't shoot," he pleaded. "You gotta know why we're here."

"Shut up and get on the floor," Adrian said as he raised the pistol again.

Brent got down on his knees and looked over at Jamie. "Please, she's got nothin' to do with this. She jus' wanted to help."

"Take her shoes off," Adrian said, stepping back and aiming down the sights of the pistol. "Now."

Brent looked down at Jamie's body and saw a slight rise and fall in her chest. *She's still alive,* he thought as he made his way to her feet and removed her shoes.

"Good. Now take the laces out and toss one of them to me."

"Son, you're making a mistake. We're not here to..."

"SHUT UP AND DO IT!" Adrian whispered loudly, flashing a face of rage as he looked from Brent to the house entry door and back.

Brent removed the laces from her shoes and threw one at Adrian's feet. He crouched down and picked it up. "Now take the other one and tie up her hands."

Brent looked down at the small pool of blood that had dripped down from the side of Jamie's head and onto the floor. He had the familiar feeling that he was once again a day late and a dollar short, having failed another poor soul. He tied her hands together and mouthed the words "I'm sorry."

"Now get on your knees and put your hands behind your back."

"Felix is in there, ain't he? He gave me the keys. He can explain all this. Now I don't care if you tie me up, but you gotta get her to a hospital. She could have a concussion." Brent put his hands behind his back and looked down at Jamie, wishing she would just sit up and light a cigarette.

Look at this asshole tying us up and not listening to a goddamn thing we got to say. What a prick.

"I'm certain he can fill us in later," Adrian said as he walked up behind Brent and dragged the shoelace through his fingers. "Jamie and I."

Brent watched as the shoelace came down across his vision and landed around his neck. He brought his hands up to pull on the cord as Adrian put his knee into his back and shoved him to the floor. The lace dug into his skin as he tried to reach behind him and swing his fist. He couldn't reach, so he brought his hands back to his neck and dug his nails into his skin, trying, and failing, to get under the lace.

As mortality swept over him in bands of grey and black, he closed his eyes and listened. He could hear his own heartbeat pumping even faster than that time he'd nearly collapsed at the police academy, and his lungs throbbing to get one last order of fresh air before closing time. His arms went limp and hit the floor in what felt like slow motion, the crash they made echoing endlessly through his brain. The sounds of the world had gone from a deafening roar to a persistent hum that pulsed through his mind, getting softer and softer until everything was perfectly quiet.

CHAPTER X:
SAFE AND SOUND

Adrian released the end of the shoelace and rolled Brent over onto his back, then reached into the pockets of Brent's jacket, pulling out the list, the lock, and the keys. He wasn't sure what the next move was, and as he checked the knot on Jamie's restraint, he heard Brent's words repeating in his head. *"Felix can explain all of this."*

He set me up, Adrian thought. *How could Felix do that to me after all these years?*

He shoved the anger down as he stepped over Jamie and opened the door adjoining the garage to the house. As he walked down the hallway, he heard Nicole speaking in the dining room and closed his eyes in disgust. *They're all against me.*

"...he wants to find out what happened to David's father because..."

"Because she killed his son," Adrian said as he walked into the dining room and put his hand on Nicole's arm. He squeezed the skin between her neck and shoulder as if he were giving her a massage, staring at Felix as his other hand raised with the gun.

"Adrian," Felix said, getting to his feet slowly and putting his hands in the air. "Easy, now. We can talk this out. No reason anybody else needs to get hurt."

Adrian smiled and turned his head to Nicole. "You hear that? Everything's going to be alright!" He pinched her skin harder, then moved his hand to her back and shoved her toward the dinner table. She flung her arms out and caught herself, knocking a wine glass on the floor, where it shattered.

Adrian produced the gun again. "Sit, won't you? We still have dessert."

Felix and Nicole looked at each other and took their seats, turning back to the table as Adrian walked to his own seat. "I knew you were weak, Nicole. You make our mother sick," he said, shaking his head and resting the gun on the table.

"Adrian, can I speak?" Felix asked, sensing Adrian's need for control.

"Please do, Pastor. As a matter of fact, tell me just what your plan was here tonight. I found your friends out in the garage snooping around. How long have they known? Have YOU known?"

"Friends? What are you talking about?"

"Quit with the act. I know you sent them. Brent told me you gave him these," Adrian said as he reached inside his pocket and threw the keys onto the table.

"Whose keys do you think those are, son?" Felix asked after a long pause.

"Come on, really? I don't know, Rick's? Morgan's? They deserved what they got. You of all people should understand that! I gave them their REAL second chance!"

"Adrian," Felix said in a low voice, "they weren't here because of you."

He looked down at the table and then at Nicole. "Those keys belong to your father."

"What do you mean, *my father?*" Adrian said, raising the gun again, this time with a slight wobble in his grip.

"Those keys went to the vehicle that killed Officer Demick—your father's car."

"There you go lying again!" Adrian said as he stood up and pointed the gun at Felix. "You son of a bitch, you're LYING!"

"It's not a lie, Adrian. Search and you will see that it's the truth. You were only a child then, but you have to remember. Your father changed after it happened; got angry at the little things. The van—the very same company van you drive around today—do you remember when it first rolled into the driveway? I do, and if you look inside, you will too. Your father was the one who killed Brent's partner."

"And, what, you covered it up until now? Why wouldn't you go to the police? If you knew he was the killer, why did you wait all these years? I'll tell you why. It was *you!*"

"NO," Felix said firmly. "I'm not the monster in all this. Your father is."

Felix reached toward his pocket.

"DON'T!" Adrian said, taking a step closer to Felix and putting both hands on the gun. "Don't you move another muscle or I'll shoot. God forgives those who punish the filth, so don't think I won't pull this trigger, *Felix*."

"I don't have any weapons, son. Just let me show you," he said as he reached inside his pocket and pulled out a little black key.

"What, more keys? Those prove nothing except the fact that you're a liar AND a thief!"

"Shut your mouth. boy!" Felix said, holding up the key. It was a small nontraditional key with a barrel tip wrapped in a black plastic sheath. "I believe it goes to your father's safe. If you'll just let me look inside, we can settle this here and now."

"I think I've heard enough," Adrian said as he raised his arm and eyed down the end of the barrel.

"WAIT," Nicole screamed out. "Adrian, you CAN'T DO THIS. At least…" she turned and looked at Felix, "…not yet."

"Why's that, Nicole? You got some keys in your pocket, too?"

"There's no going back from this. Not if you do it here, in our mother's home. If he's right, and you kill him here, you've failed me AND our mother."

Adrian's hand began to shake again as his nostrils flared and cheeks became flush. He turned, then pointed the gun at Nicole. "Do you think you're still worth saving after all of this? Do you still think there's a path that leads away from the darkness you've created?"

"If you kill him now, she'll never forgive you not allowing me the chance."

Adrian stared at his sister, steaming from the thought that she, after all these years, would have any idea of what their mother would have wanted. Somewhere, though, below the layers of righteousness, he felt that it was true.

He turned the gun again to Felix. "Get up."

"You're making the right choice, son."

"You don't know anything. Now walk. The safe is in the closet."

They made their way down the hall, passing the family room, where Adrian paused and ran his hand down the door. As they walked, Felix and Nicole heard Adrian whispering and laughing to himself behind them.

They passed through the main living room and entered their father's bedroom, where Nicole stopped and pointed at the closet door. She looked around the room and felt like she was again inside a memory—her mother's artwork was still positioned on the walls and her vanity was covered in various makeups and jewelry. Their father had left it for all these years. The only difference was a large break in the center of the mirror, the obvious mark of a punch.

Nicole opened the closet door, revealing a neat rack of suits and ties, along with four pairs of dress shoes neatly placed together. "Behind the suits," Adrian said, looking at Nicole and motioning for her to move them aside. She did. Attached to the wall behind them was a large metal safe.

It was made by a company named Sentry and had a small rubber-covered key port under a large silver keypad. Felix walked inside the closet and pulled the rubber keyhole cover off, placing it on top of the safe as he brought the key up with his other hand and placed it inside the port. He turned it slowly until he heard the bars that held the door closed move out of place. The door swung open.

"Well, where's your proof?" Adrian asked impatiently.

Felix ignored Adrian's question. His mind was instantly teleported back in time as he saw what was lying in the safe next to a golden watch and a small stack of cash. A tattered bloody shirt.

2

"What do you mean, *not yet?*" Felix asked the strange man who stood in front of him at the Shady Acre Motel. "Who are you calling?"

"I'm not calling anyone," the man said as he set the phone down, "but time is running short. That cop you killed is going to be all over the news, and you can bet your ass they're going to be showing up to shitholes like this in no time. Now come on. You need to get out of those clothes and wash the blood off you—unless, of course, you think they softened their stance on police killings lately?"

"I don't understand. Why are you helping me?"

"That doesn't really matter right now, but between you and me, that son of a bitch had it coming."

Felix got to his feet and headed toward the bathroom, his head swimming with this new information and an inability to think critically about any of it while his head still swayed from the drugs he had taken the night before. "I don't have any clothes," he said, looking at the stranger who had just given him the free pass of a lifetime.

"I'll find you something. Now go."

Felix got in the shower and washed the blood from his hands and the rest of his body, holding back the urge to scream as the dark red flakes went down the drain. He sat beneath the water and cried, imagining the full scope of his actions and wondering if his life had any meaning left at all. He finished cleaning up and got out of the shower, finding a towel on the wall and wrapping it around himself before opening the door.

"Here," the man said, tossing Felix a pair of basketball shorts and a white shirt. "Found these in the laundry room. Now hurry up and get dressed. We're leaving."

After Felix put on the baggy clothing, he looked at himself in the mirror. *What have I become?* He dropped his head in grief, and as he opened his eyes, he caught sight of something in the small trash can next to the sink. He reached inside and held the item up in the light. *Car keys.*

"Let's go," he heard from outside, the words accompanied by a fist rapping on the door. He put the keys into his pocket and took one more look into the mirror before exiting the bathroom.

He followed the man outside, then around the side of the building and into the woods. He noticed that the man had picked up the clothing he'd been wearing before and had placed the articles inside a plastic shopping bag, which he now carried under his arm.

"What about the car?" Felix asked, thinking it was a mistake to leave it behind.

"I got rid of it earlier. Follow me." Felix followed as the stranger led him through a path in the woods that ended up at a small clearing near a brook.

"I used to walk these trails when I was in school. Good to see they haven't changed."

"Who are you?" Felix asked impatiently. *Who are you, and why the HELL would you help a cop killer?*

"My name is Scott. And yours?" the man replied, reaching out for a handshake.

For a moment, he thought he could lie and somehow get away from this stranger and all of it unscathed, but he also knew there was a lot he didn't understand quite yet, and decided it wasn't the right move. "Felix," he said, reaching out his hand.

"Well, Felix, I'm sure you're wondering what the hell we're doing all the way out here. Well, I'll tell you what we're doing: we're going to get rid of these." He ripped open the plastic bag and dropped the clothing onto the ground, throwing the bag on top of the pile and pulling a lighter from his pocket. "Don't worry about the motel. The things that go on in that place don't surprise the maids anymore, and I'm certain they won't bat an eye before scrubbing the place down for the next drug deal."

"Why are you helping me?" he asked again, this time expecting an answer that made sense.

"Last night was a long one for me, Felix. See, the police officer you killed, well, he destroyed my family. That no-good bastard called himself a hero, and all the while, he was running around town making messes for everyone else. You stole my car, which I suppose is my fault for leaving the keys in the ignition, but you did me the greatest favor a man could ask for. You killed the man who was sleeping with my wife."

Felix watched as Scott bent down to the pile of clothes and lit the lighter, holding it on the jeans until they began to smoke and catch fire.

"What happens now? What do I do?"

"Nothing. You go your way and I go mine. If it helps, just know you *did* try to save him, I can tell by the blood on the shirt that you didn't just hit him and leave. And if you ever have doubts, just remember: he wasn't a good man; he was a no-good cheating hypocrite who deserved what he got."

They parted ways in the woods that day, Felix leaving first and running in the opposite direction of the motel. He heard sirens in the distance that made his heart skip a beat, and beneath the confusion he still felt, there was a deeper urge to find somewhere he could get a fix.

The days passed and turned into weeks, the story capturing the imagination of every citizen in town. Felix found himself on the verge of breaking on many occasions, inevitably drowning out the thought with a needle. A month after his clothes had gone up in smoke, he woke up in a panic again, this time at the hospital. He had overdosed and been brought back to life by paramedics. It was that day he decided enough was enough.

After months of rehab, and more close encounters of the confession kind, he finally had the strength to walk out the door. The few people he had opened up to inside had made him realize that the thing he was missing most was a higher power, something to believe in that was greater than himself. And so his first stop after being released was a local church.

Over the next few years, he worked to find the light, spending most of his free time helping with community events and studying the Bible until it became part of him. He kept in mind what Scott had told him in the woods, and though the Bible recognized adultery as a sin, underneath the progress, a lingering doubt remained about whether he could truly give himself up to a higher power without admitting what he'd done.

He contemplated the thought occasionally until, one day, a woman had approached him after an event and thanked him for everything he had done to make the day a success. It had been a fundraiser for the teen center in town, and she had been moved by the generosity of the church, and by Felix especially for spending long hours working to ensure the best turnout ever. Felix had been humbled by her words, and for the first time felt a responsibility to the town and its people to continue bearing the burden he had placed upon himself in the name of progress.

Not long after, as Felix began to work towards advancing his role within the church, he recognized Scott sitting with his wife and two children at Sunday mass. At the conclusion of the service, Felix made his way to the door and shook hands with folks as they exited the building, then headed home to turn on football games and put roasts into the oven. At the end of the line was Scott, the mystery man from the motel who was partially to credit, in a way, for his current success.

"Felix, right?" Scott said as he took his hand at the door and shook it, looking into his eyes and smiling.

"Yes, that's me. Thank you for coming. We appreciate the support."

"You guys wait in the car. I'll be right there," Scott said to his wife as she and the kids exited through the door. Felix watched as the little girl turned and smiled at him, so he smiled back and waved at her goodbye.

"Is there something I can help you with?" Felix asked, looking around to see if any stragglers remained.

"I just wanted to thank you for everything you've done for me. You know, you've really come a long way."

"Thank you," Felix said, unsure of what to say now. "The Lord guides me now, and I do follow."

"That's wonderful. Really good stuff. I was hoping we could catch up sometime soon, you and me. I have something I want to talk to you about."

"I'm not sure that would be for the best. I'm quite busy these days, as you can see." He waved his arm around, gesturing for Scott to look around the church at what his life had become.

"Sure, sure, I get it, but here's my number anyway," he said, handing Felix his business card. It had the logo of the funeral parlor on the front next to the contact information.

"I left something for you in the collection plate too. God bless," he said, then walked out the door.

Felix looked at the card again and turned around. *What could he possibly want with me now?* he thought as he made his way to the collection plate stand.

Inside was a pile of cash—mostly twenties, he was pleased to see—but beneath those was a tattered piece of fabric. He picked it up and saw that it was partially burned on one of the edges and torn on the other, as if it had been ripped off a larger piece. In the middle of the cloth was a small red drop, faded to a dark brown over the years.

His head turned sharply to the front door as he realized it was the cop's blood.

He put out the fire. And took the shirt...

3

Felix reached out his arm and grabbed the shirt, pulling it out with a dazed look on his face. He opened it up and held it out of for Adrian and Nicole to see. The shirt was missing a small portion from the bottom and was covered in patches of blood, burn holes, and soot.

He had longed to have the article of clothing back in his possession, and felt a little cheated that its return was overshadowed by the fear of his own death.

"An old, bloody shirt? What does that have to do with anything?" Adrian asked.

"This was the shirt I was wearing the day I met your father. The day he convinced me I was a killer."

"So, you admit it then," Adrian said, looking at his sister with an "I told you so" face. "It's covered in blood and who knows what else? Seems pretty convincing."

"No, listen: he TOLD me I killed him, but that wasn't the truth. He framed me. Why else would he keep it here? Locked away in a safe and not in the hands of the authorities? It was so he could blackmail me."

"He did seem a little off after that happened," Nicole added, looking at the shirt. "It makes sense. What other purpose could it serve?"

"I don't know!" Adrian yelled. "Maybe he didn't know who the shirt belonged to. Maybe he found it in his car and didn't know what to do. That makes more sense to me than our father just killing a cop out of the blue."

"He told me David Senior was fooling around with your mother."

Adrian turned and punched Felix in the mouth. "Don't you EVER talk about our mother like that. She wasn't a slut like your friend Jamie out there, you hear me?"

Felix stumbled and put his hands up to defend himself, but Adrian took a step back and raised the gun. "Tell me why I shouldn't put a bullet in your head right now."

Nicole held her hands over her face. She knew Felix had gone too far talking about their mother. She knew that at any second, Adrian would pull the trigger, and she would be right back to square one.

"Do it. I deserve it," Felix said as he wiped the blood from his nose. "I failed you, both of you. Now do it. You're never going to believe the truth anyway, so just pull the trigger and kill any chance she has of salvation."

"You ARE weak!" Adrian said, laughing now. "All these years, I thought you were the strongest man I knew! Able to hold true even when the scum of the earth stabbed you in the back over and over and over again. Well, now I know why: because beneath all of that, beneath every single truth you ever told, beneath every sermon you spewed out, was a lie. So, no, I'm not going to do what you tell me to do. That's a fool's game. But what I do know is this: once you stand back up, you're going to do exactly what I tell you, or she—" Adrian said as he pulled Nicole in front of him and put the gun against her head, "—and her little friends are going where God himself can't save them."

Nicole stared at Felix and begged him not to do anything stupid. She felt the metal tip of the gun against her temple and prayed it wasn't the last thing she felt on this earth.

Felix nodded his head in agreement, a tear streaming down his face as he looked at Nicole with immense grief.

"Close the safe. We're leaving," Adrian said, letting go of Nicole and moving out of the closet towards the door. She watched as Felix went to close the safe and instead reached inside, grabbing a piece of paper and putting it into his pocket before turning the key and locking it once more.

"Toss me the shirt," Adrian said as Felix came out of the closet behind them.

Felix looked at the tattered relic that had caused him so many nightmares over the years and begrudgingly tossed it to Adrian. He wished for only a moment or two more to explain things, but knew it would be received as well as the last batch, so he kept his mouth closed, walking after Adrian when he was given the order.

They got back into the kitchen and were directed to go to the garage. "For a fun surprise brought to us by Pastor Robinson," Adrian said.

They entered, Nicole first, with Felix behind her and Adrian last. Nicole gasped as she entered and saw two bodies on the floor.

"Adrian, why?" Nicole whimpered.

"Oh, relax. She's not dead. Only him." He kicked at Jamie's side, causing her to take in a sharp breath. She woke entirely and began screaming.

251

"Quiet now, girl," Felix said as she turned and looked at him.

"But—are you with HIM?"

"Just be quiet and listen now, ok? Its gunna be alright, child. I promise."

"I wouldn't take advice from a guy like him," Adrian interjected.

"Let me go, you motherf—" Adrian put his free hand over her mouth and squeezed, turning her head so he could see her eyes.

"You broke into MY father's house, so don't blame this on me, sweetheart. You can blame him for getting you into this mess," he said, moving her face so she could see Felix.

"Now, you, me, and my sister are going for a little ride, so I need you to shut your mouth. Think you can handle that? Do you think she can handle that, Brent?" He turned her face again, this time showing her Brent's body. She screamed, forcing Adrian to cover her mouth again.

"Is that your idea of quiet?" he asked, watching the tears roll down her face. He lifted his hand off her mouth. This time, no sound came out.

"Good. I knew I could count on you for something. Now, *Pastor*, here's what I need you to do. Help my sister get these two in the trunk. I know it's a tight fit, but I'm sure you can make it work. Then, the three of us—" he said, making a small circle in the air with the gun, "—are going to go back to our good friend Cooper for a fun little reunion!"

"And where will I go?" Felix asked after having been left out of the plan.

"You're going to clean my father's house, like we were never here. I'm sure you can manage that after all the bitch work you make the kids do. Then, you're going to go back to the church and do what you've always done: lie to the people and tell them everything is fine—dandy, in fact! Then, on Friday, I'm going to need you to stop everything and wait for my call. If I even THINK the cops or anyone else has gotten wind of this, well…" He turned Jamie's face towards Felix again. "… I think you know what happens then."

"Nobody wants to resolve this more than me, son. What happens on Friday?"

"That's when we get to hear the REAL truth," Adrian said, turning his attention to Nicole. "From our father."

CHAPTER XI:
LATER GATOR

Nicole sat in the passenger seat of her Civic as it turned onto Route Five in White River Junction, silently staring out the window and reflecting on the grim task she'd completed before the ride: stuffing Jamie and Brent into the trunk. She could feel Adrian's eyes on her, the light of passing cars and streetlamps confirming it in short glimpses.

When they finally rode past the cemetery gate and up the hill to the mausoleum, she turned to him and offered only a look of indifference. What followed was another bout of cold chills and numbness, but in her mind, the darkness had swept back over her the moment she had opened her mouth to Felix.

Adrian opened the trunk and motioned for Jamie to keep quiet, calmly whispering, "Shh," and moving a finger from his own lips to the front of the gag that now covered her mouth. He moved one of Brent's arms off her and pulled her out. "Guess he couldn't keep his hands to himself," he said with a laugh.

He ushered them into the mausoleum, forcing Nicole into the hatch first and handing her the keys to unlock the door, keeping his own free to wield the pistol. They descended the stairs and, as the echoing metal clang of Nicole fumbling around for the lock in the dark faded, entered the vault.

"Who's there?" Nicole heard from within. "Help me, please." The begging was followed by the sound of what she knew was Cooper crying. He had woken from his drug-induced trip at some point, and was now experiencing what Nicole had when she was first dragged into the hole: the sweeping darkness.

Adrian flicked on the light and placed the lantern on the table. "Cuffs," he said to Nicole in a casual, *"you know the routine"* tone. She walked to her spot on the wall and put her wrists into the handcuffs, closing them with a *click* and proving their security with a shake of her arms.

Meanwhile, Jamie scrambled over to Cooper on the floor and choked out an incoherent string of words through her gag as she saw the markings on his body. Nicole's chest was comparable to the cemetery gate as the two came together, the breathing example of Adrian's senseless destruction a cold and ominous weight.

"It's ok. He had to do it. I fucked up," Cooper said to Jamie, looking up at Adrian, who was studying their interaction.

"My deepest apologies on leaving you for so long. We had a little field trip to go on after your information on Felix, and, well, I think you were right about him after all. Well, partially."

"And her? What is she doing here?"

"Well," Adrian said as he walked to Cooper's side and knelt down, "she fucked up, too."

Nicole looked away as Adrian placed his arm around Jamie's neck and put the gun to her head.

"NO," Cooper screamed. "I told you the truth! Don't hurt her!"

"I'm not going to hurt her, Cooper; I just want her to tell you where she was the night you disappeared," Adrian said as he pulled the gag off Jamie's mouth.

"Don't listen to him! He's a fuckin' animal! He killed Brent!"

Shut up! Nicole thought as she opened her eyes again. *Either play his game or shut the hell up!*

Cooper's lip began to tremble as he looked between Adrian and Jamie. "What's he talkin' bout?"

Jamie stared back. Then, her face contorted with guilt, she looked away. "I never meant to..."

"WHERE?" Cooper screamed.

"I was waiting... for him," she whispered toward the ground. "I didn't think..."

"Why the hell would you be out that late with HIM?" Cooper yelled, his eye darting between Jamie and Adrian again.

"She thinks I'm handsome," Adrian said as he held his arms up wide in a *"soak it up"* pose.

Nicole watched his display of arrogance unfolding with a dull throb beginning to grow inside her head. *How can you parade your acts of adultery on one hand and condemn everyone else on the other?*

She wanted to shout the word *hypocrite* at him, to open his eyes to this blatant discrepancy in his judgement, but she knew it wouldn't hold any power against the twisted vines of holy justification that had grown into the bedrock of his personality.

"Stupid SLUT!" Cooper yelled, squirming in his restraints. "And you, you sick fuck," he said, dropping the act of obedient captive, "what kind of man goes and fucks around with another man's wife?"

"Oh, I was never going to go ALL THE WAY. I just needed a good excuse to get her out of the house. And, now that the air is clear..."

You cant! Nicole thought as Adrian closed his eyes and quickly mumbled something to himself.

Then he put his finger on the trigger and squeezed.

Nicole slammed her eyes shut as the shot partially deafened her and filled the room with the smell of burnt gunpowder. She opened them again a few seconds later, and through the ringing that seemed to invade all her senses at once, she watched Jamie fall on top of Cooper and begin beating her fists on his chest.

Adrian turned and looked at her, his eyes seeming to glow in the dark. He turned back to Jamie and dragged her off Cooper, slamming her onto the floor and holding her down with his foot. When she stopped moving, he took the ropes off Cooper and used them to tie Jamie's feet and hands, replacing the shoelace around her wrists with a sturdier rope.

When he finished, he walked to Nicole and took a seat next to her on the wall, placing his hand on her leg and shaking it. "I do believe that one is on you again, sis, but to tell you the truth, he's been on my waiting list for a long time now."

She refused to look at him, though she did feel something like guilt squirming around inside her. *He's the one who pulled the trigger, not you. Yes, but you're the one who couldn't keep your mouth shut.*

"I can't risk people like him ruining it for us now. We're getting so close, I can feel it!"

What about her? she thought. *Is she still alive to play some other perverted role in all this, or is she just meant to suffer the loss until it drains her?*

"Only a few more days and we can put all this in the past. But..." he said as he ran his hand down the side of her leg and stopped at her knee, "... I don't believe our mother would be pleased with you trying to sabotage her son. Is she even there anymore?"

"Adrian," she said, afraid the most recent bout of insanity may have pushed him to a new level of sick that she didn't want to imagine. "I need something for the pain."

He pulled his hand back, to her relief. "Of course." He retrieved the pouch from the other side of the room and opened it on the table, filling a syringe and tapping the side. "Her first."

Adrian knelt and stuck Jamie in the neck with the needle, squeezing the heroin into her veins. Nicole noticed that she didn't struggle or even attempt to move at all. She *wanted* it. He filled up the syringe again and brought it to Nicole's side.

"The same one?" she asked, knowing the outcome of sharing needles could be its own type of torture.

"Another old saying comes to mind: beggars can't be choosers."

She grimaced as he stuck the needle in her arm and relaxed as it released. Hepatitis was a good trade for mental escape. She had gotten used to the initial rush, and rested her head against the wall as she waited for it to take her away. Then she snapped to attention as Adrian began tugging on her plastic boot.

"What are you doing? Adrian, don't," she said, feeling the drugs starting to kick in.

He took it off her foot and felt her ankle, pulling his hand back and inspecting it more closely. He put his hand back on her ankle again and rubbed his fingers around, smudging and smearing the makeup.

"Oh, dear," he said as he stood up again, the movement making her slightly dizzy.

"It looks like you made your choice LONG before the pastor arrived."

"Adrian, I can…"

"It's a shame, really," he said, cutting her off as he began walking around the room and admiring the urns. "Here I was thinking you wanted to LIVE! That you were ashamed of the way you left me, that you WANTED to make things right for the family you abandoned, but I guess I was wrong. AND I HATE BEING WRONG!" he said as he spun around and slammed his hands down on the table.

"You're just the same STUPID girl who wants to run and hide, leaving ME to pick up the pieces!"

Adrian turned and kicked Jamie in the side, causing her to cry out in pain. "Why did you leave?" he yelled, then kicked her again.

"Why do you lie?" Another kick, this time at her face. "ANSWER ME!"

"Stop hurting her!" Nicole screamed out. At least, she thought she did. The heroin was beginning to make her head swirl, and while she knew the hallucinations were coming, she could feel that this was real. *Why is he talking to her like she's... me?*

Adrian came back and grabbed the hair on top of Nicole's head and yanked her to her feet. "I don't like the way Mother cries when I hurt you."

His face began to contort and melt like a candle, swirling around and turning every shade of red she had ever seen. He put his hand around her throat and stepped on her ankle with most of his weight. As the pain rippled through her body, he came back into focus.

"But I guess I better practice getting used to it."

2

On the following morning, Nicole woke slowly as a pounding sound invaded her dreams, getting more and more obtrusive until she finally felt the real world rushing back in. *THUD,* she heard again, then spoke.

"Jamie, is that you?" she asked, praying for a response.

"Yeah, I'm here," she heard, along with rustling from across the room.

"What's that sound?" Nicole wondered aloud, unsure if it had come from inside or outside of the vault. Her chest tingled slightly at the thought of someone trying to break down the door.

"It was me," cut through the dark, causing the tingle to die.

"What are you doing?"

"I don't know, really. There's some wood thing behind me I'm hitting. Thought maybe if someone could hear us down here, they might find a way to get us out."

"It won't work. I've tried," Nicole said as a sad matter of fact.

"Wait, when did *you* try?" Jamie asked, surprised. "I was awake before you, I think."

"I don't know. Yesterday, the day before. The day before that too, probably."

There was a moment of silence as Jamie connected the dots in her head. *THUD.*

"What are we gunna do, then?" Jamie asked a minute later. "Sit around and wait for him to come back and kill us? There's always a way out of these things. ALWAYS."

Nicole couldn't help but feel sorry for Jamie. *This is real life, dear. There's no secret potion stashed in the wall that's going to give us inhuman strength and make us capable of knocking down doors. There's no prince to break them down from the outside, either. There's just us... and ghosts.*

They sat in silence. The only sound was Jamie moving her hands around in a futile attempt to untie them. Nicole rattled her own handcuffs at one point, not because she thought they were going to come loose, but because it was the only thing that made her feel more connected to Jamie than her brother.

If I would have just stayed in Arkansas, maybe some of the innocents would have lived... She shook her head at the thought. *They're ALL innocent.*

"You know what I mean," Nicole said out loud.

"Are you talkin' to yourself?" Jamie asked. "Don't you fuckin' go crazy on me now, lady. Your brother's got that part covered, and I need you sane if we're gunna get outta here."

"Sorry," Nicole said, taking a breath and rattling her handcuffs again. "It's this place."

"Why is he doin' this? I get not wanting to see your father go to jail, but this is completely insane!"

"It has nothing to do with our father," Nicole said. "It's our mother."

Nicole told Jamie the story of their mother's suicide, adding that her own failure to cope with the stress and changing family dynamics had resulted in her leaving Adrian to absorb all the guilt himself. "It's my fault for not staying around to help him understand that her choice to die had nothing to do with him."

"Holy shit, that'll fuck ya up, alright," Jamie said after Nicole finished. "That ain't on you, though. Cooper tried that same kinda guilt trip shit on me when HE couldn't get it together. You mighta given him a few more years before it took hold, but you can't take the scars off a man's soul. The only difference probably woulda been how much time you spent in this fuckin' hole."

Nicole wished she could believe her, that it wouldn't have made a difference, but she could never know for sure, and the thought once again reminded her of a song her mother used to sing to them in the family room. *"If I could turn the page, perhaps then I'd rearrange just a day or two..."*

"OW, FUCK," Jamie yelled seemingly out of nowhere, bringing Nicole back into the present.

"What happened?" she asked, knowing the cramps from prolonged time in one position all too well and assuming they had been the cause of the outburst.

"Somethin' just poked me in the ass."

Nicole heard more shuffling sounds as Jamie moved around on the floor, presumably to get into a position where she could feel what caused the pain.

"It's some sorta pin, I think... wait." She paused as she inspected the item further. "No, it's like a badge or something? Oh, shit!" Jamie yelled, excited. "I think I can cut through the rope with this!"

"No! Don't!" Nicole yelled, knowing exactly what would happen if she did. Sure, she would be out of the ropes, but still far from out of the vault.

"What the hell do you mean, *'don't?'*"

"Adrian. He'll be back this morning—any time now. If he finds out you tried to escape, you're toast." Then, deciding to add herself to accentuate the point, she said, "We BOTH are."

"So, what the hell should I do? If we do NOTHING, we're dead, too!"

"I DON'T KNOW YET," Nicole said hurriedly. *If she cuts the ropes, there's still the door. The pin COULD unlock the door, but if it doesn't and he sees the ropes are cut—DEAD. But...* She shook her handcuffs. *If it unlocks these cuffs, I can try the door, and if the door unlocks, we can escape, and if it doesn't, I can still get back inside the cuffs—no severed rope.*

"Give me the badge," she said, then laid out the idea she had just run through in her mind. "It's the only way to make sure he doesn't kill one of us if it DOESN'T work. He'll bring us food and water, then be gone most of the day."

"Fuuuck," Jamie drew out with a harsh sigh. "But don't you dare fuckin' leave me."

Jamie began working her way across the floor, holding the badge behind her back as she moved first her legs, then her torso in short bursts. She finally made it to Nicole and took a breath. "What should I do with it now?"

"My feet," Nicole said. "Put it at my feet." Jamie made one last turn and felt Nicole's feet at the small of her back, then dropped the badge on the floor.

"Ok, it's there."

Nicole felt the badge with the sole of her foot and positioned it between her toes. She lifted her legs up above her head and stretched her hands out from the handcuffs until she finally felt the metal on the tips of her fingers and grasped the sides.

"Got it," Nicole said as she felt for the sharp pin on the back with her other hand and moved it toward the keyhole on the cuffs. She had felt the keyhole dozens of times as she had sat alone in the dark, on one occasion having wished she was Houdini and had a pocket in her skin containing the magic key. Now she pressed the pin inside the lock and began moving it around as fast as she could, being careful not to drop the badge and potentially lose precious time.

Nothing happened. No clicking sounds or release, no magic. "Come on, you piece of shit," she said as she pressed the pin in with more force. She began to feel the doubt fall over her again as the pin just made metal-on-metal scraping sounds and the handcuffs refused to open. As the cuffs dug into her skin from the furious motions, she closed her eyes again to focus. This time, David appeared to her.

"Howdy there, stranger, need help getting your little cuffs unlocked?"

"That would be the bee's knees," she responded out loud, this time not caring if Jamie heard.

"Well, you oughtta know, the key for those cuffs is bigger than a little-old pin. Maybe try one of the points of the star?"

"Well, golly gee. Ya know, I didn't think of that. You're just as smart as you are handsome."

"What the fuck?" Jamie said at the mimicry.

"I guess we're 'bout to find out, ma'am." David said as Nicole turned the badge over.

Nicole pressed a star point into the lock and twisted. This time, the cuff released.

"Don't go makin' a ruckus, now. I'll catch ya when the cows come home." David disappeared from her mind as she pulled the cuff through the loop in the wall and got to her feet.

"It worked!?" Jamie said excitedly. "Get me the hell out of these!"

"No, remember the plan," Nicole said as she felt for the door on the wall next to her. "I can't take those off until I'm SURE we can actually get out of here."

"Well, hurry up then, *ma'am*."

Nicole disregarded the mocking and turned her attention to the door. This time, she started with the point of the star, and when it was too big, she flipped the badge on its side and used the pin. For the next minute she wiggled it around and pushed every which way she could think of, each time finding the door still locked.

"It won't work," she said. "I have to put the cuffs back on before he gets here or he'll kill us both."

"Wait!" Jamie yelled. "They always have two things when they're opening doors in the movies. Find something else to go in with it—like, like, I don't know, a nail or a wire or something."

"There's only one pin," she replied. "Do you have any in your hair?"

"No," Jamie said reluctantly, "but what about that lantern he had last night?"

She added with a spark, "Isn't there some kinda wiring on the side?"

Nicole turned around and, with her arms out in front of her, made her way to the table. She gently felt around for the lantern, knowing if she knocked it over, there would be no pretending this attempt didn't happen.

"The glass!" Jamie added. "Can't we break the glass and cut his ass up or somethin'?"

"NO," Nicole said harshly. "I tried that before, too. He's prepared for that."

Her hands found the lantern, and as she began pulling at the wire on the side, she had a better idea and stopped. She felt around the bottom and the top and found the handle was also made of a thin type of metal. *I can replace it if it doesn't work. Can't fix the wire.* She followed it to the side with her fingers and felt that it was only connected through small holes, allowing her to press the sides and pop it out into her hand.

"Got something, I think." She made her way back to the door and inserted the lantern handle first, then the pin. She jiggled them around, expecting another disappointment, but after only a few seconds, the lock clicked and the handle turned.

"Holy shit," she said, her heart beginning to pump hard and fast.

"You got it! NOW cut me loose, and let's get the fuck outta here!"

"Not yet," Nicole said again. "There's still one more door up there."

"I don't care, just get these ropes off me! We already know you can open it if it's locked!"

"But what if it's padlocked from the outside?" she said, wishing she would have been paying attention the last time she went through rather than focusing on the stained-glass lighting. "I'm just going to take a look, I'll be right back, I promise."

"NO! Cut me loose you bitch!" Jamie shouted.

"LISTEN TO ME," Nicole shouted back. "If there's no way out up there and he finds us out down HERE, he WILL kill you! Just give me two minutes to scope it out. If there's a way out I'll cut you loose, if not we can wait until after he leaves and have more time to figure it out."

"URGHH," Jamie growled out in anger. "GO THEN!"

Nicole took a deep breath and began ascending the stairs, the pain in her ankle almost as fresh as the day she first came down them, thanks to Adrian's last stand the night before. As she climbed, she had a flashback of her encounter with Adrian at the top, imagining he would be there again this time, waiting to pop out with those glowing eyes just before banishing her to the vault for the last time.

She pushed through the menacing thoughts and pain, taking one last deep breath before pressing open the hatch and stepping out. He wasn't there. She pulled herself up and quickly looked around, spying the hole in the glass again and looking through it to see if anyone was in the cemetery. It was deserted, and even if it wasn't, she thought, anyone caught trying to help them was surely going to have their own trip down the stairs or worse.

She looked at the door, her heart sinking as she recognized it was indeed locked from the outside. She turned her attention back to the window, where she stuck her arm out and began gauging whether it was big enough for her to climb through. She managed to also get her head out, nearly cutting herself on the glass that remained at the bottom. *I would never fit without cutting myself to pieces,* she thought. *But JAMIE might.*

Nicole made her way back down the stairs, her adrenaline drowning out the pain she felt in her ankle and allowing her to reach the bottom in less than a minute. "You can make it through the window," she said, dropping to her knees and taking the side of the badge to the ropes on Jamie's hands.

She stabbed and poked at them, feeling the strands begin to break after a few accidental jabs that went into Jamie's hand. After another minute of slicing, she yelled, "PULL."

Jamie pulled the ropes apart with all her strength to keep them taut. Nicole continued slicing as the tension increased, causing them to fly apart one by one. "MORE," Nicole yelled, feeling the last few lines between her fingers. Jamie pulled again with all her strength, this time causing the rope to split in half.

"Holy shit, you did it!" Jamie cried out as she brought her hands in front of her and sat up to tackle the rope around her legs.

THUD.

"What was that?" Jamie asked, her words coming out fast and high pitched.

"Shh," Nicole said, then listened.

"Must be the road," Jamie whispered after a few seconds of silence. She began pulling at the rope again.

"SHH," Nicole said, this time a little louder.

Jamie stopped, they both heard it. *Footsteps.*

"Shit shit shit," Jamie said. "You gotta help me. He's gunna kill me!"

"Lay down again," Nicole said in a panic.

"You're not tying me up again!" Jamie said in a huff, "there's two of us and only one of him, we can't just roll over and die!"

270

"He's just here to drop stuff off, I'll leave it loose." She said, hoping Jamie could set aside her mortal fear for just a second and understand her cooperation was literally life or death.

"NO!" Jamie said to Nicole's dismay, "just put me up against the wall, I'll keep my hands behind my back so I can scratch his eyes out if I have to."

"Fine," Nicole said with grave defeat, "but if you have to, use this, it's sharper," she added and placed the badge into Jamie's hand, knowing she had to get back into the handcuffs and that Jamie should be the one with the pseudo-weapon.

Jamie dropped the badge into her bra and flattened her shirt, then sat against the wall leaning forward while Nicole quickly circled the rope around her wrists.

"The lantern!" Jamie whispered as Nicole started toward her own side of the room. "You have to fix it!"

Nicole stuck her arms out and rushed over to the side of the table, being careful not to blow it now by knocking things over. She then tried to slip the pin back into the tiny holes they had come out of. She heard the footsteps stop just outside the door, followed by the sound of keys. *There's no time,* she thought and laid the lantern on its side, the pin only halfway secured.

She jumped back to her spot near the wall and reached up to find the metal ring on the wall. The front door of the vault opened with a stretch of light as she got the cuffs through the metal ring and around her wrist again. She turned to conceal the cuffs as the light fell on her, then listened as the door began to close. Just as it clicked into place, she closed her eyes and pushed the handcuffs into place, a prisoner once more. A moment later, the lamp flashed on. There stood Adrian next to three bags, staring intently at the lantern.

"Good morning, ladies. What do we have here?" he said, picking up the handle.

"I think I kicked the table last night in my sleep. I'm really sorry," Jamie said, allowing Nicole's muscles to relax slightly.

"Well, it's not like you KILLED someone. Just be a little more careful. Stupidity has a price down here," Adrian replied, looking at Nicole.

"What did you do with Cooper?" Jamie asked as the light shined on the empty space where his body had been the night before.

"He and Brent had an appointment at the parlor. Seems they didn't realize I was on vacation this week. Quite inconsiderate, if you ask me."

Nicole had wondered how Adrian managed to find the time to come down and taunt her so frequently, especially with her father away. She had almost asked at one point, but had learned better than to *ask stupid questions*, unless she wanted painful answers.

"But they didn't want to be gone too long, so I brought them back." Adrian picked up the two white paper bags from the floor and dumped them onto the table.

Jamie screamed in horror as the ash carpeted the table. Nicole couldn't help but feel like she was seeing a magic trick for the second time. It left her completely unphased as the term *bone fragments* streaked through her mind in lettering a little less bold than before.

Adrian took notice of her lack of enthusiasm. "What's the matter? Getting old already?"

She looked away from him and fixed her eyes on Jamie. She knew what was next—she would have to make an urn. For a moment, she felt sorry for her, having already had to do it once herself, but then her eyes widened. *The severed strands.*

"Can I make the urn again?" she asked, praying he would allow her to be the one to sit at the wheel. "I think she's gunna mess it up if she does. They deserve better than anything that bimbo can make."

"Fuck YOU!" Jamie said, unaware that Nicole was trying to help.

Adrian thought about it for a moment, then got out the wheel and the third bag, filled with what Nicole had guessed correctly was clay. "They usually make their own before I send them to be judged," he said as he undid her handcuffs and stood her up, "but since you robbed them of that, I suppose this could work."

"Wha-what's she doin?" Jamie asked as the wheel began to spin. "What the hell is that for?"

"Just shut your mouth," Nicole said as she molded the clay, trying to go as quickly as possible so Adrian would leave, giving them another chance at escape. She completed the first and began making the second, cruising through the process with a precision that seemed both crucial and unfortunate to possess. She finished in just under fifteen minutes—probably a world record, if Guinness recognized murder and torture as legitimate criteria.

"There, it's done," she said, standing up and returning to her place on the wall. She slipped her own hands into the cuffs and clicked them into place.

"Who knew you could be so helpful?" Adrian said, beginning to move the ashes around on the table. He picked up one of the urns and began sweeping one of the piles off the table into the opening. "See ya later, alligator."

Nicole expected Adrian to pick up the other urn and do the same, but instead, he brushed the other pile into the same urn. "In a while, crocodile."

"What are you doing?" she asked, confused that he hadn't kept them separated. "I made two."

"Thank you for that, sis. You really saved me some time," he said as he placed the urn on the shelf behind Jamie and knelt down at her side.

"But, like I said before, I WON'T be made a fool of." He pulled Jamie from the wall and tossed her down on her stomach, revealing the hastily replaced rope.

"Do you think I'm stupid, Nicole?" he said as he grabbed Jamie by the wrists and dragged her to Nicole's side. "Or did you just forget the PRICE?"

Nicole watched in horror as he kicked her again and again and again, each blow punctuated with another deafening scream. A badge wasn't strong enough to slay a monster. Jamie never stood a chance.

Adrian stopped and took a breath, then reached into his back pocket and pulled out the leather pouch. He opened it up and filled up two syringes, tapping them each on the side before injecting them both into Jamie.

The screaming stopped as the drugs entered her system. Her head hit the floor and her eyes turned up and stared at the ceiling. After another few seconds, her body began convulsing.

Nicole couldn't watch, and closing her eyes didn't help— Jamie continued to make gurgling sounds as her mouth foamed up and her body rose and fell on the floor like a fish out of water. Nicole wept, thinking that if she would have just cut the ropes in the first place, Jamie could have climbed out the window and been long gone. *Maybe I would be the one on the floor, the one who deserves it.*

After another few minutes, the room was quiet again. Adrian stood up and stared at Jamie's body. "I made the mistake of giving too big a dose once, back before she and the rest of the scum," he said while tossing a glance at the wall of urns, "provided me with the tricks of the trade. It's surprising how intelligent people can be on matters that destroy their minds! I would much rather have them completely alert for their reckoning but hey, who can say no when sweet irony volunteers for their cause? She was trying to ruin it for us, and Mother."

"Stop talking about our goddamn mother!" Nicole screamed out. "She's DEAD, Adrian. YOU killed her, and she's not coming back! And she sure as HELL wouldn't think what you do is RIGHT! So stop with this stupid game. If you're going to kill me, just do it!"

"There she is, at long last," Adrian said, turning sharply on his feet. "There's the sister I remember—so full of disregard you would think she was an orphan! I may have been the one that killed her, but YOU broke her heart first."

Adrian pulled his hand back and slapped Nicole in the face. He looked at her, frantically looking for a reason to stop, and when he found none, he hit her again.

He beat her, punching and slapping her until her nose was broken and her left eye was black and blue. "Look what she does to me!" he screamed as he stood up and turned around.

He moved back toward Jamie's body and kicked her again before sitting down next to her and running his hand through her hair.

He stayed there for a while, stroking her hair and humming to himself. The beating had left Nicole too disoriented to understand what was happening, but the tune was familiar and danced around inside her bruised and bloody skull.

Don't you fuckin' leave me, joined the composition, reminding her of the price everyone but her had paid since she came to town. She began to regain focus as Adrian got up and exited the room, only ridding herself of the tune when he returned shortly afterward with a body bag in hand.

"Please, not yet," Nicole said, watching him drag Jamie into the bag and zip the top closed. Adrian surprised her with a look not of anger, but of understanding.

"They talk to you too, don't they?" She closed her eyes and nodded.

"I know you have to, but please, don't leave me here alone. Just one more night."

Adrian looked at Nicole and saw the tears streaming down her face from her bloodshot eyes and over the bruises he had made when he lost control.

"One more night," he said as he dropped the handle. "I'll be back to tend to the lawn in the morning. Then it's time…" He paused.

"… for all of us to go."

CHAPTER XII:
ONE FOR YOUR GHOST

Scott Emerson stepped out of his car at the Petro Mart on Friday morning after driving for nearly three hours from New Haven, Connecticut to Whiter River Junction. He stood up and stretched his legs before sliding his card through the payment slot of the gas pump and shoving the nozzle into the tank. He looked around and sighed, glad to be home and out of that godforsaken state.

Your motto may be in Latin, but all your people know how to speak is Hick, he thought as the pump wheel began to spin.

He pulled his phone out of his pocket and opened it to the text messages. He had hoped that at some point while he was gone, he would have received a message from Adrian to the effect of, "you have to come home right away, Nicole wants to talk to you, she's not mad anymore," but the message had never come, leaving him feeling a little puzzled about her intentions.

He saw also that Felix apparently hadn't been able to talk any sense into them either. *Worthless* was the word that came to his mind.

He decided that, rather than waiting for word, he would stop by and see Felix right off the get-go. Perhaps he had gotten it in his head that he should help THEM, rather than himself. He thought Felix was more sensible than that, having much more to lose than anyone else in town were his secrets to come out, but the lack of communication worried him.

A click came from inside of his car and the gasoline flow stopped, so he put the phone back in his pocket and hung up the hose, stretching each of his legs one final time before hitting the road.

The dash clock read 10:30 as he stepped out and made his way up to the front door. He found it unlocked. He walked to the back, where he and the other members of the lottery had spent many nights deliberating over what to do with their funds and who deserved them most. There, he found Felix, seated at the table reading from the good book.

"Sit down, Scott," Felix said, not bothering to look up as he spoke.

"Not even a 'welcome back,' eh?" Scott said, again receiving no acknowledgement. "I came by to see if there was any news on my daughter. I didn't hear from you or Adrian all week, and figured either she didn't show, or YOU decided she shouldn't."

"It's much more serious than that, Scott," Felix replied, looking up from the Bible at last. He took his reading glasses off and tucked them away in his pocket as Scott spoke again.

"What does that mean, exactly? Keep in mind, I still know how to find the collection plate, so don't feed me any bullshit."

Felix allowed the threat to bounce off him without budging. "It's Adrian. He killed Brent."

Scott's mouth hung ajar with a mixture of shock and disbelief—the look that had conned Felix many times in the past. "What do you mean, he KILLED him? He would never!"

"Before you go accusing me of making it up, Scott, there's more." Felix laid out the parts of the chaos that occurred during dinner, including Brent's garage demise and the abduction of Jamie and Nicole. He also gave Scott a variation of the story he had given about the keys resurfacing, this time naming Brent as the recipient from the anonymous source.

"Kidnap, murder? It doesn't make sense," Scott said as Felix's story concluded.

"Adrian has been taking part in sinister activities for years under both our noses, utilizing the lottery as a selection tool of sorts and going rogue. It seems that you weren't the only one interested in the lottery for the purpose of keeping tabs, Scott. He mentioned the names of two previous winners when he found the keys on Brent—Morgan and Rick—which can't have been just out of the blue. He's much more troubled than I could have ever imagined."

"Your mind's the one in trouble," Scott answered, unable at first to formulate his thoughts into something more concrete than a childish retort. "Adrian's been one of the most hardworking and dedicated citizens this town has ever had, and you think he just decided to start killing people left and right? Even if your fantasies WERE true, what does any of that have to do with Nicole?"

"I'm not exactly sure," Felix said, leaning back in his chair and lacing his fingers together on the table, "but he's holding her and Jamie hostage somewhere and promised to kill them if the authorities got involved. I do think it has something to do with Junior—Nicole may have had a part in his disappearance, so Adrian is looking to absolve her of her sins."

He hesitated, causing unease in Scott and making him shift his weight forward.

"By finding his father's killer," Felix said.

Scott listened to Felix's explanation and began to laugh. "You're insane! And even if it were true, YOU'RE the one he's after anyway!"

He shook his head and stepped one foot off to the side in a less imposing stance. "You fucked up and let him believe he killed his mother! You were SUPPOSED to fix him, not mess him up even more! Why didn't the buck stop with you anyway? God didn't command you to tell him the truth to save their lives. Pretty convenient!"

"The keys," Felix said after a long pause, astounded that Scott's paranoia would cloud his ability to think critically. "Brent found proof that the car belonged to you, and after Adrian killed him, he took them for himself. He wants us to meet him at the parlor, at noon," Felix said.

"Or Nicole and Jamie will suffer."

Scott looked at Felix with a fading grin as the deadline hung in the air, but the more he thought about it, the more it seemed like it was going to work out the way he had always intended.

He can't prove a thing, but I can, Scott thought. *It's right inside my safe.*

He stood up and began walking out. "I guess I'll be seeing you in a while, then. And, Felix," he said, stopping at the door, "I see through all of this you still haven't mentioned anything about their mother's real cause of death. Do you suppose this would be a good time to bring it up?"

2

Adrian stepped inside the vault just after nine in the morning and brought his sister a breakfast sandwich and a bottle of water. He found her still asleep and decided to leave them beside her, rather than wake her up for what was essentially, in prison terminology, her last meal. He knelt and unzipped the black body bag on the floor.

"Sorry, I didn't think you'd be hungry," he whispered, then sealed the bag again.

He walked back up the stairs to the main floor of the vault and opened the gate, then took out a stashed weed whacker and gas can he kept for grounds maintenance, setting them on the ground and locking the gate behind him. He slid on his eye protection and walked up the hill to the back of the cemetery, pulling the cord as he reached the section of stones from the 1700s and getting to work.

He weaved his way through the rows and between the headstones, returning them to a groomed state of beauty. As he worked his way across, he thought about how this would be a monumental day for him, a day when so many pieces fell together. *Nicole's sins will be undone when Father makes Felix confess, and Mother can finally accept her into the great big Arkansas in the sky.*

Though the day carried a lot of urgency, he still took the time to inspect each one of the stones as he cut down all the weeds that tried to take refuge on the holy land he served. Nothing gave him more pride than seeing the freshly cut lawn week after week. He found that the routine, structure, and attention to detail it took were all traits that mankind had lost in their quest for instant gratification via the easy route. There was pleasure in the simplicity of it all, and only those who truly had respect for the time and effort it took to keep it tame would reap the rewards of the work.

A sense of peace had sprung over him since the night before, as well—one he hadn't felt since the day his sister had showed her face at the funeral parlor.

Once the top level was nearly complete, he stopped to go around the Bacon mausoleum. As he trimmed around the sides, he made a mental note to fix the broken glass that had been there since his run-in with David. He looked inside the hole and saw that at least the birds hadn't decided to make it their home yet.

He realized something about himself in that moment as he looked at the glass he should have picked up days ago: that the sordid relationship he had with his sister had made HIM sloppy.

He finished cutting the top section and made his way back to the bottom of the hill, where he worked for another half hour before stopping to take a drink and check his watch. *Right on schedule.*

As he took a sip of water, he noticed a vehicle pulling into the entryway of the cemetery and prepared to smile and wave, continuing the façade that he was "the nice friendly man who mows the lawn at the cemetery and says peaceful prayers when loved ones pass away." He raised his hand to wave, but realized that the driver of the vehicle wasn't someone coming to pay their respects.

It was Felix.

Adrian dropped the weed whacker on the ground and stormed over to the company van he had opted to take that morning for its generous capacity, grabbing the pistol out of the glove box and turning it toward Felix. "What do you think you're doing here? I thought I told what would happen if you didn't listen."

"I know, I know. Don't shoot, please," Felix pleaded, with his arms raised in surrender.

"I met with Scott already. He'll be there at noon, just like you asked."

"So why are you here? I wasn't kidding when I said I wouldn't blink before sending you to hell with the rest of the scum."

"I have something I need to tell you—and your sister," Felix said, trying to maintain a nonthreatening stance as he raised his hands higher.

Adrian looked around at the rest of the un-mowed rows in the plot. "I don't have time for this, old man. Just meet me at the parlor, like I told you to!"

"It's about your mother."

Adrian tightened his grip on the gun and twisted it sideways at the boldness of Felix's continued resurrection attempts. "What about her?" he asked through gritted teeth.

"I think Nicole needs to hear this, too. Where is she, son?" Felix asked, with his hands now raised above his head at their peak.

Adrian thought about pulling the trigger, but he knew he needed his father to have a chance to set things straight first—a chance to wash the filth from his name. He lowered the gun.

"You want to see her?" he asked, thinking he could have a two-for-one if he brought Felix down into the vault. *I can hear what you have to say AND show you exactly how much damage your meddling caused.* "Fine."

He turned around and walked to the receiving vault door, opening the lock and waving for Felix to go inside. "Down there," Adrian said, pointing at the hatch on the floor.

When they reached the bottom, Adrian held the gun to Felix's lower back as he took out his keys and unlocked the door. "Come on in, Pastor. Don't mind the mess."

He sneered as he made his way to the lantern, turning it on with a flash and watching with delight as Felix saw the body bag on the floor.

"I'm sorry, but Jamie and Cooper won't be joining us. Turns out they both needed an express ticket to the pearly gates. Isn't that right, Ni..."

Adrian had turned his head as he spoke and stopped mid-sentence.

Nicole was gone.

He rushed over to the wall and felt the handcuffs, somehow being unable to accept the fact that they were empty.

He grabbed the handle of the door leading to the mausoleum and turned, his stomach dropping out from under him as he found that it was unlocked.

"Don't you fucking move!" he screamed. Then, after a quick assessment of the situation, he cracked Felix in the side of the head with the gun. He needed to run up the stairs and

287

see if she had made it out the door, and at Felix's age, a blow like that would immobilize him long enough to allow it.

He reached the top and crashed through the hole in the floor, jumping out and running around the casket to see if she was hiding. When she was nowhere to be found, he screamed with rage. "YOU LEFT ME AGAIN, YOU WRETCHED BITCH!"

The next thing he checked was the door that led outside from the mausoleum—it was still locked, which made his brain feel like it was exploding. He couldn't comprehend what was happening, so he swung his fists against the door until his knuckles were bloody.

Just as his knuckles felt that like they were going to break, he noticed the sunlight shining through the break in the mosaic glass he hadn't gotten around to fixing.

He quickly stepped in front of the hole and scanned the edges, then looked closer at the fresh blood coating a jagged piece at the bottom. *That sneaky bitch squeezed her way out.*

He cursed her again and ran back down the stairs, nearly hitting his head on the top of the hatch as he bolted through. *She unlocked the door somehow and squeezed out through the window, and now she could be ANYWHERE!*

He guessed she must have pretended to be asleep when he first got there in the morning and waited for him to come down the hill before escaping through the window. *Even if her ankle slowed her down, that's still close to thirty minutes. She could have gotten picked up by now, or WORSE!*

When he entered the vault again, he saw Felix zipping up the body bag with one hand and holding his head with the other. "Lord, what have you done?"

"Change of plans, Pastor," Adrian said, producing the gun again. "You're riding with me."

Adrian told Felix to grab the bag and drag it to the door-way. He explained how to attach it to the pulley, and yelled at him to hurry up when his pace didn't meet his own sense of urgency.

"I will LEAVE you down here with a bullet in your head," Adrian proclaimed with a heightening level of stern eagerness.

They reached the top of the stairs and turned around. "PULL."

Felix grabbed onto the rope and began dragging the body up the stairs. "Would it be wiser to leave the body here, if you're in a rush?" Felix asked, keeping his eyes on the rope.

"And with it, enough evidence to lock me away, is that it?" Adrian asked. "Just shut your mouth and pull."

A minute later, the bag reached the top of the stairs, where Adrian grabbed onto the handle and dragged it to the back of the company van. He pointed the gun at Felix and forced him to help load the body in the back, looking around as he did and listening for the inevitable sound of si-rens, which now pressured him like sharks circling the seal.

"Burn it," Adrian said, motioning for Felix to grab the can of gasoline from the grass. He opened the glove box in the van and pulled out a book of matches with the logo of a sleazy casino on the front. "Downstairs."

"I can't. Not again," Felix said as he rubbed his head again and leaned over to catch his breath. "It'll take me ten minutes to get back up here if I do."

"Fine," Adrian said, actually agreeing that it would be more time than he was willing to waste, "but give me your keys."

Felix reached into his pocket and took out the keys, tossing them at Adrian's feet before being herded back into the top of the vault.

"At least it's quieter in here," Adrian said as he pointed the pistol at Felix's thigh and pulled the trigger. Felix dropped as Adrian flew the stairs with the gas and matches.

After only seconds, Adrian was running up the stairs again, dowsing the wood with the last bit of gasoline and tossing the can back below. "Don't even think about playing the cripple from that muscle shot, I know you still shoot hoops with the kids on Saturdays. Get in the van."

Felix got to his feet slowly and began hobbling, and after a few steps, he heard the roaring sound of flames crashing up the stairs and bursting through the opening in the vault.

"Dear god," he said as Adrian slammed the door to the hatch closed and walked away un-singed.

Adrian knew the opening in the mausoleum would feed enough air to burn the rest of the fresh evidence inside, and while it wouldn't get rid of the contents of the urns, it would at least take care of any fingerprints and give him ammo to call it a heinous act of arson. *So what if they found ashes? They could never prove they belonged to someone I killed. Just an eccentric cremation technician who collects the unwanted leftovers. Is that a crime?*

If he was lucky, too— *extremely lucky*—and Nicole did decide to crawl back to Arkansas instead of racing the clock, the fire might die down with nobody ever knowing it existed.

He jumped into the driver's seat and put the keys in the ignition, daring the van to fuck him over and give him trouble starting. It didn't, so he slammed it into drive and exited the cemetery toward the funeral parlor. As he drove down the road, he felt a pure hatred for his sister growing inside his chest. He understood that her leaving could actually turn out to be a blessing, but with it, he felt that she had once again abandoned him when he needed her most.

He turned into the funeral parlor and drove around the building to the service door in the back, noticing that his father's vehicle, along with any sign of police, were nowhere to be seen. *Perhaps she's smarter than I thought.*

Then he took Felix out by gunpoint, handing him the keys to the parlor and instructing him to unlock the door and drag the gurney located inside the entryway to the back of the van or find out what two lead-filled thighs felt like. *I may not need you for her sake anymore, but you and Jamie still have a hot date tonight.*

While Felix hopped to the door and grabbed the gurney to support his weight, Adrian grabbed a small backpack from the van and threw it over his shoulder. They loaded the body onto the gurney and pushed it inside the parlor, through another set of doors and against the wall of the cremation room. Adrian flipped a switch and brought the machine to life, filling the space with a low-pitched rumbling noise and dim layer of light. Then he gave Felix an order to move Jamie's body onto the metal rollers.

Felix unzipped the bag, then stopped. "No, not until your father gets here."

"NO?" Adrian exclaimed with sarcasm. "Are you getting deaf in your old age there, Mr. Robinson? I SAID MOVE

HER, NOW!" He raised the pistol and stared at Felix, daring him to disobey again.

"AND I SAID NO!" Felix yelled back. "I know you think you've got it all figured out, but you're making a BIG mistake! I refuse to let you make it without hearing the truth first. If you want to kill me after that, I'll gladly hop on that roller too!"

Adrian couldn't believe this outright act of defiance was happening. There, in the place where so many before had crumbled to the epitome of obedience and learned what it meant to give yourself to the Lord, stood a man who knew nothing of the truth, nothing of obedience—only deceit and sin.

"That man knows no truth," a new voice said from behind them. They both turned, each seeing the gun before their faces.

"Father," Adrian said, with a hint of relief in his voice. "I knew you'd show. I knew you wouldn't leave me like Nicole."

"And where is *she?*" Scott asked, looking around the room.

"You didn't...?" he asked, trying to determine if Nicole was alive or dead.

"She's smarter than I remembered. She got away."

"That's good, son. Now what are we doing down here?" he said, looking around the room.

"If it's because of something *he* said," Scott added, pointing the gun at Felix, "you can bet your ass he's just trying to save his own." Scott walked up to the cremation machine and looked through the window before hitting the button to open the door, tripling the rays escaping into the room and unleashing their flickering effects.

"He told me he knows something," Adrian said, turning his own gun on Felix again. "Something about David Senior and our mother."

Adrian reached inside the bag he had taken from the van and produced the tattered shirt they had taken from the safe. "He said this had something to do with it."

"He doesn't know a goddamn thing. Don't be stupid!" Scott said as he eyed the shirt that had been missing from his safe. "Can't you see? He's just a small-town criminal. Always has been and always will be. You can't trust a word that comes out of his mouth."

"I want to hear what he has to say," Adrian said, offended his father would assume stupidity on his part. "He has to atone anyway."

Adrian looked at Felix and waited. He knew there was nothing Felix could say that would change his fate, but part of him couldn't allow him to die without hearing what he had to say about his mother.

"For Christ's sake," Scott said, then pulled the trigger, hitting Felix in the chest and knocking him onto the floor next to the gurney.

"NO!" Adrian screamed and reared around, shooting his father in the arm and making him drop the gun with a howl.

"I SAID LET HIM SPEAK!" Adrian screamed. "WHAT DO I HAVE TO DO TO MAKE YOU PEOPLE LISTEN!"

Felix fell to the floor, but instead of reaching for his chest, he reached inside his pocket and pulled out the sheet of paper he had taken from the safe. "Adrian," he squeaked out, tossing the crumbled paper at his feet.

Scott saw the toss. "I KNEW YOU WERE A THIEF," he yelled, then lunged after the paper. Adrian grabbed his shirt and threw him backward, pointing the gun at his head as he sat against the wall.

"I WILL shoot you again if you move another muscle!" He walked backward and crouched down, picking the paper up and opening it. It was a letter addressed to Scott and signed at the bottom by his mother. He looked at his father and took a step backward, hitting the gurney behind him before reading it out loud.

Scott,

By the time you find this letter, me and the kids will be long gone. I had my suspicions when David died that you may have found out about us and killed him, and your abusive treatment of us the last few years was enough to tell me I was right. You deserve to spend the rest of your life in prison, alone, if you don't get the death penalty, that is. I'm almost certain you will, after I give David's watch to the authorities, along with the shirt you're using to frame that other man. And while they're at it, they might as well know you buried the car in the cemetery! Did you think I wouldn't put it all together? If I'm being honest, I might as well tell you the whole truth, so it can haunt you as you rot away in that cell. The children you supposedly loved, but not enough to tame your temper around—you weren't their father. David was. I hope that eats you as you fry, you murdering bastard, and I hope the last thing you think about before your brain melts is how alone you always were.

Sincerely,

K.

Adrian finished reading the letter and stood frozen, unable to comprehend what he had just read.

"Now you know!" Scott yelled. "SHE cheated on ME! Biology is just a fucking science course. You're still my son Adrian!"

"What happened to her after she wrote this?" Adrian said at last, pointing the gun at Scott. "Why would she say she was going to skip town, then kill herself?"

"She didn't commit suicide," Scott said. "She didn't know what she was talking about. I tried to tell her she was wrong about me being a killer, but she wouldn't listen. That's when he found out," Scott said, motioning toward Felix, "and shut her up for good."

"Don't believe him, Adrian," Felix said as he began to choke on blood. "He called me and said your mother had to die, that he would kill me AND go after the flock if I didn't kill her."

He coughed and began to wheeze. "I went to the house to see what she knew, and she had already taken the pills, I swear."

"Liar!" Scott yelled. "You FORCED her to take the pills!"

"No," Felix said, coughing up more blood. "I went there, but she was already on the floor when I got there. She was barely alive, but she told me Scott had found the letter the night before and threatened to kill her and the kids if she opened her mouth."

"You're not going to believe any of this, are you, son?" Scott asked incredulously. "This is just the death rattle of a sad man trying to clear his guilty conscience!"

"I thought I told you to shut your mouth!" Adrian yelled, his veins pulsing with fury as the nightmare that loomed over his entire life spun like a vicious mobile.

"She told me I was innocent, that the proof was in his safe. The last thing she said was…" his throat made a gravelly croak as his head hit the floor. "… 'protect my babies, and tell them I love them.'"

Adrian began to shake as the reality that he wasn't responsible for his mother's death gripped him. He had spent his entire adult life trying to make amends for a crime he hadn't committed.

"Adrian," Felix said, surprising him as he grabbed his shirt. "Read Jamie her last rites."

"They won't do any good. She's been gone far too long."

"Not for her sake. For yours," Felix said as the hand clutching his chest inside his robe fell motionless.

Adrian stood up and realized his entire body was shaking. He couldn't focus on any of the information he had just received and turned toward the gurney with his eyes closed to pray. "Eternal rest grant unto them, O Lord, and let perpetual light shine upon them. May the souls of the faithful departed, through the mercy of God, rest in peace. Amen.

As he finished the prayer, a song from his childhood began playing from the other side of the room, a song from his childhood. He turned slightly as its melodic lines struck him like a lullaby: *Tell me lies, tell me sweet little lies.* He was immediately wrapped in a fond memory of his mother, seeing her face appear before him with a warm and inviting smile.

"Mother?" he said as he felt a hand on his shoulder and turned.

3

Earlier that day, Nicole woke up sweating. *"It's time for her, and you to go,"* she remembered Adrian saying the night before as drops of sweat ran down her face.

She'd had another nightmare, too. This time, she was standing over Jamie, cutting the ropes off her arms, when the needle slipped and landed in her throat, and she bled to death in her arms, screaming, *"CUT ME LOOSE, PLEASE!"*

She shook the sweat off her face and tried to concentrate. Her brother would be there any time now.

She heard his footsteps when he did arrive a short time later. She pulled her legs back in and closed her eyes, selling the old sleeping bit easier than she thought. After the footsteps dissipated again, she waited, this time for another sound. After a few minutes, she told herself maybe she was wrong. Maybe it wasn't going to work. But then she heard it: the low buzzing from when she'd first arrived. *The weed whacker.*

She got to work, first reaching her leg out and looping the handle of the body bag and pulling it toward her. She had been able to replicate this once before, but hadn't dared actually move the bag until now for fear Adrian would see that it had changed spots.

She used her toes to unzip the bag partway and stuck her leg inside. At first, she felt the top of Jamie's head. The hair beneath her feet brought tears to her eyes as she thought again about the decision she'd made that cost Jamie her life.

"I'm sorry," she whispered, continuing to move her foot down to Jamie's chest. *If I would have known...*

Her foot found the pin on the inside of the bra, and after sticking her other foot inside the bag, she gripped it with both feet and ripped it through the fabric.

She opened the handcuffs, then took the handle off the lantern and made her way up the stairs into the mausoleum. In Adrian's fit of rage the night before, he had missed the fact that the door was unlocked. *If he hadn't hurt me, he wouldn't have been too upset to check,* she thought.

Then she had to push out the thought of the extra beating she would have had to endure had he discovered it. *I'd be right there next to you, Jamie. No doubt about it.*

She opened the top and got out onto the floor, listening to the sound of Adrian tending the lawn less than a hundred yards away. "What am I doing?" she said to herself as the idea of making it all the way out of the cemetery without his knowledge was undermined by the pain in her ankle. "Do I really think this is going to work?"

She waited, cocooned in a state of spine-tingling fear as the buzzing grew steadily louder until it was upon her. She placed the carpet square over the hatch and crawled behind the casket, praying he didn't find her there. *Not now.* Just when she thought he may have looked inside and seen her, a slight delay in the sound told her it was over, and she heard him leave the mausoleum behind.

She carefully looked out the window and watched as he began walking down the hill. "This is it," she said, reaching one hand out the window and another through the bar on the wrought iron gate.

The plan was to open the lock and escape through the woods, something she could have tried the day before if she had thought there was enough time. Now, since the only time left to consider was her own, she reached her hands out for the lock. As she began to twist, she heard a noise from behind her.

She turned, and when she saw nothing, she gave her attention back to her escape.

She heard it again. This time, she ignored the sound and kept trying to get free, praying for help from the God she didn't believe in.

"Where are you off to?" It was a voice this time, but it wasn't Adrian's. It was the soft voice of a woman. Her mother.

"Down here," the voice said. Nicole looked down and saw her, staring back through a broken shard of stained glass.

"I'm leaving," Nicole said, knowing she must be hallucinating again.

"But what about your brother. Aren't you going to help him?"

"Don't you think I've done enough already?" Nicole asked sharply. "Every time I tried to help someone, they died. I'm done! Why would I help him, anyway? He's a monster! I'm getting out of here and going far, far away!"

"But you don't really believe you caused that pain, do you? Doesn't part of you know who's to blame? The person who deserves your help the most?"

Nicole looked at her mother, and after moment, dropped her hands when she understood what her words had meant. "You mean, help him by... stopping him?"

Her mother didn't reply, but smiled back at her as she faded away and was gone again, leaving just a shard of glass.

Nicole looked at the jagged edges of the glass and was reminded of Jamie, Brent, Cooper, the man in the box whose name she couldn't remember, and David. *I'm not the one she wants. It's HIM—but how?*

She closed her eyes and watched as the band of strangers in her mind took up arms with David and wished her luck. *They're not mad at me,* she thought. *They're ROOTING for me.* She dropped the lantern handle on the ground and pulled her hands back inside, the pain and suffering Adrian had inflicted beginning to ignite inside her as determination. "For you, ghosts. For all of you."

She placed her arm on the glass sticking out of the window and closed her eyes as she dragged it across the sharp edge, opening them again afterward as the blood dripped down the glass. She ripped a piece of her shirt off and wrapped it around the wound, being careful not to let any hit the floor, then bent down and picked up a shard of glass and ran back downstairs as fast as her ankle would allow.

When she got to the bottom, she turned the lantern on and took Jamie out of the body bag, setting them both aside gently. She then dropped to the floor and used the side of the badge to start digging into the dirt. The process was too slow at first, but sped up after realizing she could shove the point of the badge into the ground in small square patterns and pull the whole layer off with her hands. A nagging doubt tried to bring her to her senses and tell her she was going to fail, but she flicked it aside with the sweat from her brow and persisted, loosening and scooping away the soil one handful at a time.

She heard the buzzing sound stop above her as she moved Jamie's body into the hole she had created and used the bottom of her plastic boot to smooth over the earth while she waited for it to pick back up again. "I swear I'm going to make him pay," she said as she threw the boot aside.

If he sees all this dirt, he'll know something is off, she thought, looking at the mound left behind after moving Jamie's body into the hole. Then, after a flash of genius, she took the lids off all the urns and began stuffing dirt into them one by one, filling them to the brim. When all the dirt was gone, she placed the lids back on and swept the little bits of loose dirt off the shelves with her hand, sickened by the thought of a single ounce of dust being the difference between life and death.

She then moved the body bag back to its original place on top of Jamie's shallow grave. She grabbed the badge from the floor beside it, batting away one final attempt from the logical portion of her brain to just run upstairs and out the door. "I have to do this for them," she said to herself as she zipped herself inside the bag.

There, she waited a dangerously short amount of time before she heard the keys rattling, signifying her soon-to-be future as either a vigilante or a slice of toast.

She held her breath and listened as she ceased to be the sole occupant of the room, praying Adrian would fall for the ruse. She heard him talking to himself at first, then fought back the urge to jump out and run again as he fell for the ruse and stormed up the stairs. *Who did he tell not to go anywhere?* she wondered. *Does he think he can control ghosts too?* Her question was quickly answered as the zipper opened and she saw Felix staring back at her.

"Nicole!" Felix said, utterly stunned.

"Shh," she said with a finger to her mouth.

"Don't let him push me in the machine," she whispered. "Do you have a phone?"

Felix nodded his head and quickly took it out of his pocket. They both jumped as they heard Adrian scream and begin pounding on something from up the stairs. Nicole took the phone from his hand and entered a number into his keypad.

"I don't know if this will work," she whispered, "but if we make it to the incineration room, hit the green button." Nicole shoved the phone in Felix's hands as the sound of Adrian's approach echoed down the stairs. "Not all the way," she whispered as Felix closed the bag again. He understood and left a small space at the top.

As the bag moved up the stairs with Nicole inside, she felt the blood on her arm beginning to soak through her shirt. The cut was deeper than she had intended. To make matters worse, her head was slamming against each step on the way up. *My head's going to split in half.*

She held tight to the badge in one hand and the shard of glass in the other, knowing that if she screamed, she would be exposed. She thought about her mother's smile inside the glass on the floor and clamped her mouth shut as her head hit the steps. *Crack, crack, crack.*

4

Nicole remained on her back on the gurney in the body bag, listening as Scott entered the room, as the gun went off, and as the note from her mother was read out loud. She screamed silently as the news of her real parentage hit the air, and her heart plummeted in her chest like a bowling ball from a rooftop.

It all angered her more, and when she heard the ringtone she had put on her phone to remind her of her mother, she carefully pushed a finger through the hole in the bag and slid down the zipper. *Tell me lies, tell me sweet little lies.*

Nicole sprang up from the bag and dropped her hand on Adrian's shoulder, spinning him around to see his face. In the millisecond it took for the lines on his face to contort into confusion she had jammed her arms out at full force, making him explode backwards in a blind frenzy as the shard of glass and badge entered separate eyes. She lifted her legs out of the bag as he dropped the gun, then sent him to the floor with a kick to the ribs when he tried to reach for it.

"WHY?" he screamed, as he tore the objects from his body and dropped them into a new pool of blood. He put his hands to his face and looked at her through the webbing of his fingers. "I WAS TRYING TO SAVE YOU!"

She walked to Felix's side and put a hand on his head, turning it towards her. She wanted to thank him, to tell him she believed him about everything, but his hand slid out from the inside of his robe and dropped his cell phone on the floor. He was gone.

"Nicole," she heard from behind her, prompting her to stand slowly and face the man for whom she had come to town in the first place: her father.

"YOU," she shouted, raising her hand and pointing at the man responsible for every bit of the torment she had endured, "did ALL of this!"

She started towards the man she'd used to call her father, the man who used to beat her for coming home late or too early, the man who murdered her REAL father and caused her mother to kill herself.

"Hold on, now. You gotta listen to me," Scott said, picking up the silver-plated gun and pointing it at her. "I didn't mean for any of this to happen. You gotta believe me!"

"What are you going to do?" she asked as she took another step closer, forcing him to move away from the wall and into the middle of the room. "Are you going to kill me too? Just like you killed my REAL father and our mother?"

"Who are you to judge me?" Scott said, changing his tone as he got to his feet. "You've been a pretty busy girl since you came back to town, too. I heard you killed David? I was trying to protect you from that, not have you out there fucking your own brother! Your mother thought she was fooling me, but she wasn't. I killed your father, but your mother died because she couldn't handle the mess she made for HERSELF!"

"Shut up," Adrian said softly from the floor, his eyes dripping blood down his face.

"And what about Felix?" Nicole asked, taking another step towards Scott. "Did he die because of a mess HE created too!?"

"That wasn't supposed to happen!" Scott said, shaking the end of the gun and looking at Nicole with contempt.

"The cops were supposed to find me in the back seat of that car and think someone held me hostage during the hit-and-run. I didn't know someone was going to steal the damn thing! And when I walked into the motel to frame Cooper and saw HIM there passed out," he said, motioning toward Felix's body, "it just made sense. All I had to do was wipe some of my blood on his shirt and convince him the blood belonged to the cop. He was a junkie, a nobody! If I would have gone to jail, your mother would have been left to take care of you two, and hell, she wasn't fit to do that alone, running around town like some kinda whore."

"SHUT UP, SHUT UP," Adrian screamed as the insults toward his mother fueled another spark of rage. He got off the floor and jumped in the direction of Scott's voice.

Scott turned and aimed the gun at Adrian, sucking in a swift puff of air as he was met with the sound of an empty chamber. *CLICK.*

Adrian grabbed onto Scott's chest and pushed him backwards onto the metal rollers of the incinerator. "I TOLD YOU NOT TO TALK ABOUT MY MOTHER LIKE THAT!"

As Scott screamed and gave the trigger a few more desperate, fruitless squeezes, Adrian turned to his sister and smiled. "The big red one," he said as the glow surrounding the slits in his eyes grew brighter.

Nicole had no fear left inside her body as she stared into them, watching as the flames from inside the incinerator cast hungry shadows across the side of his face. She walked to the back of the room and grabbed the metal pole from the wall, then turned to the rollers and closed her eyes. Scott let out one final plea for help before she jammed the pole into the soles of Adrian's boots and pushed the two of them into the machine.

Scott screams intensified as she walked to the control box in what felt like slow motion. Then, as she hit the big red button to close the door, they were replaced again with her mother's song. "For you, Mother," she whispered as it played.

The inferno roared inside the cremation chamber, and a minute later when the ringtone that had placed itself on repeat in her mind had stopped, she was left in silence once again.

She walked to the window and looked inside. She was greeted by a face: Adrian's.

She put her hand to the glass. It burned, but she didn't care. "If only you would have known," she said, thinking of the life he might had if not for the blame he rationed for himself all those years before. "Maybe I'd be singing Mom's songs with you now instead of talking to your ghost."

Adrian moved aside, revealing the burning carcass of the man who had destroyed the world for both of them, reducing it to nothing but a pile of ash and bone fragments.

"I guess this means we're finished."

Adrian put his hand against the glass and touched hers. She watched as the glow in his eyes disappeared, leaving them whole again.

"Thank you for helping me keep my promise," she said, thinking again of David, Jamie, and the rest of those he'd stolen so dearly from in his tragically misguided fight. He took his hand away from the window and smiled at her like the little brother she once knew, then slowly fell backwards until he was engulfed in flames.

5

The rest of the day flew by in a dizzying array of flashing lights, sirens, and questions Nicole didn't know how to answer. *"How long has your brother been engaging in criminal activity? Was Mr. Emerson aware of his son's homicidal tendencies?"*

And her favorite: *"What made you return after all this time?"*

"I don't know," she said, "but do any of you smoke?"

She told the detectives about the place she had buried Jamie, and how they would find the remains of many more victims when they entered the vault. "Including... David Demick Junior."

The detectives looked at each other as the name came out of her mouth, then a female officer spoke. "Ma'am, I know you've been through one hell of an ordeal this evening, and I'm sure you're lookin' forward to getting some sleep... but after you get that ankle checked out we're going to have to ask you to come with us down to the station so we can ask you a few more questions."

She nodded her head as she put out the cigarette she had snagged off one of the "on-call" paramedics. "I know, but first..."

The officer brought Nicole back into the parlor and down the stairs into the cremation room. "It's officially a crime scene now," she said sternly, "but since you were already down here, I don't see how it could hurt anything for you to see."

"Thank you," Nicole said as she walked to the far side of the room and grabbed her cell phone from its hiding place under one of the shelves. An officer told her it was evidence and that she couldn't keep it, but one press of the power button confirmed a suspicion that had been on her mind from the moment she exited the body bag. "Thanks mom," she said as she dropped the lifeless phone into the evidence bag.

The police had turned the incinerator off before its cycle was complete, but Nicole still felt a rush of heat as she got close to the glass and peered inside.

At first, she saw only one pile of ashes. The outline of an eye socket not fully burned stared back at her from where Scott had lain just before her brother reached out to her. Her heart sped a little as she stood on the tips of her toes and looked beneath the door, subsiding as the second skull came into view.

"Ok," she said as she turned away from the machine. "I'm ready."

"You weren't fixin' to leave without sayin' goodbye now were ya ma'am?" a voice said from the end of the rollers. The cops doling out the questions had vanished, replaced with the glowing faces of David, Felix, Brent, Jamie, and Cooper. Nicole was struck with a wave of guilt as their collective loss surfaced in her memory, but that feeling was replaced with love and acceptance as they each smiled and joined their hands. She wanted to tell them all how sorry she was, how she wished she could turn back time and just stay in Arkansas, but as they offered their final silent cheers and slowly faded away she knew none of it was necessary, and there was only one thing left to say.

"Goodbye."

Reality rushed back in the form of the officer sticking her arm out, offering it to steady Nicole's walk up the stairs.

"Miss?" Nicole heard the officer say after stopping abruptly.

"While you're still here, I just have to ask—what do want us to do with the remains, you know, once we're done here?"

Nicole looked her in the face and busted out with laughter, causing the officer to feel a little uneasy.

"Miss?" she asked again, thinking she may have to take out the cuffs after all.

Nicole tilted her head back and closed her eyes, letting out one more bout of laughter before turning back.

"That's not my rodeo," she said with a smile, "and they're definitely not my clowns."